JOURNEY TO
NORA

REVISED EDITION

JOURNEY TO
NORA

REVISED EDITION

ARON FENICAL

Copyright © 2022 by Aron Fenical.

All rights reserved. No part of this book may be reproduced in any form or by any electronic or mechanical means, including information storage and retrieval systems, without permission in writing from the publisher, except by reviewers, who may quote brief passages in a review.

ISBN: 978-1-956515-85-5 (Paperback Edition)
ISBN: 978-1-956515-86-2 (Hardcover Edition)
ISBN: 978-1-956515-87-9 (E-book Edition)

Some characters and events in this book are fictitious. Any similarity to the real persons, living or dead, is coincidental and not intended by the author.

Book Ordering Information

Phone Number: 315 288-7939 ext. 1000 or 347-901-4920
Email: info@globalsummithouse.com
Global Summit House
www.globalsummithouse.com

Printed in the United States of America

CONTENTS

Chapter One 1
Chapter Two 10
Chapter Three 16
Chapter Four 25
Chapter Five 34
Chapter Six 45
Chapter Seven 53
Chapter Eight 64
Chapter Nine 76
Chapter Ten 87
Chapter Eleven 103
Chapter Twelve 112
Chapter Thirteen 119
Chapter Fourteen 134
Chapter Fifteen 141
Chapter Sixteen 152
Chapter Seventeen 166
Chapter Eighteen 178
Chapter Nineteen 184
Chapter Twenty 195
Chapter Twenty One 201
Chapter Twenty Two 206
Chapter Twenty Three 215

CHAPTER ONE

Shawn Higgins stands in front of his parents' gravesite. Truthfully, he doesn't come out here much. Today is special, he's wearing a mid-grade suit, something he never wears, and his baseball cap. Today is Shawn's birthday, the anniversary of his mom's death, twenty years ago, and his father's death six months ago in a car accident coming home from work late one night. As darkness sets, wind blows dead leaves around Shawn's feet. Tight within his fist, roses for the graves. He kneels, places the flowers into the holder nestled in the dirt amidst the two graves. He wipes the dead leaves away that lay in front of the triangle-shaped tombstone, their names, Shannon Higgins, Hoard Higgins, inscribed, dead center in calligraphy, across the face of the tombstone. At the top-most point his Mom's favorite gold-chain charm necklace has been hanging since her funeral, its last charm, a broken half lightning bolt (unbeknownst to Shawn has always been broken since his first memories. Shawn watches the charm scrape across its marble face and wonders if it might be something more.

Suddenly, a noise erupts behind him. Abruptly he turns and notices the rusted cemetery gate swings haphazard in the wind. His thoughts shift back to his parents' tombstone, yet again a noise from behind him piques his suspicion. This time he ignores the noise and focuses solely only on the gravesite. In a blink his attention shifts to his immediate surroundings where crackling leaves become more evident. He momentarily remains kneeling, digging his heels into the soft earth, then like a startled cat turns to see a large figure standing behind him wearing a long, dark trench coat. His face is shaded by the cemetery shadows. Instinctively, Shawn quickly swings his leg out, swipes the legs dropping the cryptic stranger to the ground.

Shawn springs to his feet, runs through the maze of tombstones. He glances back to see if any long, dark trench coats follow him. He tumbles head over heels. Unscathed, he regains his composure, scurries behind one of the tombstones, peering out from around the marble slab, scans the shadows for more dark trench coats. He notices three silhouette movements atop the hill. In the darkening wind the three shadows move in unison toward him. Swallowing his heartbeat, he turns, looks down the hill toward his streetlight illuminated Suzuki, leaning on its kickstand, outside the open cemetery gate.

He grabs the keys out of his jacket pocket and breathes, "Three, two, one". He darts out from behind the tombstone, charging forward, hurdles whatever obstacles he encounters. He reaches his bike, slam-dunks into his black helmet, turns the ignition key of his 2009 orange and black Suzuki GSX65 off road motorcycle, guns the throttle. He shifts into 1st gear, rapidly accelerating through the 6 gears. He leaves the men charging down the hill far behind him. As Shawn rides away he glances over his shoulder to get a better look at the ambiguous men, rapidly advancing.

Shawn rides through the back alleys of Edgewater, Florida, knowing he can't go home, these men will surely be waiting. He stops at a payphone to call his childhood best friend, Stewart Collins. He is a bit crazy in the way he does things, how he dresses, acts, but he is dependable. Shawn digs through his pockets looking for some loose change to use the payphone, empty pockets. Suddenly, from Publix an eldely lady hobbles up next to him.

"Excuse me sir, do you need change for the phone?" At first Shawn doesn't notice her. When he does he turns abruptly toward her, frustration in his eyes, "I'm sorry what, ma'am?"

"Do you need change for the phone?" Shawn stops rummaging through his pockets.

"Yes ma'am" Shawn replies.

She reaches into her small leather pocketbook.

"Here you go young man," she gingerly passes Shawn eight quarters with trembling hands.

"Thank you." Shawn replies, taking the quarters from her outreached hand.

"You're welcome, young man. Get home safe." The lady breathes walking away.

Shawn dials, waiting for Stewart to pick up the phone. He nervously looks around for any sign of being followed. Finally, through the phone a loud, "Hello?" It's Stewart.

Shawn's speech is accelerated. "Stewart. Listen. Remember where we hung out as kids?"

"Yes."

"As fast as you can, bring me a laptop, flashlights, and a cell phone. Meet me there ASAP," Shawn urgently blurts.

Stewart asks, "What? Why?".

"Just do it! and bring me a change of clothes."

Shawn slams the phone down, strolls cautiously to his bike still waiting for any of the three men to confront him. He grabs his helmet and screams away winding through the gears. He drives up and down back alleys to avoid being spotted. He races to Fairmont Ave. and his old high school. Behind, there's a rusty water tank, half above ground and half underground. Shawn parks in the surrounding bushes for camouflage, leans the bike against its kickstand and hops off. He shimmies down the ladder sprouting out of the ground running horizontally below ground he can walk upright comfortably in the vacant water tower tank. The tank dips downward slightly further into the ground.

Shawn searches through the darkness to locate the candles they brought here sometime ago along with some small furniture. He fingers the darkness hoping to discover anything beside himself occupying the darkness. He fumbles across a box on the ground.

He kneels cautiously and rummages through it. He finds a candle and a book of matches. He sets the candle on the ground, opens the book of matches, tears a match off and strikes it against the emery board, searching the ground for the candle. Finding it, he lights it. The candlelight provides ample light for Shawn to find the other candles laying about the tank. He quickly lights them, setting them about the sconce candle holders set into the surrounding walls. This light illuminates the walls, which are covered with spray paint, pictures of women, and all things young men like. Shawn sees that the mattress that they got from his house still lies at the end of the tank. He starts pacing up and down the tank looking at all the pictures, in wait for Stewart to arrive.

An hour passes and Shawn, starts getting tired, stretches out into a fetal position on the old mattress and catches some shut eye while he waits for Stewart. Within minutes Shawn yawns himself to sleep. Stewart slips his praying hands beneath his head and falls into a deep sleep.

After another hour following the same route Stewart took, Shakes Shawn awake screaming, "Wake-Up!" Shawn pops up and Stewart hands him a black bookbag.

Shawn poses, "You get everything I asked for?"

"Of course, it's all there," Stewart answers.

He's wearing his normal black pants, black AC/DC tee shirt, black Cleveland Indian baseball cap, black boots and a black knee length leather jacket. The only thing with color on him is his Irish auburn hair and freckles splattered all over his face. Don't let his look fool you though. He's not only street and book smart, computer savvy, and a smart ass with a silver tongue.

"What's all this about, Shawn? You called me up right when I was going to get my groove on, and you want all these things."

Shawn changes into a black pair of jeans and a black hooded sweater, and asks Stewart if the computer is charged.

"Yes. Why?" Stewart replies, bass in his voice.

"Listen, I don't know. I was at my parents' grave and a couple of guys tried to grab me," Shawn says, visibly shaken.

"What? Who tried to grab you?"

"I don't know. It all happened too quickly."

Shawn explains, "I'm going to stay in the tank until I can figure things out".

"What do you want me to do now?" Stewart asks.

Shawn finishes changing his clothes. "I want you to bring up the street cameras from the cemetery earlier tonight," Shawn demands, looking through the bag.

Stewart turns the laptop on and asks, "What are you looking for?"

Shawn pulls everything out of the bag. "I'm looking for food."

"There are a few sandwiches in the front pouch."

Shawn goes straight for the sandwiches. He eats them right away. Five minutes later, Stewart retrieves the footage from the street cameras.

"Wonder what this is?" Shawn's attention turns toward the video on the laptop.

"Lemme see that", Shawn swipes the laptop from Stewart, not allowing him to see the footage.

"What you're not going to let me see?" Stewart stands directly behind Shawn.

"I was there Stewart, not you so this is mine first", Shawn puts his full body in front of the screen.

"You're just being a prick", Stewart says angrily.

Stewart has become disgusted, presses his body close, breath Shawn's his ear,

Shawn closes the laptop.

Stewart, annoyed with Shawn's actions, barks, "What do you want me to do now?"

"Nothing. Go home. I'll call you if I need you. I don't know what's going on. I don't want you involved."

Stewart, unsettled, walks away grumbling mumblings underneath his breath, "If you don't need me I GUESS I'LL GO HOME SHAWN"!

Shawn tilts back against the wall viewing the footage over and again asking himself, "Who are those guys? I've never seen them before." After looking over the same footage for two hours hoping he'd be able to identify the men who followed him. "God knows what they were after," gnaws at the back of his brain when he decides to head home and see if anyone is waiting there. He repacks the backpack, grabs a flashlight, and starts to blow out the candles. He climbs up the ladder and exits the tank, covers the entry hole with an old piece of plywood, and spreads old leaves on top.

Shawn runs toward his bike with the backpack strapped to his back and the flashlight in his hand. Just as he gets to his bike his phone rings. Hesitantly, he answers.

"Hello?"

He white-knuckles the phone in anticipation of a voice. With the airwaves silent Shawn relaxes his grip.

Just as he is about to disconnect he suddenly hears a man's voice dominate the earpiece.

"Meet us at your parent's grave in an hour."

Defiant, Shawn spits back, "No!," and ends the call. Instantly, the phone rings. Shawn debates whether he should answer, delegating whether he should bring this to the police. It goes to voicemail. Seconds later it chimes again.

Shawn hits answer, listening to the same deep voice.

"If you hang that phone up we might just have to hurt your friend Stewart. So meet us at your parents' grave in an hour. If you don't show up, well, your friend Stewart won't like that decision, trust me."

Immediately, Shawn hangs up the phone feeling sick with dread for his friend. He has no other choice but to hop on his bike and ride to the cemetery earlier than scheduled to scout for an escape.

When Shawn arrives he notices a man standing at his parents' grave. Very cautiously he gets off his bike and places his helmet down, never taking his eyes off the strange man. The man has short, scruffy black hair. He's wearing black slacks and a white button down shirt over a sleeveless tee under a knee length black trench coat. Shawn carefully walks up the hill, looking around for signs of anybody else, and Stewart. Shawn approaches and the man starts to speak:

"I worked with your father. He was a good man," he begins, while looking down at the gravesites. "He showed me things about people that I didn't know. He was a smart man. He talked about you all the time, how smart you are. That's why I knew you would be here early. I thought, 'What would your father do in this situation?' So here we are."

Shawn stands listening, not knowing what to do, trying to make sense of all this.

The guy goes on, "Shawn, listen. We're not going to hurt you or your friend. We just need your help."

"My help? Who needs my help? Who are you? Let me see your I.D. if you have nothing to hide."

As the man reaches into his pocket, Shawn takes a step back. The man takes out his wallet and hands it to Shawn. Inside it shows his name is Tyler Parks. On top of the I.D. it reads A.H.R. Behind the I.D. is a picture of Tyler with Shawn's father. Shawn looks up at Tyler and asks, "A.H.R. What's that mean?" as he gives back his wallet.

"Everything will be explained. All I ask is that you trust me like I trusted your father. Look at it this way: your government and I need your help."

Shawn says nothing at first. He just looks around for Stewart. Then he replies, "If you want me to trust you tell me where my friend is."

Tyler points down the hill. Shawn sees Stewart and one other man leaning against a black SUV with tinted windows. When Shawn and Tyler get down to the truck Shawn turns to Stewart and asks him if he's okay. Stewart nods his head. You can tell he is very nervous, like he is about to wet himself.

Tyler says to Shawn, "This is Matt Franks who also worked with your father as a member of the A.H.R team." Franks is an African American man who is tall, muscular and bald. Another guy sitting in the driver's seat opens the passenger window and tells everybody that they have to go. Tyler opens the back side door of the SUV to let Franks in first. He turns to Shawn and Stewart giving them the option to get in. They both turn to each other, feeling intrigued by the situation, and Shawn wanting to see what more he can learn about his father's work. He climbs into the SUV.

Shawn and Stewart sit in the back two seats. Tyler Parks and agent Matt Franks are sitting in front of them. Stewart elbows Shawn to get his attention. Since Stewart is still a little bit uneasy about everything, Shawn starts to explain that these guys are from some kind of government agency called A.H.R. Stewart turns to tell Shawn that he never heard of them, but decides to keep that to himself. Shawn tells him that his father worked with them, and that they claim to need his help. After hopping on to Interstate 95 southbound heading towards Miami, Stewart quietly elbows Shawn.

"Where are we going? Did you ask them that?" Stewart whispers.

Shawn, with a puzzled look over his face, looks up at Tyler and calls out his name.

"Yes, Shawn?"

"Where are we going? You never told me."

"I wasn't sure if you were coming so I had to keep it quiet," Tyler tells them. "You two are on your way to NASA."

Shawn and Stewart look at each other in disbelief. Then Stewart starts to laugh sarcastically waiting for someone to laugh with him. No one does. He looks at Shawn and then out the SUV window to the big gateway of the entrance to Kennedy Space Center. His face and stomach begin to sink.

"The Space Center? I used to come here with my mother until she found something better to do." Stewart says.

"What did she find that was better than spending time with her own son?" Franks asks. Stewart, deep in his own thoughts, doesn't answer.

Franks tries to break his train of thought by asking again, "What did she find?"

Finally Stewart shamefully replies, "Local bars, bad men and a whole lot of drugs."

Franks just shakes his head and turns back around in his seat. The SUV stops in front of a small building in front of a really big warehouse. Tyler and Franks exit the SUV, while Shawn and Stewart hesitate. Eventually, they exit and the driver drives the SUV away. The four men are left standing there. Shawn and Stewart start to walk around the smaller building but are stopped in their tracks when they see Tyler and Franks enter the small shack. Shawn and Stewart stop and look at each other.

"You go first," says Shawn.

"No, no, you go first," Stewart quickly answers back.

"Rock, paper, scissors?"

They reluctantly do their childhood drawbreaker several times before.

Franks pops his head out the door and screams, "Are you little girls coming, or are you too scared to come inside?" He laughs and goes back in.

Shawn and Stewart start to push each other closer to the door, eventually Shawn wins and Stewart enters very slowly with Shawn following closely behind.

They're in a small cubicle, one desk and an oversized man sitting behind it. The man's face is all red from standing up to salute Tyler and Franks.

"If you two are done fooling around we have to go," Tyler says.

"Go where?" Stewart asks.

Just then the wall on the right of the desk glides up into the ceiling exposing a passenger elevator the four men enter.

CHAPTER TWO

Stewart smiles, "Where are we going? There is only one floor," attempting to be comically sarcastic.

Before he could say another rude comment the doors open from behind startling him.

"About time y'all got here, Tyler. What the hell took you so long?" A man dressed in full marine blues, with five bright stars that stand out on his shoulder hollers. His hand is already out to shake Shawn and Stewart's even before they exit the elevator.

Tyler and Franks push their way through Shawn and Stewart to avail themselves from the elevator, saluting the General. Then, they both are shuffled into the next room. The General turns back towards Shawn and Stewart, who are still in the elevator. He sticks his hand back towards them and says, "I'm General George T. Stone."

Shawn walks out of the elevator and shakes his hand, rudely asking, "What do you want from us? We didn't do anything and your goons kind of grabbed us and brought us here. Why?"

By now Stewart has exited the elevator. Stone turns to him and puts out his hand to shake it, showing Stewart full attention.

"Doctor Howard Higgins informed me you're good with computers, and other stuff."

Stewart doesn't respond. Shawn steps between them.

"Wait. How do you know my father?" Shawn questions,

forcing Stewart aside. "My father. How do you know him?" Shawn's face is red with anger. His fist tightens up.

"He worked here. You both sit down. I'll explain everything to you."

Hesitant, Shawn and Stewart follow behind him. Tyler and Franks are already sitting at one end of a fingernail-shaped table situated a step up to a big projection screen, which Stone stands in front of.

"Please. Sit so we can get started. We have a lot to cover," Stone commands, slightly alarmed.

"What's this all about? You got us here, now start talking," Shawn answers back, annoyed with this whole affair.

Shawn and Stewart sit at the other end of the table from Tyler and Franks. Stone turns on the screen behind him. On the screen in bold black letters:

AHR

"What is that? The men that brought us here had that on their I.D's," Shawn blurts, cutting Stone off.

"A.II.R. stands for **ALIEN HUMAN RELATIONS.** It's a section of the United States Government. Your father and I started this program over thirty years ago. We both were just starting out. I was just out of boot camp and your father was just out of college. He was a know it all, received a grant to fund his invention, a radio receiver that transmits into outer space. It was a way to make contact with other species," Stone continues, gaining Shawn and Stewart's full attention. "Your father only had enough money to have his machine operate for a year, so every night when I was on guard duty your father was in his lab, headphones on, striving to make contact. Night after night, day after day, he was doing everything he could to make it work. I felt sorry for him because he believed so strongly that his invention would work; that he could indeed make contact, even when his colleagues made him the brunt of their jokes behind his back. He always knew but, honestly, didn't care. He just went on about his business. Now months started to pass and I could see the pressure mounting from above. The brass was starting to get to him. So, while I was on guard duty, I would help. And when he didn't need my help, I would be an ally."

Stone pauses for a minute, takes a sip of water from the glass that sits on the desk to the left of him. He sets the glass down, continues talking. "Your father was on the brink of giving up because his year was just about over, when the unthinkable happened. He made contact with another species outside our solar system. We couldn't draw any conclusions if this was a practical joke or if this was the real deal, so we kept it under raps. My boss, who like many others didn't believe in the project, observed the interest I showed in Dr. Higgins's research and made me the advisor of the project."

Stone stops talking for a moment and switches the picture on the screen, which now shows a numeric formula used to decode the signal. "We discovered the signal materialized in months ending with thirty days. Still we hadn't told anybody about the discovery. We started checking where the signal was coming from and were astounded it was coming from outside of our solar system. We were floored. Still, we kept it to ourselves until we had enough transmitted recordings of a language, or pattern. Nothing came of it because we'd get the same patterns in return. Until one night we got letters back, too. They were scrambled on the computer screen."

General Stone flips the screen and shows the pattern of letters in which he just mentioned, and continues talking.

"With that, I told my superior everything. He thought I was crazy, until me and your father presented our findings."

Stewart interrupts, "Wait. You mean to tell me that you and Shawn's father made contact with aliens?"

"Yes, like I was saying, things moved very quickly. I became General and your father made one of the greatest discoveries of all-time. As time progressed communications became stronger every month ending with thirty days. Eventually, a bond was formed. At the International Space Station your father and I came face to face with these beings. Over these thirty years we have sent our people to their solar system with the help of their technology, and we've used their technology for military purposes here on Earth. They have a few of their kind mixed in with our government. Your father, myself, and the president's top advisors assimilated ourselves into their government. In time we found out that they have the ability to adapt to any environment by shape shifting. In their solar system, there are planets surrounding theirs with other kinds of intelligent beings on them. Their people have no problem adapting to our way of life. Their planet's atmosphere is almost like our own."

Speechless, Shawn and Stewart are frozen in their seats. Stone continues talking. "A.H.R. was formed with both humans and aliens on the same side, fighting together. Both leaders of each planet agreed that your father would run and make the final decision pertaining to the A.H.R team."

"Wait a minute, you mean to tell me that aliens are real, and that one could be in this room right now?" Stewart screams out, turning to face Franks and Tyler, then back to Shawn, elbowing him in the ribs. "Wow. I think it's Franks. Look at him. He looks weird already," Stewart whispers to Shawn, trying not to attract attention from everyone else in the room, but failing miserably at doing so.

Shawn looks down at the table, picks up his head and turns it toward Tyler. "No. It's Tyler." He squints his eyes as he says it again, but louder, "No. It's Tyler. Tell me I'm wrong, General Stone."

"No, you aren't wrong," answers Tyler. He gets up from his seat and moves toward General Stone. With distrust Shawn follows him with his eyes.

Stewart, on the other hand, is intrigued over all of this so he blurts out, "Wait a minute, you can change forms? Can I see your true form?"

Franks laughs in his seat saying, "This should be good." He turns to Tyler and says, "Show them, Tyler. They'll love it."

Tyler turns to Stone and in a flash the clothes he was wearing are now covering a bright blue figure. His skin is like a clear jelly substance although you can't quite see through it. It seems to move, like a bad trip. Then, as quickly as he changed into his alien form, turns back into his human form. Stewart can't even contain his enjoyment. All this has him believing in aliens again.

Shawn remains silent. Tyler walks back to his seat and finally Shawn says, "You were the one who made contact with my father. You also met my father at the space station."

Tyler nods. "Your father was a proud man. He was very trusting and caring of all who came in contact with him and I'll never forget it. I'll show the same respect to you and Stewart, just like he did me." He gets up out of his seat and walks towards the boys. He puts out his hand to shake Shawn's, but Shawn doesn't respond. Stewart puts his hand out to shake.

Shawn is in shock. He had no idea who his father really was. In a way, he feels betrayed. He looks up at Stone, and then at Tyler and says, "Ah well. You knew him better than me. I had no idea about any of this stuff." He pauses for a brief second to catch his breath and with sadness in his voice continues. "I thought my father was a traveling salesman or something. He was never home, and when he was home he would spend time with me and Stewart. He tried to be a father to me but he was always somehow distant from the two of us. He always ended up on the phone or in his office." Shawn freezes, lost in thought, in the past.

Stone tries to comfort Shawn telling him that it was top secret and he was required to secrecy. This doesn't help at all.

Shawn's temper explodes, "If it was a big secret all my life. Why did you guys bring us here and tell us this now?" adding, "My father is dead." He slams his fist down on the table, getting the attention of Tyler, Stone, and even Franks sitting at the other end of the table.

Shawn pops out of his seat and tries to leave when Stone stops him. "Wait, your father is alive. He needs you both to free him. He always said if he ever got in a jam that you can help."

"What? My father is alive? Then what or who did we bury next to my mother?"

Stewart is floored hearing Mr. Higgins is still alive. Shawn is about to lose it.

"At first we thought your father was dead, until about a month ago. We got word that people like Tyler had taken him out of protest in the junction of the two races. Your father has left many clues both here on Earth and on Tyler's planet. We need your assistance in getting him back."

Shawn, still standing by the doorway, falls back against the door frame, slapping his right hand against his forehead in disbelief. He looks at Stone. "I can't help you. I wish I could for the sake of my father, but I just can't. I'm sorry."

Shawn runs out of the room and gets into the elevator. Stewart and Tyler try to stop him but it's too late. Stone calls down the main entrance guard. Shawn has already run past him. Stone hangs up the phone and relays the message to everyone. "He's gone."

For the first time silence overwhelms the entire room. Stone turns to Stewart.

"Can you help us?"

Stewart looks up and replies "Yes. I'll help. And Shawn, he'll be back, just give him time. I promise." In his head he has doubts, he feels Shawn has been lied to and betrayed by his father, which he takes very personally.

Stone turns to Franks leaning back in his chair, his feet resting on the table. He calls out Franks name but as normal Franks isn't listening.

He screams, "Franks!" falling backward out of his seat.

"Yes, General?" Franks asks, as Stewart and Tyler laugh over what just happened. General Stone is not amused.

"Franks, take Stewart back to his house so he can get his belongings, and come back here to show him around, introduce him to the other team members."

"What team members?" Stewart asks.

"Oh, the team. You'll love them," Franks answers with a smile, walking to the elevator. He cracks a smile. Stewart is confused.

General Stone and Tyler stay behind reviewing the situation they face without Shawn in their plans.

CHAPTER THREE

Stewart and Franks return from getting Stewart's personal belongings. They enter through the same entrance they came in before and the same overweight man is sitting behind the desk.

"How is it going, Earl?" Franks says with a smile.

The man blushes with the thought of someone paying attention to him, and answers, "Fine."

"Listen. This is Stewart. He's going to be with us for a while, so give him anything he needs and give him clearance from now on. Okay?"

"No problem, sir, I understand," Earl replies with a nervous hesitation in his voice.

Franks and Stewart step into the elevator heading to the third floor living quarters. Stewart steps off the elevator into an open space. It looks like a top floor Manhattan penthouse. To the left of them is a large sitting area with a couch that could seat ten, in front hangs a fifty-inch plasma TV. To the left of the couch is a kitchen with all the appliances anyone could need. Nothing separates the two rooms but a long butcher countertop, with four bar stools on either side of it. Stewart stands in amazement at how nice the place is. Franks standing behind him gives him a push to wake him up.

"Come on, I'll show you your room."

Stewart follows Franks down a hallway that seems to follow around the living room and kitchen.

"Who lives here with us?" Stewart asks.

"Me and the other team members."

"There are other team members? How many? Where are they?"

"Oh, they're around. I'll let you meet them on your own," Franks answers with a smile.

"Why would you do a thing like that?"

"Well, because it'll be funny for me," Franks laughs, bringing a half-smile to Stewart's face.

They come to his room which is the fourth door down in a row of seven. Franks opens the door and lets Stewart enter. The room is very big. There is one bed on each side of the room, a large bathroom between the beds, and a sitting area with a TV and laptop for internet access.

Stewart puts his bags on one of the beds and looks over at the other bed wondering where Shawn is. He thinks about what he must be going through, finding out that his father is still alive.

"He'll be back," Stewart thinks, "he won't leave me. He'd want to do this for his father."

Stewart sits on his bed still lost in thought over his friend. He notices a camera in the wall vent. He walks over to it and disconnects it.

Stewart is a computer whiz. As a kid he used to build and program them from scratch. He goes everywhere with his equipment, including his personal laptop and his bug detector. He grabs it out of one of his bags and starts to search. He finds one quickly in the TV remote and another one in the laptop. He searches the whole room and bathroom and finds a total of twenty five listening devices scattered between the room and the bathroom. He throws them in the garbage, takes the bag and laptop out, and storms out of the room slamming the door behind him.

He comes across Franks sitting watching TV. He walks by him to the elevator, proceeds in and goes to the fifth floor hoping Stone is still there.

Stone is sitting in his office right off the briefing room. He is talking with Tyler. Stewart walks in.

"Excuse you, Stewart, you can't just barge into my office. We have rules and you need to learn them." Stone barks.

Stewart is not really listening. He angrily throws the bag of listening devices down on Stone's desk and hands him the laptop.

"You want Shawn to trust you and our room is wired with listening devices and cameras? You all say you knew Shawn's father, and if that's true you would know trust is very high on his priority list. You all should know that Shawn and I are just as smart as the good doctor." Stewart's face is red with anger and his heart is racing.

Stone and Tyler remain still in their seats.

"Wow, you found them quickly. We will send someone up right away to get the rest," Stone says. Stewart, still angry, replies, "Don't bother. I found all of them and the camera." He starts to walk out.

"Wait." Stone stops Stewart and explains to him that he had to test him to see if he was as smart as Doctor Higgins said.

Stewart isn't pleased, and walks out on them. Tyler starts to get up to talk to Stewart but Stone stops him. By now Stewart is in the elevator.

"Boy, that was fast," Tyler expels dumping the listening devices out of the bag onto Stone's desk. "Did he find them all?" Stone asks.

Tyler counts the listening devices one by one. He checks the records of how many devices they put in the room.

"Yeah, he found them all," Tyler says in amazement.

Stone stands up. "What if Shawn doesn't come back? Can we do this without him?"

Tyler, shaking his head, mumbles, "He'll be back."

Stone taps him on the shoulder and commands, "Now it's your turn to officially train them."

Tyler quickly answers, "Don't worry. My team will get them in shape." They both leave the office for the night.

Meanwhile back at Shawn's house, Shawn is passed out in the dark on the living room floor, until a knock at the front door wakes him. He looks down at the bottle of rum in one hand, and in the other is a picture of his parents that was taken before he was born. He looks at the picture again and is overcome with drunken emotion. Tears run down his cheeks with the thought his father is still alive. Then, there is a knock at the front door. A third and fourth consecutively louder .

Shawn stands up. His head is dizzy with rum. He stumbles toward the door and looks through the peephole noticing his neighbor holding some kind of food dish. Shawn opens the door

"There you are Shawn. I was just about to leave." Shawn's neighbor Helen Ross is a nice lady and ever since Shawn's father died she has been bringing over food dishes for Shawn time and again. She notices the rum bottle in Shawn's hand

"Here take this." She says handing Shawn the food dish. Shawn looks down and sees six stuffed pasta shells in red sauce.

"I gave three for you, and three for Stewart because he's over here all the time anyway".

"Much appreciated Helen"

She takes the bottle from Shawn's other hand in one quick motion. Helen walks up to the fireplace and chucks the bottle in, a fireball follows.

"Wooooo," Helen hollers, jumping back from the fire she created.

"You ok, Mrs. Ross?" Shawn asks, holding back his smile.

"I'm fine, now give me that food so I can fix you a plate." Mrs Ross takes the food from Shawn's hands.

"Come sit Shawn and tell me why you are drinking so much? Why are you so upset?" She puffs pulling out plates and silverware like she has done a thousand times before.

"So tell me Shawn, what's troubling you?" she asks again, handing him a plate of chicken casserole. Shawn can't tell Mrs. Ross the truth about how his father is still alive and that he worked with aliens from another planet, so he makes something up to her.

"It was my birthday today and losing my dad, I guess the loneliness got to me."

"HAPPY BIRTHDAY and I get that Shawn but you are never alone especially since you have me, your aunt, cousin CJ to help you and Stewart.

"You're right, I still have a lot of people who care for me." Shawn says with a mouthful of food. Mrs. Ross and Shawn talk for a while and after some time she leaves with a much calmer Shawn by himself. After she has left Shawn goes to his father's office and kicks open the door. He then sits at his father's desk and turns on the desk light. Everything so clean; nothing out of place. The chess board is still set up the way he and his father left it during their last game together.

With no idea what it is he's looking for Shawn rummages aimlessly through desk drawers. He notices there's no computer and one of the drawers is locked. He picks up the letter opener off the desk and starts to pick the lock with no luck. He pushes his seat back from the desk and, dissatisfied, hurls the letter opener at a picture that hangs on the wall in front of him. Instead of sticking in the wall it makes a sound of hitting metal and falls to the ground. Shawn is perplexed, gets up to investigate. He picks up the letter opener and touches the picture where it was struck. He takes the picture down off the wall and notices nothing but the paneling there. Shawn is confused but he is positive he heard the sound of metal. He pokes through the hole with the letter opener point and hears metal clashing with the stainless steel letter opener. He puts his hand flat on the wall revealing a slight recess unnoticeable to the naked eye. Shawn forces the recess in. The section of the wall Shawn has his hand on disappears revealing a small HOLLON wall safe with a turn dial. Shawn studies the dial with a furrowed brow thinking of the series of numbers that will open the door. Maybe his father's birthday, 4/14/60. Shawn jostles the handle but still the door remains locked. Shawn spins the dial three times to reset the cylinder and begins again. This time he uses his own birthday, 9/19/20. A dull thud is heard. Shawn enthusiastically grabs the handle and swings it in an upward motion. Simultaneously, he pulls the door toward him.

Inside is a shoe box. Shawn takes it out and looks inside. He finds stocks, birth certificates, and old pictures of Shawn and his mother. He throws the box down and hears a faint rattling sound. He picks the shoe box back up and turns it over. All the papers drop on the ground and a key ring with two small keys rests on the papers.

He picks up the key, goes back to the desk. He tries the first key. It doesn't work, so he tries the second key and the lock opens. Shawn takes a deep breath before opening the drawer, not knowing what he's going to find. With some force, he pulls it open quickly. He looks down and sees a small metal box and a folder with papers in it. He picks up the folder and begins to read. It contains a list of the A.H.R team members.

1. Tyler Parks -Team leader & pilot - Noraian
2. Bobby Hawkins - Co-pilot - Noraian
3. Matt Franks - Ex-Navy Seals, gunner - Human
4. James Starkly - Marine sniper, family man, Gunnery - Human
5. Samantha Stone- Computer expert, General Stone's daughter, Army brat
6. Sidney (Sid) Price -Team mechanic & inventor- Noraian
7. Crystal Washburn- Interpreter & communications works on space station
8. Brad (Scanvokia) - Pilot, in charge of Earth Base, Noraian soldiers on NORA - Noraian

Shawn flips to the next page and on it there are blueprints of the seven floor complex in which the team is stationed. It shows and labels each floor:

First floor: Supplies, armory garage and vehiclegarage
Second floor: Personnel offices
Third floor: Living quarters
Fourth Floor: Communications room and computer lab
Fifth floor: Briefing / Meeting Hall
Sixth Floor: Training, combat training
Seventh Floor: Training, swimming, exercise rooms

After that is the history of all the team members. Shawn goes right to Tyler's file, which is empty. This angers Shawn and he then tosses all the papers on his father's desk. A small envelope slides out from the middle of all the papers. He quickly reaches for it and opens it up. Inside is a letter.

Shawn,

If you are reading this letter I'm either dead or in some kind of trouble. I wish that I was there to answer all the questions you have. You are probably very confused and knowing you like I do, very angry right now.

You will meet General T. Stone. He is one of my oldest friends. We started this program together a long time ago. Tyler Parks is another friend of mine. Outside of you and Stewart they are the closest family I've got. The three of us formed A.H.R, which Stone will fill you in on. I have set you up with a very trustworthy team; they come from all kinds of backgrounds, as do you, my son. Listen to all of them carefully. They will help you become what I know you can become.

In my drawer you will find a metal box. In It is a small cyclical disk. It's the first key that will lead you to the first piece of the puzzle. The first piece will be for you and Stewart. You will find that I have left help for the both of you along the way. Hopefully, it will guide you through your trials.

I tried to keep all of this from you but I now know that I was wrong. I hope you can forgive me. Shawn, your family needs you. I need you. Remember to always have an open mind and always trust in yourself and your abilities. Tell Stewart I need him to have his thinking game on. He is very important to solving the clues that I have left for the both of you. These are things only you two need to know. I have set up free passage and living quarters everywhere for the two of you. I love you both so much. Be careful and I hope to see you both really soon.

Shawn, I left something for you, it's where both our hearts lie, and it will help you as it did me through these trying times ahead.

Love, Dad

P.S - Shawn, please give the other envelope to General Stone when you meet him. Thank you.

Shawn folds up the letter, puts it back in the envelope, and places it back on the desk. He wipes the tears from his face. Then, he gets up and goes to the hallway closet to grab a black knapsack. He heads back to the office and places all the papers and the small metal box into the knapsack and turns off the desk lamp. He leaves the office with the knapsack, and goes to his room.

Shawn is not the neatest person in the world. It's not that he is dirty, he showers and keeps his clothes clean, but he is unorganized. He walks into his room where there are piles of clean clothes everywhere. Like most days, his bed is not made. There are papers thrown all around his room. However, Shawn can find anything he needs, although anybody else would be lost. He grabs a big army duffle bag and starts throwing clothes into it. These are clothes that he frequently wears on a day to day basis. He grabs his small carrying bag with his toothbrush and other stuff like that, and then throws them in with his clothes. He zips it up and walks out to the living room. He throws the two bags by the front door, and crashes on the couch for the rest of the night.

The next morning, Shawn is woken by the sun glaring through the window. He has only been sleeping for three hours, but he pushes himself to wake up. He wipes the crust from his eyes and gets up. He grabs the black knapsack, places it over his shoulders, and picks up the army bag. Then he turns around to see the inside of the house as though it might be for the last time. He locks the front door on his way to his motorcycle. He places the army bag right inside the garage and then calls Stewart to have someone come and pick it up for him. He doesn't get Stewart, so he leaves him a message on his voicemail. He hops on his bike and heads to the place where both their hearts lie.

Shawn pulls up to the cemetery where this madness began. He walks up to his mother's grave and sits next to her tombstone. He says a quick prayer that his father taught him, which he says every visit. He then slides his hand over his mom's name, wishing like always that he had the chance to know her, and then starts to dig a hole for the flowers he bought yesterday. About a foot down he comes across the feeling of plastic. He realizes that it's a plastic bag wrapped around a small wooden box. He finishes digging out the box and notices that it's the box he made for his father when he was in school.

Shawn takes the box out of the plastic bag and opens it up. Inside is a titanium round disk with symbols and a weird picture on it. Shawn turns the picture over and realizes it's a picture of his mom holding him for the very first time. On the sides of her is his dad and Tyler, which brings tension into his heart. This is the only picture Shawn has seen of him and his mother, and with Tyler being in it, it pisses Shawn off.

He rests against the tombstone for a while, looking at the picture and going over everything that he has learned in the last twenty four hours. Dark clouds start rolling in from the south. Lightning is flashing from far away. Shawn stands up and walks to his bike to head towards the NASA compound.

CHAPTER FOUR

Stewart wakes up and notices that Shawn didn't sleep in his bed. He gets up in a state of panic, in fear of his friends' whereabouts. He runs out of the room, running into Franks.

"Have you seen Shawn?" Stewart asks.

Franks doesn't know what to say so he burst out with, "No, Why?"

"Because he didn't sleep in his bed."

Stewart rushes back to the bedroom. He finds his phone and as he picks it up. The phone is beeping letting Stewart know that he has a voice message. He calls his voicemail. The message was from Shawn simply stating to have Stone send one of his men to his house to pick up his belongings that sit right in the garage, and also to tell General Stone that he will be there later today, He has to do something first. Stewart is relieved that Shawn is coming back. Now Stewart can get comfortable in his new surroundings, which means getting under the skin of his new housemates.

Outside the complex Shawn pulls up on his motorcycle. Waiting there is Tyler. He is leaning against the small building. Shawn pulls right up in front of Tyler and takes off his helmet.

"Don't worry, you don't have to send your attack dogs after me, I'm here," says Shawn.

Tyler looks up at Shawn and says, "I wasn't worried, after all you are your father's son, are you not?"

"Yes, I am."

"If you want me to call and have your bike put away I will." Tyler tells him.

Shawn answers back quickly, "Nobody rides this bike but me."

With a small smile on his face, Tyler replies, "What? Not even Stewart?"

"Oh no, Stewart's good with a lot of computers and all that geek stuff, but he lacks hand eye coordination."

Tyler shakes his head and laughs. "Well then let me show you where to put your bike."

Tyler hops on the back of the bike and Shawn takes off in a wheelie. They drive around to the side of a big warehouse to the garage. Tyler points Shawn to the garage door that is slightly open. Shawn races the bike through the door, which gets the attention of two nearby guards. He parks the bike with a guy working on a truck. By the time they stop the bike the two guards are right by their side. Both are very built and well groomed, with shaved faces.

"EXCUSE ME. EXCUSE ME. You can't be in here," one of the guards says as Tyler gets off the bike. "Oh, sorry, Mr. Parks, we didn't know it was you, sorry." The two guards walk away quickly.

"O.K. I guess you do have pull here." Shawn says, which brings a small smile to his face.

With all the noise and commotion, it gets the attention of the man working on one of the SUVs. A medium size man with tattoos on his arms, full of meaning only to him, walks up to them. His face is slightly elongated with big white teeth that show even when he's not smiling, which go well with his big green eyes.

"I told you, Tyler, the guards are going to get you one of these days," the man says as he approaches.

"Shawn, I want you to meet someone," Tyler says.

Shawn cuts Tyler off and says, "You must be Sidney Price. I'm Shawn Higgins." He puts his hand out to Sidney.

Sidney looks at Shawn. "Oh right. You're the doctor's son. Glad to meet you". Sidney is a medium built man, but he is fast thinking and a fast mover. He talks really fast due to all the energy drinks he throws down his throat.

Tyler, totally blown away that Shawn knew who Sidney was, taps Shawn on the shoulder.

"How did you know his name?"

Shawn turns his head back to Tyler and simply says, "I've done my homework. You'd be surprised to know what I know." He turns his attention back to Sidney, leaving Tyler baffled in thought.

"So, Sidney, what are you working on?"

"Wait, don't tell me, you are into cars?" Sidney asks with excitement that someone else might share the same interest that he has.

"Well, let's put it this way, I won't get lost down here."

Sidney looks confused over Shawn's remark.

"Yes, Sidney, I'm good with cars," Shawn says bluntly and to the point.

"Cool!" Sidney has a huge smile across his face showing off all those pearly white teeth.

The three men walk over to the SUV. Shawn looks over the building as he walks with Sidney. This building has a 30 foot high ceiling inside and about 200 vehicles, ranging between motorcycles to tractor trailers. While Tyler and Sidney talk about the repairs on the SUV Shawn starts to wander around looking at everything. The first cars that Shawn walks up to were a row of twenty 2011 Black Dodge Chargers. As he looks at the cars, Tyler walks up behind him.

"Like what you see?"

"These cars are nice!" Shawn's mouth hits the floor. He's like a kid in a candy store.

"Come with me, you haven't seen anything yet."

Tyler walks Shawn around the building showing him SUV's, jeeps, a mess of dirt bikes, four wheelers and motorcycles. He explains to Shawn that they have a vehicle for any conflict. But by now Shawn has already stopped paying attention to Tyler because he is checking out the bikes, one by one.

After Shawn stops drooling over the bikes he catches up to

Tyler at the elevator doors. Tyler scans his eye and the elevator opens and both of them enter. He asks Shawn to follow him to get clearance for the complex. Shawn didn't mind because he figures where there were computers there would be Stewart. He wants to see him and tell him about what he found in his father's office. The doors opened and sure enough Stewart was sitting right in front of the computers.

Stewart turns around in his chair to see who was coming in.

"About time you got yourself here. Everybody's so worried that you jumped ship, but I was like, 'No, relax he'll be here'."

"Sure you did buddy, you were probably the first one to grab the phone book to start looking for my replacement," Shawn says.

Tyler starts laughing as the two friends joke back and forth. Shawn gets all the clearances for the complex from Tyler. Meanwhile, Stewart is starting to get the subtle hints of Shawn's body language, signaling him to leave.

"Hey man, have you seen our living quarters yet?" Stewart asks Shawn.

"Wait a minute, I have to share a room with you? This should be fun," Shawn jokingly says out loud, as the two of them head towards the elevator door. Shawn and Stewart exit the elevator where Franks is still sitting on the couch watching television.

"Didn't I leave you in that position three hours ago?" Stewart asks Franks.

"Hey look, you found Shawn. I guess you can stop worrying that he won't come back," says Franks.

Stewart, laughing as he turns to Shawn, says, "He's joking." His face turned bright red; brighter than his hair.

"Got my back," Shawn jokes. "You knew I was coming back to the compound right?"

Stewart just keeps saying over and over, "He's joking."

Franks then says to Shawn, "Are you staying?" Shawn shows him his ID badge. He then tells Franks that he's here to get his father back, dead or alive. He shakes Frank's hand and follows Stewart to their room.

Shawn walks right to his bag that sits on his bed. He throws the black knapsack down onto the floor. "Feels like I've been carrying the kitchen sink in there".

He looks at Stewart who is scanning.

"What are you doing?" Shawn says.

"Scanning for bugs. I found over twenty of them here last night."

Shawn, shaking his head, asks, "Did you say anything to Stone?"

"I did, but he said he wanted to test me."

"Do you believe him?"

"I'm checking tonight, what you think," Stewart says.

"So, did you find anything?" Shawn asks, with hesitation in his voice.

"No," Stewart says. Then he asks Shawn where he was last night.

"I went back to my parent's house."

"So what did you find?"

Shawn is now busy unpacking, throwing clothes all-around his bed. He grabs some clothes so he can take a shower. He hands Stewart the black knapsack and tells him to look over the computer files to see if he can open them. Stewart laughs at the fact that Shawn thinks he might have problems opening any computer files. He starts looking through all the papers first to understand what he might be looking for on the computer. Then he tries to open the computer files, as Shawn heads into the shower.

A half an hour passes, Shawn exits the shower wearing black cargo pants, like most days. He is a creature of habit. He likes certain things, like these cargo pants, and shorts, and T-Shirts of any kind no matter what they say on them. He also wears flannel jackets all the time. One thing he always wears or keeps on him at all times is a ball cap of his favorite sports team.

Shawn throws the towel he was using to dry his hair on the floor next to his bed. Stewart gets up and picks up the towel behind him. Shawn pays no attention to this while he puts on his shirt and sits down on the spot where Stewart was sitting. While Stewart hangs Shawn's towel off the hook behind the door and tells him, "Yes, I got into one, it had no password of any kind. You are not going to believe it but-"

Shawn cuts him off. "After the things I read in those files, nothing will surprise me."

Stewart sits down next to Shawn, and grabs the laptop. He opens up the file. In it are plans for a spaceship that seats ten, has a medical room in it, and a small computer room. It can travel through space without a problem.

"Do you see that?" Stewart's pointing out that the plane looks like a mini stealth bomber.

There is a knock at the door. Franks pops his head into the bedroom and says that he has finished making dinner.

Stewart closes the laptop quickly and blurts out, "Great! I'm starving. Be right out."

Franks leaves the room as quickly as he came in. Shawn goes over to his bag and begins throwing more clothes on the ground while looking for a pair of socks. He finds a pair and puts them on. When he finishes throwing his clothes around, his half of the room looks like a bomb went off. Stewart just stands there shaking his head in disbelief. They both leave the room and head down the hallway where Franks is in the kitchen fixing his plate of dinner.

"It's good to see you got off the couch, way to go," Stewart says sarcastically.

"What are you doing?" Shawn asks Stewart. The two of them are on one side of the counter, and Franks is on one side. "Stop trying to be funny Stewart. He's a lot bigger than you."

"You're right, Shawn, I'm a lot bigger than him, but for some reason he just doesn't care," Franks says, as Stewart fixes his plate of food as though nothing has happened.

"That's him trying to be funny. Trust me, he could be a lot funnier than you think."

"You mean he can be even funnier than now? I can't wait," Franks says sarcastically.

"Hey, what are you two talking about? Me? Please let it be about me," Stewart says.

"See what I mean? A whole lot more fun." Shawn gets up to get his food and slaps Stewart in the back of the head as he walks past. Stewart sits down next to Frank's at the counter.

"So, when did you get off the couch and cook a mean dish?"

"This is my day off, I only get two. As the both of you will find out really soon training is a bitch and it takes a lot out of you. So on my days off I watch football when in season, or baseball."

Stewart sits there eating his food and listening to Frank's.

"I know you're a computer geek and probably don't know what sports are, so never mind."

Shawn sits down listening to the conversation and laughs. Then, Stewart starts throwing sports stats, teams, and players, blurting them randomly at Franks.

"I hope gambling is not a deal buster because if so Stewart should just go home," Shawn says. He has a smile over his face as Stewart continues rambling stats.

"You are full of surprises, Stewart," Franks says. "Having you on my side I might break even this football season."

"Probably not with Stewart's help. He isn't that good," Shawn says to himself.

"So, where are all the other team members?" Shawn asks Franks.

Franks finishes what he was chewing, and then he takes a sip of his beer and says, "Sidney is in the garage, he should be here soon covered in grease. The others should be back tonight, and James Starkly will probably be here late tomorrow. He wanted to spend time with his family before we started training."

"People keep talking about training. What kind of training? I'm not a runner," Stewart says, making sure everybody in the room hears him loud and clear.

"You better learn how to be a runner." The loud but stern voice is heard from the background. General Stone startles the boys causing them to nearly fall out of their seats. In the meantime

Franks is standing, and saluting the General. Shawn turns to the General.

"General, I have something for you, can you please come with me?"

General Stone follows Shawn down to his room leaving Stewart and Franks talking in the kitchen.

"Next time let me know that Stone is behind me. He is like a ghost. I didn't even hear the doors open," Stewart says to Franks. Franks has no response other than laughter.

Back in his room, Shawn hands Stone the letter his father said to give him. "What's this?" Stone asks, as he takes the sealed letter

"Last night I was rummaging through my father's office trying to make sense of all this." As Shawn is talking he goes and sits on his bed. He takes a deep breath and a good look around, then says, "Hell, the people around this place seem to have known my father better than me."

Stone walks over to Shawn and sits right beside him.

"You don't know us, but everybody here knows you and Stewart because you two were all he could talk about. How he wished he could show you both all of this." Stone places his hand on Shawn's back. Shawn slumps over in disbelief.

"I read last night how you helped my father start all of this."

Stone laughs. "Your father started it. I just stood there at my post talking to him, probably disturbing him more than helping him."

Shawn looks Stone right in his eyes. "How did you learn to trust the aliens, and how do they treat us on their home planet?"

Stone takes his hand off Shawn's back and stands up.

"I'm not going to lie to you Shawn. At first it was hard. Their planet is different from ours. We can breathe on some of their planets and on some of the other planets we need breathing devices. Tyler's planet is much smaller than Earth. They pretty much have one, maybe two civilizations on their planets. On some of the other planets if we are seen we will be tortured and publicly killed."

Shawn cuts him off. "Are you sure my father is even alive?

And if so, what can Stewart and I do? We're not trained. I know my father thought we could do this but even he made mistakes." Shawn stands up with his back to Stone.

"Don't worry, your father has put a great team together and if I think you or Stewart won't be able to do this mission I will pull the plug until you both are ready."

Shawn turns around. "Stewart is a computer person. He's not really strong in the athletic department anymore."

Stone smiles. "Don't worry about Stewart in that department because Franks has become quite fond of your friend Stewart. He's going to pay a lot of attention to him. Besides, your father trusts in the people around you and they will get both of you in shape and ready for this mission."

Stewart walks into the room. "Sorry, am I interrupting anything?"

"No Stewart, I was just leaving. You boys need to get plenty of sleep tonight. The next month or so is going to be very tough, but I think you both will do fine," Stone says as he leaves the room.

Shawn turns to Stewart and tells him to take this all seriously and learn everything he can.

"Don't worry, Shawn, my game face will be on. He was like a father to me, too. I want to help bring him back just as much as you do."

Shawn puts his hand on the back of his head. "I know you do. Let's get some sleep because I'm tired."

Shawn pushes the clothes off his bed. They land in a pile upon the floor and he is able to lie down to go to sleep. Stewart throws his arms up in disgust over the fact that Shawn is such a slob, but says nothing. He turns the light off.

CHAPTER FIVE

The alarm goes off at six in the morning. Shawn gets up right away, while Stewart puts his pillow over his head to try to muffle the sound of the alarm.

"Get up, Stewart!" Shawn screams as he throws his pillow at him. Stewart takes Shawn's pillow and puts it under his head. Shawn heads to the bathroom.

"You better be up by the time I get out of the bathroom or I'm going to get you up."

After twenty minutes in the bathroom Shawn comes out only to see Stewart still lying in bed. Stewart has to be one of the hardest people to get out of bed. If you try to wake him up he will at first get angry, and then as you continue to try to wake him up he begins to throw punches, as well as kicks.

Shawn, knowing this, walks up to the side of Stewart's bed, grabs the two handles on the side of the mattress, and flips Stewart over.

Stewart pops up in shock. "What the hell, Shawn, I was getting up." His face was as red as his hair.

"I know you were, I was just helping you," Shawn smiles. "That's what friends do."

Ten minutes later Stewart finally meets Shawn in the kitchen area.

"There you are! About time you're ready. Wait. You're wearing that to workout? Blue jeans, a leather jacket and your black boots?"

Stewart says nothing at first and goes to get a cup of coffee.

"Wait, workout? Oh no, I'm not working out. I'm going to watch you work out and I'm going to drink my coffee."

Stewart finishes making his coffee and follows Shawn to the elevator. They both enter and go to the seventh floor. Once there, they walk down a small hallway to get to the gym. The gym is divided into two sections. The front section has exercise bikes and elliptical machines. In the back part sits weight benches and treadmills. The twelve foot deep swimming pool is on the other side of a glass wall, with a glass door as the entrance.

Shawn notices Franks over at the weight benches. Stewart notices a dark haired girl in a tight black jogging suit on the elliptical in the front of the room. Stewart watches her as they head towards Franks, who is in the middle of one of his reps.

Franks stops as Shawn and Stewart approach. He sits up from under the weight bar and the soldier that was spotting him walks away.

"Oh my god, tell me you did not wear jeans to work out?" Franks says as he sits there staring at Stewart.

Stewart is not paying any attention to Franks. He is still watching the dark haired girl.

"Are you even listening to me, Stewart?"

"What? Yeah, I'm listening." Stewart turns to Franks.

"Is that a coffee? You have to be in the worst shape ever. You probably don't even care. Hell, you probably smoke cigarettes, too," Franks says as his temper begins to flare. He takes working out seriously, and Stewart is making a mockery of it.

"Yes, but I roll my own, so that's good, right? Who is the girl, Franks?" Stewart asks.

Franks shakes his head and laughs. "Player, you got no chance with that one."

Stewart takes that as a challenge, and with no fear he walks over to her. He introduces himself, but there is no response. He notices she's wearing headphones so he taps her on her shoulder.

She jumps and almost falls off the elliptical. She turns to him with her green eyes, her black semi curly hair is parted in the middle and she has a firm, but skinny body.

"Can I help you with something?"

Stewart starts to introduce himself, but she cuts him off and walks away.

"Hey! Where are you going? Oh alright, then go take your shower or something, we will talk later."

Stewart watches the girl leave, her hips swaying back and forth with every step. He knows he's going to catch it from Franks and Shawn and that they're going to give him grief. He doesn't really care though. All he can think of is that beautiful girl. He walks with his head held high looking at both Franks and Shawn, ready to take whatever they can dish out. Before they can say anything he blurts out, "Well, that didn't go exactly the way I planned, but hell, I just met her. The game has begun."

Franks laughs as he puts weights on the weight bar for Shawn.

"So the game begins. What's your first move, playa?" he says to Stewart, spotting Shawn.

Shawn finishes and sits up all out of breath. Stewart starts to chuckle.

"What's so funny? He just lifted over a hundred and fifty pounds, ten times. You probably can't lift it once," Franks confidently says.

Stewart just stands there drinking his coffee. He says nothing, but puts a half smile on his face between every sip.

"What? No witty comeback, that's what I thought, you can't even lift it once."

Once again Stewart says nothing. He just drinks his coffee then blurts out, "I'll bet you fifty dollars that I can do ten just like Shawn." Stewart pauses and looks at Franks. "So, what do you say? Put your money where your mouth is, Franks."

Franks answers quickly. "Sure. You got a bet. Do you even have fifty dollars to pay me when you lose?"

Stewart pays no mind to that comment. He puts his coffee

down on the bench next to them, and takes off his leather jacket and hands it to Shawn. The other soldiers working out in the gym hear what's happening and surround the three of them as Stewart finishes up stretching. He sits down on the workout bench and the soldiers start making side bets with each other. The noise level escalates. Franks is standing with his chest pushed way out so he can brag to the other soldiers. Stewart gets in place as Franks gets behind him to spot.

Stewart begins as everybody is talking, some cheering Stewart on, and some wishing him to fail. He pretends to struggle on the first two, giving Frank some confidence of winning their bet. Franks even starts to mock Stewart. Thanks to the mocking Stewart is able to knock out the last eight very quickly, just like a professional weight lifter. The soldiers are blown away and they start handing money back and forth to each other. Stewart stands up, grabs his jacket from Shawn, puts it on, grabs his coffee and starts to walk out. He then turns to Franks and says, "Hey, give the money to Shawn and I will get it from him later." The soldiers are pointing and laughing at Franks, who is looking at Stewart not paying any attention to everyone else around him.

Stewart leaves and Franks is just floored. He turns to Shawn and says, "I just walked right into that one, didn't I?"

Shawn smiles and wipes his face with a towel. He sits nearby as the soldiers go back to what they were doing. "Yes, yes you did, and hey you even lost fifty dollars."

Franks, shaking his head, says, "Looking at him I would bet every time that he wouldn't be able to do that."

"And you would lose every time, Franks," Shawn says.

"So tell me, how did he do it? Look at him! What is he, one hundred and thirty five pounds soaking wet?"

Shawn, who is using a dumb bell, starts to laugh and looks up at Franks, "He used to be on our high school baseball team. He was one of the best players on the team, had a mean slider and the fastball was really fast. He always worked the hardest; he even pushed me at times," Shawn says, starting to run out of breathe from lifting the dumb bell.

"What happened? He drinks coffee like water and he smokes," Franks asks him.

"In a game he took a line drive to his knee and shattered it, and he never played again. He even stopped working out. He got into computers and all that stuff."

Franks sits down on the bench next to Shawn, takes a sip of his water and says, "Is he still hurt? Because that could be bad for us?"

"Nah. He's fine. I just think recovery was really hard on him, and I don't think he ever wants to go through that again." Shawn continues by saying, "Besides, he already has fifty dollars, thanks to you. Do you want to underestimate his abilities again? I'll go get him."

"No, that's ok, I like my money," Franks says with a chuckle to follow.

Meanwhile, in the computer room Stewart is playing games, when he suddenly hears a woman's voice say, "What the hell do you think you are doing?" He turns in his chair to see who it is. Then she says, "Oh my god, what are you following me now? Get out of my chair."

Stewart says nothing, and gets up. After a few moments he says, "Hi, my name is Stewart, and you are?"

"Well, Stewart, do you know you're playing video games on a United States Government computer?" The woman seems to be very upset and still refuses to give Stewart her name, but this doesn't stop him.

"So, what are you working on that's so important that it couldn't wait until I was done playing? I was just about to beat my game, what is more important than that?"

"Playing your video game is not allowed." She turns around to face the computer.

"Wait, do you want to play?"

The girl, obviously agitated, replies, "What? No, I don't know what to play! Haven't you been listening to me?"

Stewart is having a tough time listening to her; as he has been distracted by staring at her in her light green sweatpants with the word ARMY down one side of the pant leg. She has a white t-shirt on with a black sports bra. The girl is still trying to turn off the game when she accidentally un-pauses it.

"You better defend yourself before you die," Stewart says to her.

The girl tries to play, but she ends up getting killed. "Ok, how do you play? There's no way I'm dying like that."

Stewart shows her the controls, and she tries again, and again, and again.

"So, are you going to tell me your name?" Stewart asks again.

She then says, "When you earn it." A gentle smile stretches across her face.

"Ok, it's like that," Stewart answers. The girl nods her head as she plays the game, and becomes overjoyed like a kid at the candy shop.

They both continue to play the game until the General walks in. "What's going on here?" He screams at both Stewart and the girl. She jumps out of her seat to salute the General.

"Nothing sir. I'm sorry sir." She nervously says.

Stewart stands up and doesn't salute General Stone, but he takes the blame for playing the video game.

"Ok, whatever, I don't care about that. You two need to get on the same page. Stewart, you listen to her and learn the computer programs." Stone leaves the room, leaving the two of them alone again.

"Ok. What are you working on? Maybe I can earn some brownie points with you?" The girl starts to blush a little, but turns from Stewart to keep him from noticing. However, Stewart does notice, but he keeps it to himself.

"Looks like you have been trying to break this code for a long time?"

"How do you know that?" she curiously asks.

"Well, it seems like you can't get past the second stage, and that you run out of time on the others."

The girl nods her head, but says nothing.

"How many stages are there?" Stewart asks.

The girl hesitates at first, but then quietly says, "Four."

"Excuse me? What was that?" Stewart asks.

"I said four stages, and the first one was easy but then a timer starts, and I keep getting locked out."

"Can I try?" Stewart asks her. Again the girl hesitates, but gets up. Before beginning Stewart turns on three other computers.

"What are you doing? The computer is already on, why are you turning them on? Get up. You don't know what you're doing," she says as she tries to get Stewart out of the chair.

Stewart is not paying any attention to her, and he starts typing really fast. He starts rolling the chair to all the computers, almost running over the girl in the process. Behind them enters General Stone again, and just then Stewart screams out, "and…DONE!"

"What? What do you mean, 'done'? There's no way you broke that code," she says, pushing him and the chair out the way.

Stewart says nothing. He just gets up, and starts to leave, when General Stone says, "Good job, Stewart."

Stewart nods, smiles, grabs his jacket and continues out of the room when he hears, "Hey, my name is Sam."

"See? Now was that so hard?" Stewart says.

"Wait, are you going to tell me how you did that?" Sam replies.

Stewart turns back to her and simply says, "When you earn it. Thank you, and goodnight." Stewart then walks out to the elevator smiling, leaving both Stone and Sam behind. Sam is smiling at the response, and Stone just looks at Stewart and Sam staring at each other. Stone says nothing, and Sam doesn't either.

Stewart exits the elevator. Sid is sitting on the couch watching cartoons. "Cartoons. Way to go Sid, not caring what everyone thinks."

"You know Sid?" Shawn sitting on one of the bar stools asks Stewart.

"Of course I do, I probably met him before you, right Sid."

Sid throws one of his hands up to respond.

"If he wasn't into his cartoons he would tell you." Stewart says.

Stewart walks over to Shawn and Franks who is eating a big old bowl of his pasta.

"You know Stewart, you really surprised me today. Not only did you do ten reps in the gym, you also got fifty dollars of my money." Franks says as he sucks a long spaghetti noodle up in his mouth.

Stewart takes off his jacket and sets it on the chair. He then grabs a can of soda out of the refrigerator and while opening it he says to Franks, "I feel really bad about that, I kind of took advantage of you."

Franks responds quickly, "So you are going to let me keep my money?"

"Well maybe, how about this: We will go double or nothing."

"Now, what do you have in mind?" Franks asks with some hesitations in his voice.

"I bet you fifty dollars that I can get Sam to go out on a date with me, and yes, I know her name is Sam," Stewart says.

"Is that all you know?"

"I know her first name. That's all I need to know to get a date with her." Stewart says with confidence.

"You know what, it's a deal. If Sam agrees to go on a date with you, then you win." Franks laughs, and says it again. "Sam."

Just then Sam enters the living quarters.

"Did you say my name, Franks," she asks.

"No, Sam." Franks says back to her. She goes over and sits on part of the couch.

"Come on Sid, not cartoons again. All you ever watch is cartoons."

Sid ignores her while she talks.

Franks sees what kind of mood Sam is in, and then turns to Stewart. He whispers, "Go ahead, playboy. Go ask her out; win the bet."

Stewart looks at Shawn, and gets up and heads over to Sam, but this time he's feeling a little bit more comfortable compared to the first time in the gym.

"Hey. Can I speak to you?"

Sam looks up at Stewart, and looks over at Sid and tells him to get lost. Sid listens and goes over to sit in the kitchen with Franks and Shawn.

"Watch Sid, loverboy is about to strike out with Sam for the second time today, and I'm going to get my money back." Franks does a little dance of happiness over the fact of getting one over on Stewart, which sweetens the bet between the two.

"So, are you going to tell me how you broke the code?" Sam asks Stewart, as she begins to get a little flirty with Stewart.

"I don't know. I'm not sure you earned it," he says back to her. Stewart looks back at the guys in the kitchen, and back at Sam. "Let me think. Will you go out with me one night and let me show you my part of town?" He again looks back at the guys, and back at Sam.

"How much is the bet?" Sam asks.

"Hundred dollars, but I was going to ask you out anyway, this way Franks just pays for some of the date." He smiles, and even gets a smile from Sam.

She sits back on the couch, and sits up again. "Fine I'll go out on a date with you, but I get half, and you tell me how you broke that computer code."

"Deal, but I will tell you on the date, just in case we have nothing to talk about you know if i find you boring" Stewart says with a big smile on his face. Sam slaps him in his chest with the back of her hand

"You're bad Stewart." she says flirting a little bit back at him.

Sam pops up out of her seat, which makes Franks throw up his hands in joy. Then she starts to walk away, right as she gets to the three men in the kitchen area, she turns to Stewart

"Stewart Saturday we'll have that date ok." She turns to the three men, smiles and walks down the hallway to her quarters.

"Nooooooo! " is heard throughout the room. Sid and Shawn start laughing.

Stewart walks over to them. "Ok, big man! Pay up!"

Franks pulls out his wallet, and starts counting out the hundred dollars, tearing a little bit off each dollar as he drops them down.

James Starkly walks in. He is a stocky man with a marine buzzcut and a tightly shaved face. Today he is wearing green camo cargo pants with a t-shirt that reads, "Fishing isn't easy, but marriage is harder." He also has on newly polished boots, and there is a very large duffle bag on his back, and another that he's holding. James sees Franks counting his money.

"What are you doing, Franks?" James asks.

"I'm counting out a hundred dollars," Franks tells him in a sad voice.

"I see that but why?"

"I lost a bet to Stewart today." Franks says to him.

"Who's Stewart?"

"Hi, I'm Stewart, and this is Shawn." Stewart introduces them both.

"Right, Doctor Higgins's son, it's nice to meet you both. Shawn, your father is a great man." James puts his bags on the floor and puts his hand out to both of them.

"I promise Shawn that we will get your father back." Both Shawn and Stewart extend their hand in return.

James asks everyone in the room "Tell me again how you, Stewart, won a hundred dollars from Franks?"

As Franks hands Stewart the money he tells James the situation, about how he lost one bet earlier, and another when Sam agreed to go out with Stewart.

James says nothing at first then says. "You might be strong Franks, but you're not the sharpest pencil in the box." Then he turns to Stewart, and says, "You, my new friend, must have giant balls or maybe a death wish, asking Sam out on a date."

Stewart is pleased with himself once again. Shawn, on the

other hand, has his doubts and asks, "James, what's the big deal if Stewart goes out with Sam"?

"Wait Franks didn't tell you guys about Sam"? James says while laughing.

"No, I wanted it to be a surprise. You know, for my personal entertainment," Franks says.

"What is she an alien or something?" Shawn asks, as he looks at both of them waiting for an answer.

"No, she's way worse than that. She is General Stone's daughter!" James blurts out in a joyful laughter.

Shawn looks at Stewart with disbelief and says, "Great. Stone's daughter. Of course she has to be Stone's daughter." He sits on one of the stools and puts his head in his hands saying Stewart's name over and over again.

"What are you so worried about? The General and I are like this." Stewart says as he crosses two of his fingers.

Shawn picks up his head out of his hands and looks at Stewart.

"What are you talking about? He makes fun of you and he also calls you a wise ass."

"You are right, Franks, this is going to be good," James says as he picks up his bags. "If nothing else you two will make it a lot more entertaining around here."

Stewart smiles and agrees to James's comment. Shawn just shakes his head.

CHAPTER SIX

The next morning Stewart and Shawn meet another team member when Franks brings them to the motion simulator. Waiting there is Bobby Hawkins. He is all decked out in his flight simulator suit. His solid jet black hair is combed to the left, and it matches his dark black eye color. His face is covered with tiny pieces of toilet paper from his morning shave.

Bobby turns to the three of them.

"You are looking at a machine that will test hand and eye coordination, and if nothing else, your ability to handle motion sickness." Shawn looks through the clear glass window. Five feet down is a one man pod that is spinning around at a rapid pace.

"What you are looking at is a one man operated pod attached to a big beam which allows it to avoid foam obstacles that appear in different places." Stewart now begins to look at the spinning pod through the same window as Shawn.

"To make the pod avoid the obstacles one must control it by going up or down as it spins. Shawn and Stewart watch as the pod races around avoiding the foam walls.

"Who's there now?" Shawn asks, cutting off Bobby from speaking, not caring who answers his question. He gets his answer from General Stone, who walks in wearing his army cargo pants tucked into black army boots, an army green t-shirt, and a green ball cap.

"Actually, Tyler is in there right now. Next I want either you or Stewart to try it." He hands them both flight simulator suits. Stewart grabs his and quickly throws it on, announcing to everyone that he wants to go next.

"Now remember the object is to avoid the foam walls," Bobby tells him. "Tyler will show you both how to control the pod when you are down there."

Franks cuts Bobby off this time and says, "Tell them about the game we play."

"Game? What game?" Stewart asks.

"The game is simple. We keep a record of who can avoid the most foam walls. The walls pop out in different places every time around. We keep track of how many times a team member can miss the walls out of fifty times, each one a different scenario." Shawn, who has been watching Tyler control the pod the entire time, asks, "Who has the record?"

Bobby blurts out, "Tyler has been on top since we started this game four years ago. He is 38. I'm in second with 24."

Stewart then turns to Franks who is off to the side sitting on a brown couch.

"What's your record big guy, you are on the bottom, right? Well? It's ok, you can tell me."

Franks stands up with a slight bounce in his step, and says with pride, "Yup. I'm behind Sam. She has 13, and I have 12 misses." Then Franks allows a great big smile to come across his face. He puts his hand on Stewart's shoulder and simply says, "Until today, when you go and finish behind me."

Franks tries to mock Stewart but, as always, Stewart gets the last laugh. He says nothing at first. Then he shakes his head and says, "What do you think, I'm going to score lower than you big guy? You're wrong. I'm going to break Tyler's record, and I'm going to be on top."

Nobody in the room says anything until Franks starts laughing.

"Stewart you make me laugh, you think you can beat Tyler's record?" Franks continues to laugh as he sits back down on the couch.

"That's the attitude I like to hear son," Stone says, "I like that confidence."

A loud siren sounds from the air lock chamber. Shawn, still looking down at the pod, watches it as it rises from the half dome area. It takes some time for the centerpiece to lift up the pod. The beam bends like a crane as it lifts the pod out and sets into place. The red light goes on above the door that leads into the air chamber and the door automatically unlocks.

"Ok Stewart, head down stairs to Tyler." The scientist says. Stewart walks to the door with no problem. He grabs the doorknob but hesitates slightly as he begins turning the handle. Eventually the door does open. By the time Stewart reaches the area where you enter the pod, Tyler has already climbed out, and is ready to help him in. Stewart climbs in and Tyler buckles him down with two straps over each shoulder and one around the waist. Tyler explains the way the controls work, and then seals him in. The pod pulls away from the ramp that connects it to the platform. Tyler leaves the airlock chamber. As soon as the door closes the red light comes on and the door locks. The siren sounds again, and the machine starts up. The pod rises up from the platform and starts to lower into the dome. It begins to spin. It starts off slow to give the pilot the chance to get used to the controls. Then, Stewart starts bragging over the radio how he missed the walls so far and how easy this is. Tyler tells the scientist to speed the machine up to the next level. After the next cycle starts, the pod begins spinning faster.

You can see the pod going up and down, hitting the foam walls, and near the end of the cycle the pod stops moving up and down and it just goes around in circles. Finally, after all fifty walls have been displayed, the pod comes to a stop.

Stewart started out good by missing the first ten walls, but when the machine went faster he hit the rest of the targets because he was unable to keep up with the foam wall changes. Stewart is on the bottom of the standings, but at this point he doesn't care. He doesn't wait for anybody to come and help him out. He disconnects the harness belts, and hops out of the pod.

As soon as Stewart exits the pod he throws up in a nearby garbage can. He sits on the bottom of the stair that leads up to the control room. His face is as pale as a ghost and he is out of breath. Shawn and Tyler come down the stairs behind a sick Stewart. Shawn is the first to reach him. He sits down three steps above where Stewart is sitting.

"You ok?" Shawn asks Stewart as Tyler hands Stewart a bottle of water to give him a chance to recover from motion sickness.

"How was it?" Shawn asks a very dizzy Stewart. After some time Stewart answers him very slowly, and quietly.

"It was fun in the beginning, and then the foam walls started to get blurry, and then I didn't see them at all." Stewart stops talking to catch his breath, and takes a sip of bottled water, and then he says,

"I think I blacked out there for a second."

"You did because the pod stopped going up and down."

Shawn pushes past Stewart on his way to the pod. Tyler checks on Stewart one more time, then follows Shawn to the pod. Shawn climbs into the pod and Tyler begins to explain the controls as Shawn buckles himself in the seat.

"Oh great, you know how to buckle yourself in, that's step one that I don't have to tell you," Tyler says as he continues explaining the controls to him. After some time Tyler finally closes Shawn in the pod, and he and Stewart head up the stairs to the control room.

Stewart opens the door to a room full of cheers from the team, which is now joined by Sam.

"Everybody give it up for the new record breaker, the champ of last place," Franks screams, and the cheers get even louder. Stewart, being the person he is, plays along and throws his arms up in joy to feed off the crowd. Franks walks over to Stewart and hands him another bottle of water.

"Don't worry, Shawn is going to be just as bad as you were," Franks says to boost his confidence.

"Everybody does poorly their first time," Bobby Hawkins says.

Stewart drinks the water and replies, "Not Shawn. If anyone can do good on their first try, and beat Tyler's record, it would be him."

He takes another sip of water and tells everybody in the room that Shawn will break Tyler's record. Bobby is busting a gut from laughing so hard. Tyler says nothing about the rant going on with everybody, the standings, and what Shawn might do or not. It doesn't really matter to Tyler, he just cares that Shawn and Stewart get trained.

"What's happening here?" Tyler asks.

"Stewart bragged to everyone that he was going to beat your record, then he failed. He's now telling everybody that his buddy down there is going to break it," Bobby says, trying to kiss Tyler's ass.

Stewart turns to face Bobby, but by now they all have huddled in.

He boldly says, "Well, Bobby, you're so certain that my good buddy won't beat the record, why don't you put your money where your mouth is." Stewart places his hand on Bobby's shoulder, but Bobby has no response.

"Come on, I'll bet fifty dollars that Shawn can beat Tyler's record."

Bobby still doesn't say anything.

"How about one hundred dollars? Well, what do you have to say Bobby?" Stewart says, trying to get in Bobby's head.

"I'll take that bet, son." It didn't come from Bobby, but from General Stone.

"I'll take you up on that bet. There's no way", Sam blurts wanting in on the action.

"Me too, you fool", Tyler smirks to join in on the bet. In the back of his mind he hopes his record still stands.

"Me too" Bobby finally joins in to accept the bet.

Stewart, knowing he bit off more than he can chew, turns to Franks, who backs out of the group once Stewart starts making wagers.

"How about you big guy? You what in on this action?"

"No, that's okay. You took enough of my money for one week," Franks says calmly.

Down Inside the pod there's not a whole lot of room to move around for Shawn. The single level that moves the pod up and down comes through the floor in between the pilot's legs. As Shawn is lowered into the pit he closes his eyes and takes a deep breath. He sits all the way back in his seat as he prepares for the machine to start. The pod starts to spin.

Stewart has his face pressed against the window like a little kid. Shawn gets past the first ten with ease. Then the machine picks up speed. He hits three walls right away. Stewart is really nervous, wondering how he is going to pay everyone off. Then, Shawn hits another wall. Stewart's heart is pounding out his chest, the sweat dripping down his brow.

Inside the pod Shawn is not worried about hitting the walls. He works on focusing his eyes on the foam walls. At this speed it takes him some time. Then, Shawn gets into a groove, as he misses wall after wall. He hits another three at the end of the run. The machine starts to slow down. Everybody is on edge waiting for the final score. Stewart is absolutely ready to have a heart attack waiting for Shawn's score.

Then, in a really low voice the operator announces, "Wow! I can't believe it, 43 walls missed! Shawn did it, he scored a 43!" The whole room is shocked, like they just got punched in the stomach. Not Stewart, though. He's jumping up and down, collecting the money he just won from everyone, but doesn't take the money from Sam. The red light goes off and Tyler hands Stewart the hundred dollars. Stewart hands Tyler a new bottle of water. Then, Tyler heads down the stairs to Shawn.

By the time Tyler reaches Shawn the pod is just locking into place, and Tyler hooks up the ramp. He opens the pod, and Shawn, with his helmet off, is sitting with his eyes closed, still buckled into the seat.

"Are you ok, Shawn? I brought you some water."

Shawn takes a deep breath, and opens his eyes slowly.

"I'm okay, just a little dizzy, that's all."

He takes the water from Tyler, opens it, and drinks most of the bottle in one gulp. Tyler unbuckles the seat belts, and helps Shawn up and out of the pods.

Stewart pops his head out of the control room door. "You're the man Shawn! Way to go, I knew you could do it," he exclaims.

"What's that all about? Why is he screaming like that? What did he do now?" Shawn asks. Tyler just laughs as he follows Shawn to the bottom of the staircase.

"Stewart's just happy since you just won him four hundred dollars."

"What? How did I do that? The guy always seems to make money off me."

They both share a laugh and Tyler says, "He bet that you would break my record, and he bet against everyone in that room, except for Franks."

"Wait, I beat your record?" Shawn questions with excitement in his voice.

"Yes. How did you do it, anyway?"

"I focused my eyes on the walls, and visualized the walls at high speed."

Tyler shaking his head smiling replies, "You're something special, Shawn."

Stone calls the both of them up. As they walk up the stairs Tyler says, "I want to train you to become a pilot. I think you would be great at it."

Shawn says nothing at first, but then says "yes" to Tyler's request.

Meanwhile, upstairs Stewart has found himself in a very tight situation. As Sam left the room she ran her finger against Stewart's cheek and said to him that she can't wait for their date. Stewart has a great big smile across his face, but can feel the General staring a hole into the back of his head. He turns his head slightly in the General's direction and smiles at him, and then quickly leaves the room to get in the elevator. The General is ready to bust. His face is red, and his fists are clenched tightly. Tyler taps Stone on his shoulder.

"What?" Stone screams as he turns to Tyler.

"Sorry Tyler, I just found out that my daughter is going out on a date with Stewart, of all people."

Shawn starts laughing aloud which doesn't help Stone's temper.

"Hey, at least he has a lot of money now to take your daughter somewhere nice," he says, "Didn't you give some, too, General? What was it? Oh yes, a hundred dollars."

Stone's face drops, but he does smirk at the thought. Tyler starts laughing because he just can't hold it in any longer. This starts the three of them laughing and from behind, Bobby starts to laugh, even though he has no idea why they are laughing. Stone turns to Bobby.

"Why are you laughing?"

Bobby stops laughing and doesn't say anything. He just turns, and leaves the room. Stone turns back to Tyler, and Shawn, and asks, "What did you want again, Tyler?"

"Well General, I would like to teach Shawn to be a pilot."

Stone doesn't say anything, he just looks Shawn up and down which creeps Shawn out a little.

"That was a good show, beating Tyler's record, which has been in place for about four years. You know what Tyler, train him. I have a feeling that you're going to be a really good pilot, Shawn."

"Thank you sir, I know one thing, I will give it my best." but right before he leaves he tells him,

"If it means anything, General Stewart is a real good guy, very smart, and caring. Besides, he was raised by my father, so he can't be that bad, right?" Shawn leaves Tyler and Stone in the room, with a lot to think about.

CHAPTER SEVEN

Shawn finds himself on the second floor, standing outside his father's office. He grabs the handle, but doesn't turn it. He takes a deep breath, and then finally turns the knob. He flicks a switch on the wall, which happens to be on the left side of the door, and the light turns on.

The office has papers all over the place. Files are stacked on top of each other; a complete unorganized mess, unlike the office at home. He starts to pick up the papers and folders at his feet hoping to find something that will point him in the right direction. Shawn is looking for the next clue he and Stewart are supposed to follow. He starts looking through the folders in the filing cabinets, looking over everything before placing them down. Desperate to find something, he rubs the belly of a Buddha statue for luck, that sits on top of the filing cabinet. thinking that his father believed in luck, and maybe it would work for him. As he rubs the stomach, he notices a circle indent on the wooden base. He moves his finger over it, and just then remembers the metal object he found in his dad's safe. He grabs it out of his pocket, and places it in the indent, and it fits perfectly. Nothing seems to happen, and then he spins it around, counter clockwise like a dial. A draw opens up, and inside is a USB thumb drive with a leather journal book. He picks it up, ``and sits at his father's desk. Then, he opens it, unsure of what he will find out. He starts reading from the first page of the book.

ENTRY ONE:

I just made the biggest discovery in the history of mankind. Unfortunately, I can't share it with anybody outside this complex. My radio transmitter that I placed on the space station made contact with another race, located in another galaxy. My government is making me keep this a secret from the public, from my son, and the people I hold close to me, and it's just killing me inside. They are sending me to the space station to meet our newfound friends. I would be crazy if I said I wasn't scared, but this is something I've been working on my whole life, and I must complete my life-work.

-Doctor Higgins

Tyler is nearby, and sees that the light is on in Doctor Higgins's office. He pokes his head in, and sees Shawn sitting behind his father's desk.

"Oh, it's you Shawn. I saw the light on so I came to see what's up." Tyler's voice startles Shawn.

"I know you and the General think I have the key to solving everything, but I don't. Hell, for months I thought my father was dead." Tyler takes a seat and listens to Shawn vent as he continues to slide things around his father's desk.

"Then I find out that the guy standing in front of me is an alien! An actual alien! And yet, everyone thinks I have the answer to solve the problem of my dad being taken." Shawn takes a deep breath after venting his true feelings.

"Are you done?" Tyler asks.

Shawn puts his hands on his face and answers " yes." He sits up in the chair and says, "I don't even know what's really happening." Just then Tyler starts talking

"Over thirty years ago, your time, I thought I made the biggest discovery, not only for my fellow men, but for yours as well. Some thought it was a big deal, but others didn't. Some were even in my family. The day I made contact with your father Shawn.

I thought it was the greatest thing, because at the time my galaxy was in the middle of a war with one of our planets called Kincho. So at the time I did not want to start another war with a foreign planet which would be big enough to bring all the planets down, including mine. But when I met your father for the first time, he gave me a sense of hope again. When he put his hand out to shake mine with that big smile on his face I felt so much better. I believed good things could happen. I first thought everyone from earth was like him. Boy, was I wrong."

"Did you say someone in your family was not happy?" Shawn asks.

Tyler puts his head down in shame. "My older brother."

"What?"

"Yes, my older brother. I don't know if he was jealous or what, but he set up allies with some of the other planets, and they set the wheels in motion to start a major war that brought our home planet involved in the war. It didn't take them long to overthrow our high priests and force them into hiding. Most of our people, and your father, tried to help, but after a while, we were powerless. Your father, along with fourteen other humans and Noraians, were taken from their homes. Your father was on a patrol run one night when his pilot was shot and killed. Many of my people were killed in this war, all due to my brother Brackeo. He started this. Brackeo is hated by many, and by me. Because of my discovery I was loved by many.

My home planet NORA is the smallest in its galaxy, but with the material that we produce, it makes us one of the strongest planets around. Metal is the strongest in our galaxy, and since all the planets need it, we were left out of the conflicts, until my brother made a deal with another planet to take the metal for them and the power for my brother."

Shawn stops Tyler. "How many out of the six planets have life on them?"

Tyler was happy to answer all of Shawn's questions. "Well, let me see, there's our planet, then there is the planet Kincho, where there is a giant city named Kincho City. It is made up of tall, enormous buildings made from material from all the planets. It's a gathering place where all creatures can get anything they want without waiting. There's also lounging areas everywhere. The weather is like earth, but it gets very hot on some days. Kincho is one of the planets that wants peace, but it is not a fighting planet anymore. Not after the big war between the upper and lower cities. There is no government as you would call it. It's like a safe haven for creatures that want to hide out, never to be found by anyone that may be looking for them."

Shawn is just trying to take this all in and then asks, "What planet did your brother, Brackeo, make a deal with to help take over the high priests?"

Tyler hesitates, but eventually gives Shawn an answer.

"Brackeo first went to the planet Fir Tango, which is a gas ridden planet because of an asteroid that hit it, destroying everything. It left the planet filled with gas and lava, destroying itself."

"How do creatures still live on it?" Shawn asks, waiting for Tyler to continue with the history.

"Well, it's believed that the creatures that survived the asteroid blast were left deformed. Their bodies have no hair. Certain parts of their bone structure, such as the kneecaps, elbows, and their spinal cords, now show all the way down their back. Their heads are perfectly rounded because their ears were burnt off, and they are the only creatures that can breathe, other than the Noraians, on the planet, which gives them an advantage on Fir Tango."

Shawn sits there, stunned. He does not say a word until Tyler stops talking and then he asks, "Why did your brother pick that planet to make a deal with, when there are obviously much better planets out there, right?"

Tyler, impressed with the questioning, says, "Well, he picked that planet because Fir Tango has the best opportunity to make deadly bombs with all the raw material available. The day when my brother left home I was so crushed. It hurt me more than the day I buried both my father, and then my sister." Tyler looks up at

Shawn who is listening to everything.

"I looked up to my brother. He was my hero until he walked out on me and my mother. Brackeo broke my heart, until your father helped me gain back what my brother took from me."

"What's that?" Shawn asks.

"My honor. But just when I was starting to feel good about myself, my brother kidnapped your father, and word got out that he made some kind of deal with those vile creatures. Your father told me that if he was killed or captured that his son would be the answer to everything. I will help you just like your father helped me."

Shawn rests his head and arms on the desk in shock. He sits up and then asks Tyler, "What's the next step?"

"First is training, and then getting you and Stewart up to speed on the situation. We need to get you both ready to fight in a war that is not yours, and to rescue your father, as well as the other prisoners, and hopefully bring them all home safe and sound."

"What if we fail? What if Stewart and I can't help my father? What will happen to your home, and to Earth?"

Tyler says nothing at first, but then he says, "You and Stewart have been here for about a week, and you both have made great strides. He cracked a computer lock and you broke my record in flight simulation, which I will get back." Tyler stands up. "Are you coming?"

"No, I'm going to stay here, look around, and see what I can find."

"Shawn, listen to these guys are behind you and Stewart, one hundred percent. I hope you two can trust us, and that you both are behind us one hundred percent, as well." Shawn says nothing as Tyler leaves. He picks up his father's journal, opens it up, and continues to read.

ENTRY TWO:

I just returned home from my first visit to Tyler's home planet called NORA. It's similar to our planet, Earth. It has trees, water, wind, rain, and even snow. Although, there are some differences; their sky is red, but the air is so clear, almost crystal clear. Each of the planets contains a different race. The planets rotate around the sun, but each rotates differently. Think of two key rings spinning inside one another, but in the opposite direction. When two planets rotate near each other, it's like you can reach out and touch it. It's quite scary at first, but it only happens once every other month. The Noraians are so nice and welcoming, as I walked through a small town square outside a giant volcano. The Earth compound is starting to get built today. I just found out I gotta stay another month or so. Shawn is going to kill me when I get back. I hope he and Stewart are safe and staying out of trouble. What am I thinking they're with CJ. She'll keep them out of trouble? I miss them all.

-Doctor Higgins

Shawn turns the page to the next entry, reading on and trying to get into his father's head and to understand how his father dealt with all this information. He is also hoping to make his father proud.

ENTRY THREE

I saw a beautiful woman today. She has long brown hair, a smile that melted my heart. She smells like sweet morning dew. Stone told me that her name is Shannon. He said for me to try talking to her, but I always chicken out. What would I say? She probably wouldn't want anything to do with a guy like me. But Stone is right the next time I see herbuity I will approach her

-Doctor Higgins

"Holy crap this is about my mom." he blurts out. Shawn is completely blown away that he is getting the chance to read things about his mother, things that he wanted his father to tell him in person, but this will have to do for now. Shawn is eager to learn more. He continues to read.

ENTRY FOUR:

I tried talking to Shannon today, but once again I chickened out. She must think I'm some kind of stalker. I don't mean to come across like such a creep, but I don't know what to say. I've always been into my work, not girls. Oh, but she makes me want to forget about my work. Makes me want to sweep her off her feet and treat her like my queen. She is so gorgeous. She has a beautiful smile, mesmerizing eyes, and a perfect voice. When I see Shannon I want to disappear, holding her tight within my arms. I just wish I could talk to her, like I'm writing in this journal. Maybe I can do it tomorrow.

-Doctor Higgins

Shawn is excited to learn about his past, about his mother, and as he reads his heart begins to pound after every word in his father's personal notebook. Not knowing always bothered him, but he went on with his life. Shawn turns the page wondering how his parents met; how they fell in love.

ENTRY FIVE:

I cannot believe it! I was working at my desk today, on my report of Tyler's planet, and Shannon walked up to me and introduced herself. I completely froze at first, but finally blurted out my name, and tonight we are going on our first date. I'm taking her out for pizza. She told me that she has never eaten pizza before. It should be fun. I really hope that I don't make a fool of myself because I really like her

-Doctor Higgins

Shawn starts to get hungry, decides to leave. He grabs the thumb drive, and gets up from his father's desk. He closes and locks his father's door and heads off to show Stewart what he found to explain what he was told by Tyler. He walks out of the elevator and sees Franks, who is sitting on the couch watching TV with Sid. James Starkly is there too, but he's talking to his wife on a cell phone. Shawn, not seeing Stewart sitting with them, walks past and heads to their room. When he opens the door he doesn't see Stewart. He screams out, "Stewart, where are you?"

Stewart hears Shawn, and jogs from the sitting area into their room.

"What are you screaming for? You're like a baby."

"Good, there you are." Shawn smells cologne in the air, then looks at Stewart who happens to be leaving soon.

"Where are you going? I solved my dad's first clue," Shawn says with joy in his voice. He is showing a little bounce in his step; a sense of achievement.

Stewart doesn't seem to care at the moment, and for once he has no idea what Shawn is talking about.

"Stewart, I found a letter at my parent's house. Inside the letter, my father left me a circular disk, which opened up a secret drawer in a statue he has in his office."

Stewart is listening to him as he continues to get ready for his date.

"Wait, where are you going? Didn't you hear me? I have a thumb drive for you, from my father. It was in the drawer too."

Stewart is sitting on his bed tying his boots. He stands up and tells Shawn, "I'll look at the drive when I get back." He puts on his leather jacket, then puts his ball cap on, and places his hand on Shawn's shoulder to say.

"I'm going on my date with Sam tonight." His face turns red, and a smile grows.

"Wait, you're still going out with her, even though she's Stone's daughter?" Shawn questions Stewart's thinking.

Stewart stops smiling, and looks at Shawn, and simply says,

"Yes. For one, she's hot, two, she is good with computers, and three, she has spunk. Plus I really like her. She is different from the others. I feel a connection, not to be corny."

Shawn stops him and says, "And four, she's General Stone's daughter." Shawn is trying to put some sense into Stewart's head, but it's too late. Stewart has already made up his mind. He tells Shawn, "I don't care that she is Stone's daughter. I'm not like everybody else. I am not scared of him. Besides, he likes me."

Stewart is about to leave the room when Shawn stops him.

"Wait, what about the thumb drive our dad needs you?" Shawn now tries guilt which makes Stewart pause for a second. Then Stewart says.

"I'll look at it when I get back." Shawn wishes him luck. Stewart darts out the door.

Stewart heads to the living room area to find Stone waiting, not Sam. There is a sense of tension in the hallway now. Stone is standing like a statue at the end of the hallway. Stewart notices him, but walks by without saying a word. Meanwhile, Stone's eyes follow Stewart as he walks by. Then, he follows Stewart to the kitchen. Franks, Sid, and James secretly stop watching the television and start to watch the confrontation.

"I hear you are taking my daughter out on a date tonight." Stone is standing in Stewart's personal space, trying to intimidate him.

Stewart, being his normal self, goes about his business. He grabs his can of soda from the refrigerator. He sips the soda, looks at Stone, and before he can say anything, Sam enters the room.

"Daddy, please leave Stewart alone. We talked about this."

She is wearing black women's cargo pants with a sweater that reads, US Army, her white adidas shoes completes the attire. Her black hair is back in a tight ponytail, with a slight part to the left. The General hears Sam's voice and backs away, giving Stewart his space back. Stewart walks over to Sam. They both head for the elevator doors, get in, and right before it closes she screams to her father.

"Love you dad, and we're taking one of the Chargers, bye!"

The doors shut, and there is silence throughout the room. The General stands there, and a low giggle is heard in the background.

"I hope you three are laughing at the TV."

The three men quickly turn back to the TV and Stone stands there looking at them.

Stewart and Sam race out of the elevator. Each is going in two different directions. Stewart races towards the Dodge Chargers. Stewart tries to open the driver's door of the charger but of course it's locked.

"Hey what number is on the parking sign?" Sam screams over to Stewart. Stewart starts looking for the number

"Number 16." Stewart screams back. Sam grabs the keys for the car out of a metal box. Walks over to Stewart tossing the keys up in the air catching them

"Can I drive?" Stewart asks.

"I Don't know, can you handle this car?" Sam says back, still tossing the keys in the air as she walks to Stewart who is standing in the back of the car. As she gets close to Stewart he catches the keys mid-air. Sam walks to the passenger side. Stewart goes to the driver's side. Quickly Stewart notices Sam not getting in the car so he quickly runs around the front of the car. He opens the door for Sam. She slides into her seat jokingly saying,

"Are you getting soft on me?"

Stewart shuts her door gently and continues back around to the driver side.

"Better?" he says, getting into the car.

"Yes, very amusing," Sam smiles back. They both begin laughing. "So, where to on the team's dime?" Stewart smiles into Sam's eyes.

"You'll see." He throws the car in gear and races off so fast that it tosses Sam back into her seat, leaving tire marks on the garage floor. He hops onto Interstate 95 North.

"So, Stewart Collins, you won't tell me where we're going. Then tell me about you."

Stewart doesn't answer her question. In fact he changes the

subject back to her.

"I know three things about you, Miss Samantha Stone."

Sam turns her head toward the window, slowly rolls her eyes realizing the shift in conversation. She turns back to Stewart subtly letting him charm his way into her life.

"I can't wait to hear about these three wonderful things you know about me." Sam turns in her seat to face Stewart.

"One, your father is a U.S. General, and is very protective over you. And again, he is a U.S. General." Sam laughs over the first of the things he knows about her. Stewart continues.

"Two, you're good with computers and exercise to stay fit. Almost as good as I am." Sam stops laughing and slaps him lightly on his shoulder.

"Three, you seem to be a no nonsense girl that takes no shit from anyone. Which is a trait you get from your father. Who again is a U.S. General and absolutely loves me."

Sam places her hand in front of her mouth and begins to laugh.

"He loves you alright, you should have heard what he was saying about you earlier."

Stewart, quiet at first, finally says,

"He's a good father. He is just protective of his beautiful daughter. You can't blame him for that. At least he's still around. That's a good thing, right gives out a low pitched laugh while blushing in her seat.

"So, Stewart, my father is a U.S. General, what does your father do for a living?" Stewart doesn't reply and continues driving.

CHAPTER EIGHT

Stewart pulls off Interstate 95, exit 244 Edgewater.

"Edgewater...what's in Edgewater?" Sam asks. "What's in Edgewater?" She asks again.

Stewart finally breaks his silence and says,

"See I'm not too good at speaking about my family and my life. There's not much to talk about, so I think it would be better to show you." Sam turns back around in her seat to look at everything that is around her.

"See, this is where Shawn and I grew up. It doesn't look like much, but we had a blast here."

Sam says nothing. She is looking at everything as Stewart points out different things to her. She glances at Stewart from time to time, enjoying how much he in fact seems to love talking about his hometown. They pull off the main road into the town of Edgewater, and to a small bar called Jan & Lib's Hi-Tops. There are about eight cars in the small parking lot, and there is a live band playing inside.

"Where are we?" Sam asks.

"This is Shawn's Aunt's bar," Stewart says. "Inside there, people would love to tell you everything about me and Shawn."

Stewart opens the door for Sam to enter the bar. The local band is up on the small stage playing a set. There are a few people dancing in the small open space in front of the stage. To the right of the stage there is a pool table, which is divided by a half wall near the back entrance. There is another entrance at the front of the building, and the bar takes up the rest of the space. Stewart and Sam zigzag through the crowd up to the bar.

"This place is packed for only six or eight cars in the parking lot," Sam comments. With the band playing so close, Stewart doesn't hear everything she says.

"What? I couldn't hear you." He is up to her ear speaking.

She repeats herself again this time closer to his ear so he can hear her over the band.

"Oh, that is mostly because everyone in the bar lives within walking distance," Stewart says.

Sam sits at one of the stools near the end of the bar. Stewart is standing next to her. Behind the bar Benny walks up. Benny was Stewart and Shawn's classmate throughout high school. He is a skinny, lengthy guy, with brown short straight hair, and some light freckles on his face. He is wearing long legged shorts and flip-flops. His skin is tanned because he is at the beach when he is not bartending.

"Stewart. Where have you been, man?" Benny says. He gives Stewart a quick, half-hug. Stewart starts to introduce Sam to Benny, "Sam this is my friend from school, Benny Morgan." Sam puts out her hand to say hi, but Benny grabs her hand and kisses it trying to flirt with her.

"Okay Benny, that's enough. Sorry about him. He's the clown of the group," Stewart says to Sam.

From behind Sam and Stewart, a girl's voice announces, "That's funny; I thought you were the clown of our group." The girl walks around the other side of the bar next to Benny. She puts out her hand toward Sam and says, "Hi, I'm Carissa Jaime, but you can call me CJ. Everybody else does."

"Hi, I'm Sam. It's nice to meet you, CJ."

CJ has always been full of energy and very outgoing. She is semi-short, but not the slightest bit frail. She has medium, straight, dirty blonde hair and light freckles on both cheeks. She says to Sam,

"So be honest. Did you lose a bet? Is that why you're here with Stewart, blink twice really fast if he is holding you against your will" Sam starts laughing, almost falling off her stool and says, "Something like that." She looks at Stewart and sees that his face is getting red with embarrassment.

"Stewart's a good guy when he wants to be," Sam says, as she smiles towards Stewart to make him feel better.

"Hey, listen, can I get you a drink since Benny is off talking to the band, and not here doing his job?" asks CJ, complaining about her co-worker as usual. She gets Sam a Coors Light. Benny finishes his conversation with the band, and comes back over to them.

"Hey Stewart, the band asked if you want to play a song with them."

"No thanks, maybe another time Benny." Stewart replies. Benny shakes his head toward the stage, signaling to the band. Stewart turns to Sam, but before he can say anything, a man with dark long hair and a handlebar mustache taps his shoulder from behind.

"Hey Stewart, play the next song I have to use the bathroom." Stewart tries turning down the offer like he did earlier, but the guitarist, and even Sam, encourage him to play. He hesitates, but when the singer introduces him, he has no choice. Sam sits at the bar drinking her beer, watching Stewart get ready to play the guitar. The band's drummer starts the song off, then the singer starts to sing with the beat of the drums and Stewart starts playing the guitar along with the band. Sam is shocked that Stewart has no problem going up on stage and playing in front of everybody. Stage fright is something she could never deal with. She is thrilled, and begins to cheer Stewart on. She has a large smile plastered across her face as she claps louder than everyone else. She can't believe what a different guy Stewart is compared to what she thought. When the song is over Stewart passes the guitar back to a band member and gets cheers from the crowd. The entire bar chants his name asking him to play another song, even Sam is screaming for another song. Although everyone is exclaiming their thoughts, all Stewart can hear is Sam out of them all. He walks back to Sam waving his hand to everyone saying thank you to them all as he walks by. He asks Sam if she wants to play pool. Before they walk over to the table CJ stops the two of them and jokingly says, "Watch out, Sam, this one has a silver tongue."

"Very funny CJ, don't listen to her." He pushes CJ away gently. CJ is laughing and having a blast at Stewart's expense. Sam puts her hand on CJ's elbow and says,

"He has a silver tongue alright, but I can handle him." CJ holds up her beer bottle, and Sam clicks her bottle to hers. Stewart is trying to break up the two girls that are talking about him. As he's pulling Sam away from CJ he is saying, "Alright, that's enough bashing poor Stewart." He pulls Sam to the pool table in the back of the building, and starts to rack up the pool balls. CJ comes back and asks them,

"Sam, do you want another beer? Stewart, do you want your one beer?"

"Sure," Stewart replies to CJ as she walks away to get them there drinks.

"So one drink, what's that all about?" Sam questions, as Stewart hands her a pool stick.

"Oh, nothing much, my mother is a really bad drunk, so when I got injured I turned to my mom's pills and alcohol. Shawn and his father and CJ and her mom all helped me get cleaned. So I try to limit it to one or two and I still can have fun in the process," he says.

"Good for you. That's great Stewart."

Sam steps around Stewart and heads to the head of the table, rests the pool stick inside her right palm elevating her stick off the table, pulls the stick back breaking the balls scattering around the table. She sinks three solid colored blue, #2, Orange #5, and black, # 8.

"Ok, I guess you have played this game before." Sam walks around the pool table next to Stewart. She bumps him away with her hips and sinks the #1, yellow. Just then a couple walk into the bar and say "Hey Stewart. Long time, no see".

Sam stands up from the shot she was taking, and says, "Popular guy around here, aren't you?" She bends down to sink another shot.

"No, I am not popular. Half of these people I went to school with. Like I told you, Shawn and I hung out here a lot."

CJ comes back with their drinks and puts them on a small round table that sits in the corner adjacent to the pool table.

"Are you kicking his ass, Sam?"

Sam sinks the maroon, #7, pops up, and walks over to the table where CJ is standing. She picks up her bottle and says, "Of course I am." She takes a drink off her bottle of beer and places a flirty smile across her pretty face.

A few hours go by, Sam and Stewart continue to play pool. Stewart even gets a chance to dance with her. After a while they say goodbye to Benny and CJ, and sneak out the back door.

"Where are we going now?" Sam asks, walking back to the car.

"It's a surprise?" Stewart says slamming the car door behind him, adjusts the rear view mirror and drives to a new location

" I don't like surprises, but so far tonight they have been surprising and pretty fun.

Stewart takes Sam to the New Smyrna Beach Boardwalk. Once there, their first stop is to a small

Mini golf course which, unlike the pool table, Sam destroys Stewart.

"I'm pretty much getting tired of being destroyed at games I thought I was pretty good at. Good enough to beat the local yokels but Sam, you're different. You've got your game on".

Sam smiles as Stewart pulls into the Ho Chi Min chinese restaurant.

Stewart jumps out and darts around the car to open the door.

"After you, mi lady", Stewart says, extending his arm out allowing her passage into the parking lot.

"What a gentleman you are Stewart", Sam winks.

The restaurant is very small. It only has four, dark red booths that sit on either side of the restaurant. They both take a seat at one of the booths, sitting opposite of one another. After a few minutes, a small Chinese woman walks over to them. Her black hair is a large ball held up by a pencil.

"Do you want something to drink?" She hustles to ask the both of them, and then she hands them both a menu. Stewart and Sam order sodas and the waitress leaves the two of them.

"You have some crazy friends," Sam says, trying to break the ice.

"Yeah, sorry about them, they get a little out of control," he answers back.

"No, really, they're great. Benny and CJ were funny. Benny hasn't had a girlfriend in a while though, huh?"

"How did you know?" Stewart answers while laughing. Sam starts laughing too. The waitress comes back with their drinks.

"Are you ready to order?" She says,

"Shrimp Lo Mein dinner with white rice, with a shrimp egg roll please." Sam says to the waitress

"How about you sir?"

"I'll have the same as the lady." Stewart says, looking at Sam's green eyes and smiling face.

On this date they seem to keep finding things in common with each other, which gives them something to talk and laugh about. After some time, their food arrives and they both enjoy their meals, talking, and joking around with one another, enjoying each other's company. After finishing their dinner, Stewart suggests they take a walk on the beach. Sam loves the idea. She runs down the ramp to the beach's white sand. Once Sam hits the sand she plops down and takes off her shoes and socks. She rolls up her cargo jeans to right below her knees. Stewart is only half way down the ramp because he stopped to light a cigarette.

"Come on, hurry up, Stewart!" Sam yells back to Stewart. She has never walked on the beach at night. This night is a perfect time to walk down the beach shores; the moon is full and is reflecting off the ocean water. There is a light breeze coming off the ocean.

Stewart chooses to leave his boots on as they walk to just

where the water can hit their feet.

"Are you sure you don't want to take off your socks and boots?"

"No, I'm fine. These boots are waterproof." Stewart says, but just then a wave hits his feet, and soaks them right to the skin.

"Boy that water is cold," Stewart says as he hops out of the waters. He quickly decides to take off his boots as well as his socks, while he sits up away from the water. Sam continues splashing around and playing in the waves.

"This is probably the most fun I've had in a long time." she says to Stewart as she walks back to him, just as he is done taking off his socks and boots. They start to walk down the beach. In one hand are their shoes and socks, and with the other they hold each other's hand.

"So how long have you and Shawn been friends?"

"Shawn and I have known each other all of our lives. Shawn and his father are like my family." Stewart says.

"Where are your real parents?" Sam asks. At first Stewart hesitates with an answer, but Sam says,

"You don't have to answer if you don't want to." She senses he might be uncomfortable with this subject.

"No, it's not a big deal. People tell me all the time to talk about this, so here it goes." He takes a deep breath and lights a cigarette before starting.

"My father ran out on me and my mother when I was really young. My mother handled it by becoming the town's drunken whore. Shawn and his father gave me a bed at their house and fed me whenever I needed it. Shawn and I helped each other through rough times. He did not have a mother and I did not have any parents worth speaking about. We shared Doctor Higgins as a father figure and we both tried figuring it out as we both grew up."

Sam just smiles at Stewart as she squeezes his hand and says,

"That's funny because everyone back at the compound leans on Doc Higgins as a father figure, too."

"Okay it's your turn for questions." Stewart says. "Where is your mom? I know that she is not around because your father is not wearing a ring."

"No. My mom ran off, like your parents did so I can relate with you there. She couldn't handle the army life; moving from one base to another. The last time I knew where she was living, it was somewhere in the midwest. I haven't seen or talked to her since she left my dad and me five years ago."

Stewart is visibly saddened by her story, until a wave brushes up against their feet. He can relate to how she is feeling and asks, "O.K. one more question. Are you in the army like your father? I mean, being in the army isn't a bad thing, but I was just wondering." Stewart tries to fix what he was saying, and then tries to change the subject.

Sam starts laughing at the way Stewart is mumbling and at his question. After letting him panic for a little while, she replies,

"No, I'm not in the army. Shawn's father convinced me to join the AHR team because he saw how good I was with computers. My dad was standing guard when Dr. Higgins first made contact. When the government found out about the discovery, Dr. Higgins told everybody that my father was a big part of it all. The President of the United States made my father a General. He then put both Dr. Higgins and my father in charge of the AHR program, but ask my father, he will tell you everytime that Doc Higgins is in charge of the AHR team. I heard that this made certain people angry, but they were powerless to do anything about it." She finished in a funny, evil sounding voice to try to lighten the mood.

"How does Tyler play into all of this?" Stewart asks, trying to learn everything he can.

"It's funny, Tyler is the one that both Dr. Higgins and my father made contact with. See, Tyler is not his real name; it was a name that he picked out himself. Tyler is one of three people who are in charge of the soldiers on the base on NORA, he is also one of the leaders of AHR team"

"Wait, NORA? What is NORA?" Stewart asks in curiosity.

"Shouldn't you know all of this, didn't my father tell this all on your first day?"

"He probably did but my first day here is a blank. I just found out Doc Higgins is alive and aliens exist."

" Ok I'll give you that one. Ok, Well, NORA is the name of Tyler's home planet", Sam answers.

"Have you ever been to NORA?"

"Yes, I have been there twice."

"What is it like?" Stewart asks, curious to hear about life on another planet. Sam looks at the moon as she explains NORA to Stewart.

"It's not so different from Earth. The weather is a little rougher, and they only have one big landmass with oceans all around it. NORA also has a planet that you can see in the sky, something like our moon."

"How are the people in NORA?" Stewart asks with excitement in his voice.

"They're really inviting and very nice, at least the ones I have met. See, Earth built a base on NORA. It has apartments, training equipment, and also athletic fields for drills and other exercises. I was never allowed to leave the base. The only way you are allowed outside the base is with Dr. Higgins or any member of the team."

"Have you ever wanted to leave the base, and really see NORA? See how they live there, and meet the Noraians?"

Sam pauses, not knowing what to say at first. "Well the people I met so far were nice, and leaving the base alone is not allowed. Besides, I had no reason to go outside the base. Maybe, when you're there we will see it together." By now they both had walked up and down the beach, and then back to the car.

"First one to the car gets to drive back," says Sam as she knocks Stewart's boots out of his hands and runs towards the car.

"No fair, you're a cheater!" Stewart screams to Sam, who is now halfway to the car. He starts to run after her, but now it's too late. She is almost to the car. As Sam reaches the car she screams, "I win! I won!" Moments later Stewart, out of breath, comes up behind Sam and wraps his arms around her waist. He gently pulls her close to his chest. Sam turns around in Stewart's arms. She stands up on her tippy toes wrapping her arms around his neck and kisses him very gently on his lips. Then she says, blushing from the kiss,

"I won, give me the keys." Sam slips on her socks and shoes and Stewart puts on his socks and then his boots, but he doesn't tie them. They both enter the car and Sam puts the keys into the ignition as she talks to Stewart.

"Now I'll show you how an army brat drives and you can sit back in your seat and tell me how you broke those codes?"

"Damn, I was hoping you forgot about that." Stewart says as he is thrown back in his seat. Sam throws the car into gear, and peels out of the parking lot.

Sam races back to the base swerving in out of cars on Interstate 95. Stewart is holding on for dear life trying to tell her about the codes the entire way back to base. He is trying to play it cool, trying to play it calm and making sure not to scream out loud.

"Wow, we got back here a lot faster than I thought we would." Stewart said.

"What, did I scare you?" Sam laughs. Like always Stewart shows no fear on his face. Full of confidence in his voice he says,

"No, not at all, it was kind of fun". They both get out of the car and walk to the elevator holding hands.

"I had a nice time tonight with your friends, they were wild." They both enter the elevator and head to the living quarters.

"Sam, I had a really nice time tonight, too. I'm really not this open about my family to most people." Sam grabs both of Stewart's hands, pulls him close to her, and softly kisses him again.

"Don't worry, Stewart, your family is a secret, I won't tell anyone. I promise you." Stewart is so happy with everything, he pulls Sam back towards him and kisses her more aggressively.

"Oh sorry I didn't mean to..." Before he can finish what he was saying she kisses him the same way he just kissed her. Meanwhile, the elevator doors opened and closed. The doors open again and Stewart says,

"We should do this again sometime."

"I would like that, Stewart." Stewart walks Sam down the hall to her room.

"Guess Shawn is up?" Sam says as they pass the their room

"Yeah, we will be working on stuff late tonight. Wait, are you tired?"

"No not really, why?"

"Because Shawn has a thumb drive he wants me to look at it from our father, want to come look at it with us?" Sam is intrigued.

"Ok lets go." Stewart and Sam walk back to Stewart and Shawn's room right before Stewart was going to enter, pulls Stewart close to her and kisses him longer than they have kissed in the past."

"What was that for? Not that I didn't like it.

"I'm earning the privilege to hear how you cracked the codes?"

"You're still on that huh?" He says as he enters the room with Sam, meanwhile Shawn is lying across the love seat with the reading light on right behind his head. He has his father's journal on his chest. Stewart walks over to Shawn and picks up the journal, and reads what is written down.

"What's that?" Sam asks

" Our father's journal Shawn found it from the first clue in finding him."Stewart sits down in one of the chairs and Sam sits on him so she can read the journal with him.

ENTRY 18:

I just returned from NORA. I've been gone for two Earth months, but on NORA I was there for only a month. Shawn is either worried or pissed. I guess he is pissed. I wish I could tell him. Maybe one day when he is older and can handle it like an adult. When I feel that he is ready I will tell himl. I hope he won't be mad that I kept all this from him knowing that he should know.

Stewart stops reading for a second to smile and look down at a sleeping Shawn,

"The funny thing is, he was pissed every time." Stewart says as he continues on reading the entry in the journal.

He'll get over it. I hope so. All that matters is his safety. I can take him being mad at me. I love him so much. He is my life, the reason that I'm doing all this, and someday I will share all of this with him, hopefully sooner rather than later, when I know he will be safe.

"Maybe we should do this in the morning. I'll feel bad if we wake him up." Sam says as she quickly kisses him again. Stewart taps Sams but as she gets off him. Stewart closes the journal and puts it on the coffee table.

He gets up and goes and grabs a blanket off Shawn's bed and lays it across him. He turns off the light on the nightstand

"Can I walk you back to your room?"
"Of course." They both quietly leave the room and back down to Sam's room door

"I Really had a great time tonight. You really surprised me tonight, Stewart collins." She says as she once again is standing on her tippy toes with her arms around his head,

"I Understand if you want to run away now?" Stewart Says Sam laughs,

"No I'm good, I like a challenge." She kisses Stewart again before she walks backwards to her door and enters her room looking at Stewart. Once the door closes Stewarcan almost be seen as floating back to his room because he is so happy, Stewart enters the room, kicks off his boots, and climbs into his own bed. He is happy, and can't stop thinking of Sam as he falls off to sleep.

CHAPTER NINE

Sam sneaks into Stewart and Shawn's room early in the morning. She is wearing black jogging pants and a blue t-shirt, and her hair is tied back in a ponytail once again. She is startled when she notices Shawn sitting on the love seat staring at her.

"What are you doing here this early in the morning?" Shawn asks with a smile on his face.

She walks toward him and sits down in one of the seats next to him.

"What are you doing up? I wasn't expecting either of you to be up. I thought I would sneak in and wake up Stewart to go to the gym with me." Shawn sits back in the love seat laughing,

"You think Stewart's going to go to the gym, and please be careful when you wake him up"

"Come on, what's so funny?" Sam asks.

"Nothing but let me give you a word of advice. Stewart swings and kicks and gets very angry at people when they try to wake him up in the morning."

"Come on, he can't be that bad in the morning," Sam quickly replies.

"No, he is, and I can't wait to see him get up this early and go to the gym, of all places. I wish you luck," Shawn says as he sits back, getting comfortable in the love seat, and ready to enjoy the show.

Sam again tries to defend Stewart, not knowing Shawn is telling the truth about how Stewart acts when someone tries to wake him up.

"So, I take it that you both had fun last night," Shawn asks. Sam is starting to blush and says,

"Yeah, we had a good time. He took me to Jan & Lib's Hi-Tops and then to New Smyrna Boardwalk. Then we walked the beach and talked." Sam is now gloating, instead of blushing, while talking about their date last night.

"So I guess you met Benny and my cousin CJ," Shawn asks.

"Yes I did. They were great, me and CJ got along really well, but I didn't realize until now that she was your cousin."

"Yup, CJ, she is a great person, did you meet my Aunt Libby? Well, it's really Elizabeth Humphrey."

Sam cuts off Shawn, "Oh no she wasn't there. Do you get along well with CJ?"

Shawn laughs and says, "We get along when we're together, but don't piss her off."

"That's funny, she seemed way too happy to get pissed off," Sam laughs.

"Oh, trust me, CJ is a real firecracker when she wants to be. See, that one will rip you a new one if you piss her off enough." Sam gets up to wake Stewart, but Shawn stops her.

"Hey, listen I'm glad you two are trying to date. He is a good guy and he's a computer geek just like you, but not joking he needs someone good in his life."

"Very funny. Leave us geeks alone," Sam says back at him, picking up the pillow from the chair and throwing it at him in good fun. She walks up to Stewart's bed standing back from the bed, and then she starts to call his name. When that doesn't work she kicks the bed from a distance, shaking it. Like normal fashion Stewart kicks out his leg like he always does. Sam turns to Shawn.

"Boy you weren't kidding." Shawn is laughing his ass off on the loveseat.

"Come on Stewart, wake up now." Again she kicks the bed

from a distance, but it doesn't work. She throws her hands up in the air in defeat.

"Okay, what's the secret to getting him up?" she asks Shawn, who stands up, and walks over to Stewart's bed. He grabs the two handles on the side of the mattress and flips it once again, with Stewart still on it,

"What the hell man, I told you not to do that again," Stewart screams at Shawn, not knowing Sam is standing there. Shawn walks past Sam back to his seat and says, "That's how I've been waking him up lately."

Sam laughs her ass off.

Stewart pops up from the ground to yell at Shawn, but he sees Sam standing there laughing. Sam helps Stewart fix his bed, and then she sits down on it waiting for Stewart to fully wake up. She gives Stewart a quick kiss to help him wake up a little quicker.

"Come on, get ready. We're going to the gym," Sam says to Stewart.

"The gym?" Stewart's face drops, "No way. I'm not going." Sam gives him a wink and a smile and Stewart gives in. "O.K., on one condition. You play World Take Over with us later. Sam is unsure of what World Take Over is but she says yes anyway.

"Hurry up, and go get ready. Make sure you put comfortable pants and sneakers on."Stewart wasn't moving too quickly until Sam says,

"Come on go faster! The faster you go the quicker you get to see me work out and get all sweaty." Sam shoots Stewart a flirty wink.

He thinks about it at first, but then hops out of bed, and asks Shawn for a pair of Adidas jogging pants. He goes into the bathroom to change. Sam walks out of the room.

"That was easy," she says to Shawn, "That's how I do it." She says walking away, Shawn shakes his head.

Minutes later Stewart comes out of the bathroom in Shawn's Adidas pants and black John Lennon T-shirt. He starts ripping through his drawers and closet, not sure where to find his sneakers since he is always wearing his boots. His sneakers are never out in the open. Finally, he finds his sneakers still packed away in his bag stuffed in the back of the closet.

"We've been here for almost two months now," Shawn says, "and your sneakers are still packed away in your duffel bag." Shawn is amazed. He begins to get ready to leave, meanwhile Sam has already left for the kitchen.

"I can't believe you Stewart! You are getting ready to go work out."

"Are you kidding me, Shawn? Do you see what she is wearing? I'm basically going to watch her work out."

Shawn and Stewart leave the room to a crowded kitchen, which contains Sam, Franks, Sid, and Bobby Hawkins. When they both enter the crowded kitchen area Sam walks over to Stewart and gives him a quick kiss on the lips. No one in the room noticed it but Shawn and Franks.

"What's this one date and you're kissing?" Franks says. Now everybody in the room realizes the relationship between Sam and Stewart.

"Oh yeah, by the way Franks, thanks again for paying for our date last night!" Stewart says, with Sam's arm around his waist.

"That was very funny!" Franks smiles, "Good one Stewart. Oh, by the way does the General know of this new found relationship?"

"No, he does not and it's going to stay that way for now"", Sam says, "Right Sid? Right Bobby? Now if anyone is going to tell him it'll be me and Stewart." Sam is aiming most of her frustration in the direction of Sid and Bobby, because they are the two that tell the General everything that goes on in the compound. Both Sid and Bobby stand up, planning to say something, but before they can Sam continues, "And if I find out that one of you spoke to my Dad about this before me, I will kick your asses. That includes you, Franks."

Everyone laughs over the threats.

"I would love to see you try to kick Franks ass," Shawn says, "You would need a bat, and I don't even think that would work."

Franks is sitting at the counter eating his breakfast and taking everything in. He starts to speak, spitting food out of his mouth in the process, "This one knows I won't hit her back, but that doesn't mean jokes won't be placed on her."

In the past Sam always seemed to be the brunt of Franks jokes.

"Sam would get so mad she would throw things. Then she wouldn't speak to anyone for days." Franks continues on about the past.

Instantly Sam exclaims, "Okay, time to go, are you ready, Stewart?" Stewart just gets done fixing his bagel with cream cheese and coffee before he is being tugged away by Sam so that she doesn't have to listen to Franks talk anymore.

"It works every time," Franks laughs, "All you gotta do is bring up some of the past with Sam and she runs to the door." Franks is still laughing about it while Sam tugs Stewart out the door.

Shawn is fixing his own breakfast of eggs and toast. He asks Franks what he is doing today. Franks, still stuffing food down his throat, says nothing, so Shawn continues on by asking Bobby and Sid.

"Actually, Stewart and I wanted to know what you were doing."Bobby and Sid are at the kitchen table. Sid is eating his bowl of cereal. He eats a different kind each week. He likes to embrace what people do in their everyday life, like food, TV, cars, and sports games. He tries so hard to be one that fits in, but he will always know he comes from NORA. Shawn takes his breakfast to the kitchen table to join them and then asks again, "So what are you all doing today? Stewart and I wanted to see if you wanted to play a game."

Instantly, Franks turns around on his stool. "I'm not losing any more money to Stewart, no way, not again!" He hits his fist on his leg out of disbelief.

"Don't worry, you can't lose money. You lose countries, not money." Shawn says to Franks. Now Sid's focus had shifted from his cereal to every word Shawn was saying.

"You know the board game World Take Over? Roll a dice and

take over the world board game. Total world domination. I figure it's something to pass the time." Nobody says anything at first. Then Sid almost jumps out of his chair in excitement,

"I'll play, I'll play," he screams, in his high energized fashion, jumping at the opportunity of something new to do. Shortly after Franks commits to playing, once Shawn told him that they can play in front of the T.V.

"Sam said she would play," Shawn goes on, "and I'll convince Tyler to play." As soon as Shawn mentioned that Tyler was playing, Bobby instantly wanted to play.

"Great! That will be seven people. Wow, that's a lot. We will make Stewart and Sam a team." Shawn explains to all of them the rules of the game. Then he tells them to be back in three hours.

"Well at least I don't have to worry about you Franks. I know you will be right in front of the T.V." Shawn says as he gets up to put his dishes away.

"You know that's right," Franks yells out smiling and still spitting out food in the process.

A little while later Shawn runs into Tyler working on his personal car. It's a 2000 Cobra Mustang painted jet black throughout.

"How did you learn to work on earth cars so well?" he asks Tyler, who was wiping grease from his hands.

"I learned from this guy Alex Kovacasta. He was from California. He taught me about Earth engines and all the different cars."

"Where is he now?" Shawn asks, because Shawn is always trying to learn as much as he can about Tyler, because he just doesn't know enough about him which bothers Shawn. Tyler says nothing at first then he answers,

"Where is who?"

"Alex," Shawn quickly blurts out.

"Alex died in action. A battle broke out between the Tri-Vinn soldiers. They attacked the Earth base on NORA and Alex died in the fight." Shawn puts his head down for a second.

"He was the first human to die on the AHR team." Tyler goes on, "Your father took it really hard." "How did he die?" Shawn asks, while he pulls his bike out.

"When NORA made contact with Earth," Tyler explains as he sits on a nearby stool, "they were seeking out help. Years later Earth put a base on NORA. People on my planet started to listen to one man. This man started to rant and rave how earth was taking over NORA. Over time, a lot of my people on NORA started to believe him. He formed a rebel group called Tri-Vinn Soldiers." Tyler stops for a second to think of what to say next.

Shawn is finishing up looking over his bike and climbs on to it. Before he puts on his helmet he asks Tyler, "What was the leader's name?"

Tyler hesitates, and in a low, almost shameful voice, he says, "My brother." He pops up off the stool and is definitely bothered about Brackeo-Vinn. Shawn pushes Tyler for more information. Tyler takes a deep breath and with his back turned to Shawn, goes on.

"He was in my training class to protect NORA from the other planets in the NORA solar system. When we finished with training, he went to fight in the wars, and I went into communications. When my brother came home from war, he was different. Then my sister died, and he left me and our mother."

Tyler picks up a nearby screwdriver playing with it nervously in his hands as he continues talking.

"That's when I made contact with your father. I thought it was the greatest thing. The leader of the planet thought it was a God sent message. Through time the leaders of NORA and the leaders of Earth began to work together and help each other out. NORA started to gain power against our other planets. Earth was more involved, and through time a lot of my people were happy, except for my brother and his followers. They attacked my leaders and the Earth compound killing Alex Kovacasta. It was hard on your father. I hate to say this is what made him a strong leader."

Shawn zips up his leather jacket, and puts on his leather gloves. Before starting the bike he invites Tyler to the World Take Over board game, seeing that he could use some cheering up. He agrees to play, and Shawn speeds away. Shawn pulls into his driveway and notices CJ's car parked in the driveway. Shawn walks in the house and screams out "CJ where are you at?"

"I'm in the kitchen, stop screaming." she screams back.

Hey, how come you can scream then?"

"Because I'm older"

"Only for two months." CJ has been using that card all their lives.

"What are you doing here?"

"I came by to see if you are ok, because you weren't with Stewart and Sam. Who I really like. She is good for Stewart. Then I saw the kitchen was messy so I started to clean it and you came home."

"I agree with you Sam is good for him, and thank you for cleaning."

"I should start charging you."

"You won't because we are family," Shawn says looking for the board game, making more of a mess doing so. CJ turns and sees Shawn throwing everything out of the hall closet onto the floor.

"What the hell Shawn, I just cleaned there. What are you looking for?"

"I'm looking for the World Take Over board game."

"Do you have to throw everything everywhere?" CJ screams.

"There it is," Shawn says as he takes the board game down from the top shelf in the hall closet.

"Are you going to pick all that up now?' CJ asks angrily. Shawn walks to the kitchen placing the board game on the counter grabbing something to drink out of the refrigerator.

"Don't worry Shawn, I will clean this mess up for you." CJ says throwing everything back into the closet.

"Please don't mess up the kitchen now."

"I'm not. Listen CJ. Can you do me a huge favor?"

"Sure what do you need?" she says without hesitation.

"Me, Stewart and Sam are taking a trip. I was wondering if you can watch the house and put flowers at my mom's grave."

"Not a problem but where are you three going?' Shawn doesn't know what to tell CJ so he tells her the truth

"Ok this might sound crazy but Sam is actually part of a secret government agency, a team my father started. Plus I just found my Dad is alive and they recruited me and Stewart to go rescue him." Shawn waits for a response from CJ who starts laughing .

"I'm sorry Shawn, I know you are still grieving but that is the craziest story I have ever heard." CJ starts gathering her stuff to leave and as she is about to leave, she says, "Listen we are family and I love you but keep that story to yourself before they lock you up for being crazy." She closes the door to leave. Shawn screams out,

"Hey promise me that you will watch my house and continue putting flowers on my mom's tombstone?"

"Yes" she returns.

"Thank you, love you" Shawn hollers out.

"Be safe wherever you're going. Keep in touch if you can?" CJ says shutting the door behind her.

Shawn washes the glass he was using before putting the board game in another backpack. He puts it on and looks at his home before he leaves alone. Shawn hops onto his bike and jets away.

A few hours later back at the Nasa base, Shawn begins to set up the World Take Over game. Sid is reading the rules to Bobby and Franks who are sitting on the couch right next to Shawn. They are all startled by Sam who is out of breath, and then in comes a sweaty Stewart hunched over, and gasping for air.

"What the hell Sam, you killed Stewart!" Shawn says walking over to the both of them.

"He's fine," she says walking over to him and kisses him on the cheek. Stewart, so tired and sore, has no reaction. Sam runs off to the shower.

"She's tough," Stewart begins, gasping for air, "When it comes to working out." He drags himself to take a shower.

Tyler walks over to the couch holding drinks for everyone and asks, "So can anybody here tell me when Stewart and Sam got so close, and does the General know?"

The four men look at each other without saying a single word. Then, they all look at Shawn who finishes setting up the game.

"Last night they went on that date that they have been putting off for the last two months, and well, they hit it off. About the General knowing, well, that's a no."

"That should be fun when the General finds out," Tyler says, sipping his drink.

By now Stewart and Sam are coming into the room together. Sam is in baggy sweatpants, and a hooded sweatshirt, Stewart wearing blue jeans and a T-shirt. Sam overhears Tyler and asks, "Be fun when my father finds out about what?"

They both go sit together by the board game, Stewart sitting on the couch and Sam sitting on the floor between his legs.

"That you and Stewart are dating," Tyler says as he sits next to Stewart.

"Stewart and I are a couple now," Sam says, "and if any of you have a problem with that, too bad. As for my father, it might take him time. He loves me, so when we decide to tell him, he'll accept it."

They start playing, and as time passes by all of them start to understand the rules of the game. It is apparent that everyone is having a good time. Bobby is the first one to be eliminated. Franks is holding on by a thread until the team of Stewart and Sam knock him out, thanks to Sam rolling the die. The next to go is Tyler. Shawn attacks Sid in Asia from North America, which weakens him and allows him to be taken out by Stewart and Sam. There's only Sid and the team of Stewart and Sam left in the game. The game has been going on through three DVD movies that Shawn brought from his house. It even lasts through dinner. Eventually, Sid wins the game and starts jumping up and down from his win.

James Starkly walks in as Shawn and the rest of the group help clean up the game.

"What's that, World Takeover game?" he questions.

"Yes," Stewart says to him.

"My kids love that game; they always beat me in it. Who won this game? Sid jumps up chanting,

"Me, me, me!" over and over.

James shakes his head and smiles as he walks to his room for the night. The group starts to laugh, and they finally finish cleaning up, and then go to their separate rooms for the night.

CHAPTER TEN

The next morning the group meets in the briefing room, like they do every Monday morning. Only this time, for the very first time, they all walk in together; all of them talking to each other, and laughing amongst each other, like a team. They all sit down at the table, in order, from left to right; Bobby, James, Franks, Sam, Stewart, Shawn, and Sid at the end. Tyler is standing up by General Stone.

"Well look at this, for the first time in months I'm starting to see a strong team," Stone says, full of joy over the team unity. But, as normal, his joy is only for a second or two, and he gets down to business by yelling at them all.

"Stop talking. That's enough."

The group doesn't hear him until he picks a book up off of his desk and throws it on the floor, startling all of them.

"Are we all done talking? Can we all start listening now?" Stone is yelling loudly and finally he gets the attention of the team. He calmly continues.

"During the first two months we tested Shawn and Stewart, who just barely passed, by the way." They all laugh at the comment, except Stewart.

"That might be so, General," Stewart fires back, "but your daughter and I are kicking some ass together." Everybody laughs, except for Stone. Sam kicks Stewart under the table.

"On the computers, that is, sir, General, sir." Stewart finally finishes his sentence, trying to cover his ass, but everybody is still laughing.

Stone says to them, "Okay let's stop laughing, we have three months to get Shawn and Stewart able to handle space travel. We have to get them used to no gravity conditions and educate them about NORA. I also want you all to work as a team, to look after each other, and that means you too, Sam, because you are going on this mission, and I want you ready."

Sam is taking this seriously, as she normally does. This mission is important because she just found out that she has to leave the Earth compound on NORA for the first time. In order to free Dr. Higgins and the other prisoners, she and Stewart will have to break into unfamiliar computers and unlock their security system. Sam starts to tremble, and Stewart grabs her hand under the table where nobody notices. For Sam it instantly brings a quick calming sensation. So much so, that she doesn't realize her father is talking again.

"Like I said, we have three months. We will launch to the space station on September 29. In September, like every other month that only has thirty days, the space warp will open up right past our Milky Way galaxy. That's how we get to NORA. However, the tricky part is that our side of the warp is only open for one minute, whereas on NORA's side, it's open for an hour." Stewart raises his hand.

"How do we get from the space station to the warp?" Stone calls on Tyler for this one, who is standing off to the side. Tyler takes the clicker from Stone, and clicks the screen to a mock plan of a spaceship that kind of looks like a stealth U.S. Jet, but a lot larger, and has air locked hatches.

"This ship is at the space station and being prepared for our arrival," Tyler explains, "Once we get to the space station we have about eight to ten hours of work, where we will need to switch the gear and equipment from the United States Space Shuttle to the Blackbird Shuttle. We must clear your Milky Way, and make the warp by 11:11pm September 30, and remember we only have one minute to get through the space warp. If we don't make it we have to wait at least three months more until the warp opens again. So as I said, we must make the space warp." Everybody is taking notes and listening to Tyler speaking.

"But we have three months to go and a lot of training to do before we worry about all that. The closer we get, to the time we take off. We will talk about it again."

"Can I be trained in how to fly the shuttle or even be a pilot?" Shawn asks.

Initially, Tyler doesn't answer him. Instead, he gives a glance first to Bobby, then he looks over at General Stone. Stone is shaking his head yes.

"If you want to learn how to fly," Tyler says, "it will take extra time in training with me and Bobby." Stone agrees with that, and then dismisses everybody from the meeting except for Stewart and Sam. Everybody walks out, wondering if the General knows about their new relationship. The one person that is truly worrying is Sam.

General Stone waits until everybody has left the room and is in the elevator before he starts to talk to them. Sam's heart is pounding by now, waiting to see what her father is going to say next.

"The computer program that you both have to learn is tough and you need to know how to use it quickly to free Doctor Higgins and the other prisoners."

Sam is relieved that her father doesn't know about her and Stewart's relationship yet, but she knows she has to tell him quickly. Stone also tells them, "The new program is already in the computer room, and I think you two should get started in learning it right away."

In the elevator Sam realizes that Stewart is being very quiet for the first time since she has known him. She turns to him and grabs both of his hands.

"Hey, what's wrong with you? You haven't said anything for

a while." Stewart's hands are clammy, and sweat forming on his forehead. He takes a long, deep breath.

"I'm worried and starting to get scared." Sam squeezes his hands and comfortingly asks, "What are you scared about?"

Stewart, probably for the first time in a long time, says something honest and with no bullshit mixed in.

"I don't know if I can do this."

"Do what?"

"Be the hero and save Shawn's father. Hell, you can even save my father. Learn an alien computer program in less than three months plus train to actually fly in space?" Stewart exclaims with true emotion pouring out.

By now the two of them are off the elevator and entering the computer lab. Stewart sits in a chair and Sam sits on his lap. She puts one of her arms around the back of his neck and brings her face really close to his face.

"Hey, calm down. You'll be fine. I'll be right next to you the whole time." She gives him a kiss and a hug to try to calm him down, because Stewart is really shaken up over everything.

In time, they start to go through everything that was brought to them, including a box of binders, computer CDs, and thumb drives. Everything was brought back from NORA; computer software downloaded from computers on NORA technology, and information seen by only a handful of people on earth. The both of them prepare for another long night in the computer lab.

Meanwhile, Shawn is with Bobby and Tyler. He is being shown the controls and instruments of a simulator flight machine. He listens to both Tyler and Bobby explaining things for about two hours. Each shows him a different simulation. Shawn, eager to try it, jumps into the seat. He starts out alright, but crashes the plane because he is not fast enough in keeping up with the controls. This happens a lot over some time.

September 1st comes around very quickly. The first two of the three months flew by for Shawn and Stewart. Each of them has been learning individual tasks, but they are also learning team tasks. Plus, in order to get used to being in zero gravity, as well as space conditions in general, they are going to the swimming pool a lot.

Shawn has learned the controls, and has become much better at piloting the aircraft. He has worked late with Tyler and Bobby, after team training and debriefings. He has picked it up very easily and quickly. He's not ready to fly the real thing, but he is close to it.

Meanwhile, Stewart and Sam have come a long way in the last two months, with both the new technology and working well as a team. Stewart would meet Sam every night after training. Their personal relationship became really strong, and they are very happy together. Sam's father still doesn't know about them, which is really weighing down on Sam. She has almost told him on many occasions, after almost being caught together, but they always find a way not to tell him.

"I'm going to tell him tonight, I promise," Sam says, Stewart is sitting in the chair next to her. They are both in the computer room working late, like they usually do.

"Listen, tell him or don't tell him, I don't care either way." Stewart turns in his chair towards Sam.

"The only thing I care about is you. The whole thing is, when you're ready to tell your father, I'll be with you through it all, if you want me there"

Sam is flattered, but a beeping sound coming from the computer screen averts both of their attention to it. The screen is flashing red and behind it are strange symbols racing across.

"What's this stuff on the screen, Stewart?" Sam asks.

"I don't know. I have never seen this before. Let me take the warning off." Stewart stops the flashing warning light so that only the racing symbols appear. All kinds of symbols, including circles, squares, and different lines in different sequences together, fill the screen moving from left to right.

"We should call my father. Maybe he can make sense out of all this."

"That's good, call him here right away. I'm going to start to record this," Stewart says frantically to Sam as he tries to make sense of this. Sam calls her father, and it takes him no time at all to get to them.

"See dad, it's exactly what I told you it was." General Stone looks as though he has seen this before.

"I don't get it. I want Tyler in here now. Get Tyler."

Sam and Stewart are looking at each other. They are stunned, because they have never seen the General so rattled before.

"He is probably with Shawn," Stewart answers, "but where, I don't know."

General Stone's face is turning red and he starts to yell. "Did I ask you, Stewart, where he is? I said to find him now!"

"Daddy don't yell at Stewart! He didn't do anything wrong." Stewart is reaching for the phone to make an announcement for Tyler to report to the computer lab, when the General grabs the phone from him and screams through the intercom, "Tyler, this is General Stone, report to me in the computer lab immediately!" He follows that up with, "Now. Right now," and slams the phone down.

"Dad, what's wrong? I have only seen you like this once, and that was when Doctor Higgins was captured by the Tri-Vinn Soldier's." Stone is pacing back and forth, not listening to anything Sam has said. Back and forth, back and forth he paces, waiting for Tyler. Tyler steps out of the elevator and enters the room. Shawn follows right behind him both are still in there flight suits. Stone gets right in Tyler's face.

"Look! Look! What's that on the screen? You told me this would not be a problem again." Tyler is looking past Stone towards the computer screen.

"Wait, you told us you had no idea what this is," Stewart says. He stands up to allow Tyler to sit. Tyler wastes no time, and begins typing really fast.

"How did you come across this?" He is looking at Stewart and Sam.

"We were scanning programs like we have been doing for the

past two months. Then the screen started flashing red and those symbols appeared." Stewart answers.

Tyler continues typing. Shawn starts tugging on Stewarts arm to find out what's going on. Stone, still pacing and mumbling under his breath, utters,

"I thought you took care of this."

"Can one of you tell us what this is? What do the symbols mean?" Stewart yells out.

Stone is not answering. Hell, he is not even listening. Tyler is also not paying any attention. He is just staring at the screen like he is trying to read what is going across the screen.

"Screw this! If you don't tell me, I'll figure it out myself." Stewart blows past Shawn, who is still looking confused. He waits for the elevator doors to open so he can leave. He is getting even more frustrated because the elevator is taking too long to get to the floor he's on, so he decides to take the stairs. Just as he leaves the elevator doors open.

Shawn leaves the room and gets into the elevator to catch up to Stewart, but sees he wasn't there. Sam starts to follow Shawn out to the elevator when her father stops her and says,

"I would like to see you later in my office. It is important." Sam agrees and runs to catch the elevator doors, which she does in the nick of time.

"What's going on, Sam? What did you find?" Shawn asks her.

"I don't know, Shawn. Something is not right." Sam says, the elevator doors open. They ask Franks if Stewart was here. "Just blew by here. He didn't look too happy." They both run to the room without saying anything else to Franks, who continues to watch the T.V.

Stewart is sitting in one of the chairs with his feet resting on the table, and lighting a cigarette.

"What's going on, Stewart? What happened? You seem a little more nervous than normal." Shawn says to him, as Stewart inhales.

"I don't know what is happening, but I hate to say this to you, Sam, your father is hiding something, and I'm going to figure it out." Stewart stands up and says to himself,

"He knew what those symbols meant, he was reading them." Shawn stands in front of Stewart trying to get something out of him.

"Who knew? Reading What?" Stewart turns around and walks the other way saying the same thing again. Shawn is starting to get frustrated now, over not knowing what is going on, and waiting for Stewart to explain.

"Your father was acting like he saw those symbols before," Stewart says to Sam.

"Even Tyler, he was reading the symbols." He looks at Sam and asks her,

"Didn't it look like Tyler was reading the symbols also?" Sam says nothing. She just shook her head yes.

"What symbols?" Shawn says, as he is trying to get anything he can from Stewart and Sam. The two of them continue talking among themselves, talking in riddle form, keeping it from Shawn. Stewart is just trying to understand things before he explains it to Shawn. Finally, Stewart finishes his cigarette, and tries to explain everything. He picks up Shawn's father's diary while he speaks, and starts flipping through the diary's pages.

"Sam and I were scanning through flies like we have been doing for the last two months, and then, all of the sudden, a red warning light started flashing. Then all of these symbols appeared."

"What symbols?" Shawn asks.

"These are the symbols," Stewart throws Shawn's father's diary on the table, opened to the page that displays some of the symbols that appeared on the screen. He slides it across the table where Shawn is standing. Shawn picks up the journal from the table.

"What's that?" Sam asks.

Shawn doesn't answer her, and instead looks at Stewart.

"It's okay, she won't say anything, I told her about the diary already" Stewart says to Shawn. Shawn trusts Stewart and his word, so he starts to tell Sam more about the diary, and what he has learned from it and the clues they have been solving in it. Shawn reads out loud the entry that is under the symbols.

ENTRY 218:

I've come across something very strange today. A lot of different symbols came across my computer screen as I was checking files on the earth compound computer. Tyler told me it was a secret code by Tri-Vinn Soldiers; something like marching orders. I have to figure out what it says; I have to crack this code.

- Doc Higgins

Shawn stops reading all of a sudden.
"What does it say? Why did you stop?" Stewart asks. Shawn begins flipping through the pages and says,
"I didn't stop, that was the end of the entry." Shawn continues to turn through the pages. Finally Shawn comes across a page that has the same symbols all over them, like Shawn's father was trying to figure out a pattern. After about ten to fifteen pages of nothing but scribbles of symbols, Shawn comes across another entry.
"Okay here is another entry."

ENTRY 219:

I've been trying for weeks to crack the symbols and what they say and I think, I think, I finally did it.

-Doc Higgins

"Hey, look! My father created a chart of the symbols next to letters and numbers". Shawn gets a paper and pen and copies the symbol chart for Stewart so he can figure out what it says across his screen. Sam asks to see the journal. Shawn hands it to her, and she starts flipping through it.
"I can probably decipher the symbols on the screen with this paper." Stewart was just about to go when he saw Sam clutching Shawn's father's diary to her chest and she had a big smile on her face.

"What did you read, Sam?" Stewart asks.
"Listen to this," she says.

ENTRY 115:

General Stone's daughter is starting today. I'm sure she was very nervous, but she never showed it, not once. She is turning into a beautiful young lady. It's funny, I think she would be great with Stewart, they have a lot in common. Maybe one day they can meet. You never know, they just might hit it off. Which would be good for Stewart, he needs a special someone in his life. He has so little of that special connection in his life, and I think someone as strong as Sam could be good for him. It may be good for both of them.

- Doc Higgins

Sam is smiling, as she is glistering with joy and happiness. Stewart reaches out his arms to Sam and he lifts her from the couch.

"Come here, you."

"Well," Shawn interjects, "you can say one thing about my father: he can read people very well."

Shawn grabs the journal from Sam's hands. They all head to the computer lab. As they were exiting the elevator, Shawn notices that Stone and Tyler are still in the room and he quickly puts the journal in a side pocket of his cargo pants before either one of them can notice it.

"What are you three doing back here?" Stone asks.

"Sam and I are going to continue to look through the files tonight," Stewart quickly responds.

Tyler, still looking at the computer screen, is not paying any attention to what Stewart is saying. Stone, who is much calmer now, says,

"Maybe tomorrow, Tyler is still trying to figure this out."

"Can I help him?" Stewart asks. "I'm really good with

computers and figuring out patterns."

Stone is not bending on his decision. "No thanks, you better let Tyler do it. You both can get started again in the morning." They all start to leave when General Stone stops his daughter to say,

"Sam, can you stay? We need to talk for a minute."

Sam turns to Shawn and Stewart and says,

"I'll catch up with you both later."

Shawn and Stewart leave in a hurry to get back to their room. In their room Stewart jumps on one of his computers.

"What are you doing?" Shawn asks,

"We need to figure out what the code means."

Stewart, already in his zone, is typing. His eyes are going back and forth along his computer screen.

"Almost got it, there I am in. Now I can see what Tyler has been looking at."

Shawn hands Stewart the diary so that he doesn't have to read the paper he copied before. Stewart starts trying to decipher some of what is being said in this code.

"That's cool how you got into the computer Tyler is working on," Shawn says from behind him,

"Can he tell you that you are on with him?"

"No he can't, I'm sharing his screen without him knowing. It's very easy, since Tyler is on the computer. I created a back door so I can see everything he sees."

"Does he know that you are doing this?" Shawn asks Stewart again, just to make sure, because Stewart has been wrong before. Stewart didn't answer him this time because he has started matching up symbols to the chart in the diary.

After a while Stewart reassures Shawn by saying,

"Trust me, Tyler has no idea that I'm doing this. I'm like a ghost. When he shuts off his computer, this one will disconnect as well, that's why I have it recording to my computer."

Once again, Shawn is blown away by Stewart's ability on the computer.

"Okay. This is what I thought, and it isn't good. We have to go tell them," Stewart says.

Stewart races to the elevator with Shawn right behind him. They race by a sleeping Franks on the couch.

"What's up? What does it say?" Shawn asks Stewart.

"What I figured, is that it's a countdown of some sort and countdowns are bad."

In the computer lab, Tyler is still on the computer, and General Stone and Sam are talking to each other in the hallway.

"I don't want you to leave," Stone says to Sam. "It's not safe to go on this mission."

Sam can't believe what she is hearing. "What, daddy? I'm going to NORA in a month. I'm part of this team, and they need me, Stewart needs me." General Stone is not happy with Sam's decision.

"Why now?" Sam continues on. "Why all of a sudden now, do you have a problem with me going? Does it have anything to do with these symbols? What do they mean?" General Stone doesn't answer her, but Stewart does as he and Shawn exit the elevator.

"It's a countdown. The symbols on the screen are counting down at certain parts."

Tyler hears this and gets up from his chair and walks over to them.

"You're a smart kid, Stewart," Tyler begins, "and you're right, it is a countdown."

"Countdown to what?" Shawn quickly asks.

Tyler doesn't hesitate at all with an answer.

"Somehow Brackeo, the leader of the Tri-Vinn Soldiers,

"Yes we all know he's your brother." Shawn blurts out in a very angry tone.

" Wait, his brother, I didn't know that." Stewart says.

It is a countdown for what I don't know but they must have found out about our rescue plan. What I can't figure out is there timing is off for about a month, and they don't say anything about Shawn or Stewart."

General Stone is still trying to insist that his daughter stays off this mission, but she is not listening to anything he has to say.

"Why is it so important for you to go on this mission? You're still a part of the AHR team whether you go or not."

"I'm going. I'm part of this team and I'm going with Stewart when he frees Doc Higgins and the prisoners on NORA." Sam is yelling this so everybody can hear at least half the conversation.

General Stone positions himself between his daughter and Stewart.

"You don't have to go. Stewart can handle it without you. Right, Stewart?" General Stone turns to Stewart, hoping he will side with him due to his intimidation.

"No Daddy!" Sam blurts out, "I want to be there. I want to be with Stewart. We have been dating for the past two and a half months." Sam blurts out of conflict.

General Stone looks like he has just been punched in the gut with the news of Sam and Stewart dating. He doesn't say anything at first.

"Well, then I see you have made up your mind," Stone eventually says. "I guess we're done here. I'm going home." General Stone says nothing more; he just leaves.

Sam is pissed at her dad's actions, but over time she becomes sad over her dad's reaction, and is surprised that she feels like this.

For the next week the team goes on with training. It's business as usual, but for Sam there is something missing. Her father hasn't been in sight since their fight. That night, she decides to go to her childhood home after training, in Jacksonville florida, to see if her father is there. She pulls into the driveway of her family's ranch style home. She is hoping that her father's car will be visible, but it isn't. Now she's hoping that her father is at home and okay.

"Daddy? Are you home?" She announces. She searches the backyard because her father likes to sit out back and look at the sky. He is not there, so then she checks his bedroom, and his offices, but there's no sign of him. She is now starting to worry, but then she hears a noise from her bedroom. He peeks her head into her old room and sees her father sitting on the floor with a bottle of scotch between his legs. She walks over to him and picks up the empty bottle from between his legs, and places it next to him.

"Here, let me help you." Sam helps her father sit on her old bed.

"Daddy, what's wrong? I haven't seen you this drunk since mom left."

The General, for the first time in a long time, is showing a sign of weakness. Before he shows anymore he gets up.

"I'm going to take a shower." He says nothing else and walks out of the room, leaving Sam alone in the dark room.

A half hour later General Stone meets his daughter in the backyard where she is bundled up with a blanket. It is a cold night for early September.

"Here, I made you hot chocolate just the way you like it, with a lot of marshmallows," the General says to Sam. Sam takes the cup from her father as he sits in the chair next to her and says,

"I used to love sitting back here with you, looking up at the sky, just stargazing."

"What's going on dad? Why are you drinking so much?"

"I don't want you to go up this time," he replies, as he puts his cup on the table and grabs Sam's hands.

"Why?" Sam pulls her hands away and gets up. "What's going on, Dad? What are these symbols? Are they important?" Sam sits back down. Her father takes a deep breath.

"You are not going. I don't care what you say, I'm your father." The General's temper rises, and his tone of his voice is up.

"I've been there twice, what's different this time? What's with those symbols, Dad? I want to know!" Now Sam is getting mad because her father has never kept any secrets from her. He takes another deep breath, puts his hands together, looks down at the ground, and then looks back at Sam.

"There's a lot that's different this time. I'm not going with you." He puts one of his hands out for her hand, but she doesn't take it.

"I'll be safe. That's why I have been training with the team for the last four years." Her voice is low but raising in tone. "I'm going up with the team you helped create, remember you were the one that convinced me to join the team in the first place." Her father doesn't have a response right away, but eventually says,

"Because this time you all might be walking into a trap, and I'm your father first, then I'm a General to you."

Sam looks up at the stars. "I don't care, I've gotten close to the team,

"You mean you got close to Stewart?"

"Yes, I got really close to Stewart, do you have a problem with that now?" She is firmly standing her ground with her father probably for the first time in her life.

"No, I just wish you told me and not have me find out like I did."

"I know I'm sorry that that's not how I saw that going, I tried, we tried telling you so many times but I stopped it from happening. Stewart always wanted to tell you Dad, he is a really good guy and I think he loves me but hasn't said it yet."

"Do you love him?" Stone asks his daughter.

"Like I said it's not all about Stewart, I have gotten close to them all, part of a team. A team you begged me to join, so you got your wish because, I'm one of them now. If they go and I don't, and they walk into a trap and get killed, I won't be unable to live with myself." She grabs her father's hands, then makes him look at her.

"I'm going and that's it. I will not let my friends die if that's what's going to happen. Then I will be dying alongside them." She looks right into her father's eyes. They are slowly beginning to tear as the thought sets in. He wipes the tears from his eyes then stands up, and says,

"It's because of Stewart isn't it? Are you willing to give up your life for a boy you just met?" He is standing close, showing his power over her, trying to intimidate her.

She doesn't back down once again; she stands up, faces her father, and says,

"It's not only Stewart. I want to save Doctor Higgins and the planet. I'm doing it to save your life."

General Stone can't stand it anymore, the emotions are beginning to overwhelm him, and he turns from his daughter taking a few steps away from her.

"Those symbols are binary codes sent out to the Tri-Vinn Soldiers. It's given only by one person, Brackeo Vinn." He looks at Sam trying to scare her, but it doesn't work.

"He is dangerous, and he will kill you on the spot."

"Dad, I truly understand why you are so afraid, but I've been trained. I know what I am doing because of Tyler, Doc Higgins, even Stewart. I'm ready, the AHR team is ready. You should be ready too. Please give me your blessing, and let me go fight with a clear head, let me fight for our planet."

"Do you love him?" he says with his back still turned from his daughter in a low voice. Sam walks over behind her father putting her hands on one of his shoulders.

"It might be love. I don't know, but he makes me really happy, and I want you to like him, too."

General Stone grunts then takes a deep breath.

"And I want you to give him a real chance, not like the other boyfriends I had as a kid."

"If he makes you happy, then I'll give him a chance. Under one condition, you must stay focused on this mission, and if you do that I give you my blessing"Sam hugs her father.

"He makes me stronger, just like you, and I will never lose my focus." She hugs her father even tighter, and he hugs her the same way back while looking up at the dark sky lit by bright stars.

CHAPTER ELEVEN

The team has a little less than three weeks before they launch to the International Space Station. General Stone and Tyler are explaining to the team members

"Ok, it is my duty as a General, to inform you all that you could be walking into a trap. We have intercepted a Tri-vinn Soldier countdown, and we figure the countdown ends around the time we start the mission." General Stone pauses for a second and then says "I would understand if any of you want to back down and skip this mission for your safety." Stone looks at Sam while speaking, hoping that she has come to her senses. No one comes forward and after some time James Starkey says.

"I have a family, wife and two kids," everybody looks at James wondering where he is going with his speech and if he is going to back out of the missing. " With that all being said Doc Higgins is also family and I know the risks I will be going to save him, who is with me?" With that being said the rest of the team raises their hands screaming out "WE ARE WITH YOU!" together. General Stone on the other hand is upset and worried about Sam's safety. General Stone says,

"Okay, then I want you to go through all the drills again. I want all of you to be sharp and alert. Not just for me or even for Doc Higgins, do it for yourselves, your family, and your planet." While he says this he is looking at Sam, which brings a smile to both of their faces. After the General stops talking the team gets up to leave. James Starkly is the only one left. He approaches Stone and Tyler.

"I want to spend the last week with my family if that is okay with you, General Stone," Starkly requests.

"Franks already said he is willing to continue training both Stewart and Shawn."

"Are the two young men ready for what they will be walking into?" Stone questions Starkly, who happens to be standing at attention, with his arms at his sides,

"Sir, they are both determined, both extremely smart, and I truly believe they will do fine," Starkly answers firmly. "General Sir, I want to be with my family since this could very well be the last time."

"Be back the day before the launch for Quarantine."

Starkly thanks them both before he walks out he says, "I know the drill." Then he leaves the compound.

With the team down a man General Stone steps in to help with the rest of training. They go through all the things they have been working on. They swim in the pool with their space suits to portray low gravity. General Stone and Franks bring them to the shooting range, and on Fridays they all take a spin in the flight simulator where Shawn still leads in the standings. Tyler has been putting in a lot of time preparing Shawn for piloting and teaching Stewart and Sam the Tri-Vinn soldier's signals. The last Friday before they launch General Stone has one last briefing. They go over all the details.

"Okay, let's go over the launch first," General Stone says with the attention of the whole group. He is basically running through a checklist. "It takes eight minutes to break earth's orbit. It will be a total of three days until you reach the Space Station."

"Wait a minute," Stewart says, "We have to be tied to a seat for three days until we get to the International Space Station?" Stewart's face is shocked and it's definitely not happy at all, until Sam tells him that once they leave Earth's orbit they can float around the shuttle, which makes Stewart a lot happier.

The next thing they talk about is their mission. Tyler explains, beginning with Stewart and Sam.

"When we start, Stewart, Sam, and Franks, the three of you go with forces that are mixed with men from earth and people from NORA. You have the entrance of the mines where you will enter. The computer room is easier to get to from the second entrance. After you disable their security, Shawn, James Starkly, and I will free Doctor Higgins and the other prisoners." He then explains that Bobby will be waiting to get us out of there with the Blackbird Shuttle.

"Listen, I know you guys are scared, but we have an advantage. They think we are coming a month later then we are." Tyler is trying to give a speech of encouragement, but they all know that this is going to be tough and life threatening to them all.

Stone notices they are all very tired from training. "I want you all to take this weekend and have fun. I want you to rest and be back here Monday for Quarantine because we launch at nine a.m. Tuesday."

Back in their living quarters Franks is already packed for the weekend. "Where are you going, big guy?" Stewart asks.

"I'm going to be with my friends, and even go to see my mother before we leave." Franks says.

"Wait a minute, you have friends? That's not true, stop lying." Stewart replies to Franks.

Sam back-hands Stewart. Franks laughs and thanks Sam for hitting Stewart for his remarks.

"Boy, I love that you two are together. She can keep you in line," Franks says as he waits for the elevator. The doors open. "About time someone will keep him in line," Shawn says from the kitchen.

"Don't forget about Shooters Sunday," Sam screams to Franks as he enters the elevator, right before the door closes. Franks sticks his head out and says that he would be there.

"Shooters? What's that?" Stewart asks. He is always looking

for another good time.

"Oh, it's a bar right down the street from here. My Dad knows the owner and we get free drinks. So the whole team meets there before we go to the Kennedy Space Station for Quarantine." Sam answers Stewart, still standing in the kitchen.

"Quarantine? What's that?" Shawn asks.

"The day before we launch we have to all stay in an air locked room to get our bodies ready for entering orbit. We also have to do it when we land back on earth." With that, Sam heads back to her room to grab her bags that she has put together.

"So how are things going for the two of you?" Shawn asks Stewart.

"Great," Stewart answers back as he grabs the soda can from Shawn's hands and starts to drink from it.

"How are things with her father?" Stewart stops drinking and hands Shawn back an empty can.

"Well, he hasn't said two words to me in a one-on-one encounter, and he leaves the room when it's just me in it." He takes a deep breath and continues to say, "Things are going great."

Shawn smiles as he grabs another soda from the refrigerator. Sam comes back and walks behind Stewart who is sitting at one of the stools. She puts her hands around his waist and rests her head on his back.

"So where are you going this weekend Miss Sam?" Shawn asks.

"I'm spending tomorrow with my father and I'm picking up Stewart Sunday morning and we are going to spend the day together. Where am I picking you up, anyway?"

Stewart, smiling from ear to ear, quickly responds, "I'll be at Jan & Lib's Hi-Tops."

"You mean passed out," Shawn says out loud. Behind them you hear a very loud and deep grunt.

"Daddy, I didn't see you behind me," Sam says as she quickly releases her arms from around Stewart's waist. "Are you ready?"

Her father's face is flooded with a deep red color before a low deep voice says, "Yes. The car is ready and waiting on you, sweetie."

Shawn is trying not to burst out in laughter. Stewart's face is beet red and looking down as he fiddles with his fingers.

Sam swings Stewart around on his stool and gives him a long kiss with the General standing right there watching them, breathing very deeply and loud. Sam stops kissing Stewart and begins to pull her father away tugging on his arm.

"Come on dad, let's go. I'll see you both on Sunday," Sam calls back to Shawn and Stewart.

"You knew he was standing behind me the whole time." Stewart places his hand on his face. Shawn is laughing and shaking his head up and down in a yes gesture.

"He heard the passed out comment?" Stewart asked.

"Yes, why do you think I said it?"

Stewart takes the empty can of soda that sits on the countertop and throws it at Shawn.

"That's not funny," he yells.

"Do you need a ride somewhere?" Shawn asks.

"No. Sid fixed me up with a car. It is already in the garage waiting for me." The two of them continue to talk, and before saying their goodbyes, agree to meet the following day at Jan & Lib's Hi-Tops.

The next day, each member of the team did their own thing. Some did fun things with family and friends, while others got some work done. James Starkly was still with his family. Franks visited his mother and also spent time with his friends and older brother betting on sports. Tyler, Bobby, and Sid spent it at the complex because they don't have earth ties yet, other than the AHR team members. Tyler stepped out for about an hour to handle personal matters, but he was mostly in the compound. Sam and her father spent the day together and had a nice father-daughter dinner.

Saturday night, around 8:30, Shawn arrives at Jan & Lib's Hi-Tops. He walks in from the back door. The place is unusually dead for a Saturday night, but that's fine with Shawn.

"Well, look what the wind blew in," Benny screams out,

getting the attention of everyone at the bar.

"About time you got here," Stewart says, drunk as a skunk.

"I see someone broke their one drink rule," Shawn answers.

"I tried to stop him, but he continued to insist on drinking more tonight. I took his keys from him already," CJ said. Shawn takes the keys from CJ then hugs his cousin.

"What can I get you Shawn?" CJ asks as she walks back around the bar.

"Give me a shot of tequila, a beer chaser, and follow that up with a rum and coke." CJ is surprised that Shawn just ordered so much to drink.

"Make that two rum and coke and two beers, CJ," Stewart says slurring his words.

CJ looks at Shawn almost to see if he was going to stop him from ordering yet another drink.

"You heard the man, two rum and coke, two beers," Shawn yells out un-pausing a frozen CJ. This gets the attention of Libby, CJ's mother from the other side of the bar.

"Look who finally came back," Libby says in her dominating voice. She comes around the bar and gives Shawn a big kiss on his check followed up by a really tight hug.

"I'm glad you are all here," Shawn says to Benny, his cousin CJ, and his Aunt.

"Stewart and I are celebrating tonight. I would first like to ask if the three of you can check on our homes for about two, maybe three months."

The three of them are all listening in anticipation to what's coming next. Even Stewart is wondering where he is going with this.

"Stewart and I are going on a road trip to find his real father." Shawn is making up some bullshit story to cover up the real story. Stewart is too drunk to realize anything. He was lost on Shawn's first sentence, and is just going off everybody else's response. Shawn holds up his glass in salute.

"Cheers to Stewart and I for our luck, as well as safety. And cheers to his father's safe return home."

As Stewart is holding up his glass, he says, "To all fathers." They all click their glasses together in salute. The rest of the night they all party. A few of them got drunker than others, but overall it was a wonderful night.

In the morning, Stewart wakes to Sam's voice, as he lies asleep in a booth within the bar.

"Did you have a rough night," she asks as she holds a cup of coffee for him.

"What?" Stewart is just waking up; he sits up and gives Sam room to sit next to him.

CJ, who opened the bar this morning, walks over to them.

"I'm glad you got him up. I was going for the house soon." She leans down and hugs Sam. Stewart, who is still waking up, just keeps drinking his coffee.

"Are you going with Stewart and Shawn on their trip?" CJ asks Sam.

Sam has no response at first but then says yes.

CJ replies, "That's good, Stewart needs everybody around him when he meets his father." Sam agrees and plays along, realizing the cover up.

"Come on, Stewart, let's go, we have to get ready to leave tomorrow morning."

Stewart, although dealing with a really bad hangover, agrees with her. He stands up, gives CJ a hug and says his goodbyes. The two head out the back of the bar, to Stewart's car

" I'm driving." Sam screams out "Besides, CJ gave me the keys." They both get in Stewart's car and head to his apartment. "How did you get here?"

"My best friend Amanda dropped me off. I had breakfast with her this morning." The two of them spend the rest of the day snuggling together and watching movies at Stewart's apartment.

"Where are we meeting Shawn?" Sam asks.

"I don't know. I've been calling him all day, but he is not answering. I figured we would stop by his house."

"Well the rest of the team will start to gather at Shooters around six tonight," Sam explains to Stewart as they figure out their final day on Earth. They finish the movie and head over to Shawn's house. As they pull into the driveway, Sam's expression changes. There is a metal gate that surrounds the house.

"Wow, this is a really nice house." Sam says.

"It was his father's house. He left it to Shawn in his will, well I guess it would have been his fake will," Stewart says as he unlocks the front door, and they enter the house. Stewart starts calling out

"SHAWN SHAWN YOU HERE?" He screams out a few times over. As they walk around They start to notice that there are no lights on in the house and no televisions on, anywhere. There is no sign of Shawn or any one.

"I don't think he's here. Maybe he went to Shooters already," Sam says as they check all the rooms in the house.

"See, his bike's not here. He told me that we will go to Shooters together." Stewart is standing by the doorway trying to figure out where his friend is.

"Wait a minute, I know where he is." Stewart says out loud. They both get in the car and drive off. Stewart directs her to the cemetery where Shawn's mother lays to rest.

"See, there's his bike," he says as they pull up next to it. They both get out of the car and look up at Shawn standing at his mother's tombstone.

"Is that his mother's grave?" Sam asks. Stewart shakes his head yes. Shawn realizes they are both standing down the hill, and Stewart brings Sam up to the grave site. Stewart kneels on one knee and says a quiet prayer like he always does when he comes here. Sam stays back out of the way. Once Stewart is done, he goes to stand with Sam, as Shawn kisses his mother's picture that is on her tombstone and touches her necklace that hangs. He follows Sam and Stewart on his bike back to the compound garage. They walk to Shooters from there.

Shooters is a small bar, which has a rare design. One could sit at the bar inside and outside. Shawn, Stewart and Sam meet the whole team in the back of the bar. James Starkly is also back from spending time with his family. Sid, Franks, Bobby, Tyler, and General Stone are all there in their street clothes.

Sam hugs her father and they all sit down in the corner booth. Franks pours them each a beer from the pitcher that sits in the middle of the table.

"None for me, thank you though," Stewart says. Franks gets on his case. Sam turns to Stewart and says, "Just one."

Stewart smiles and copies her, "Just one."

They all raise their glasses and toast to their mission and come back safe with Doctor Higgins. After that General Stone stands up from the booth and asks for silence.

"There's something else we are celebrating tonight," he begins, "James can you, please stand up next to me?" James stands up next to General Stone like he was asked.

"James, I'm honored to stand here tonight and announce that you have been promoted to Major James Starkly of the United States army." Starkly is floored as the General hands him a Major Flower Pin. "Let me be the first to say I'm proud of you, Major James Starkly."

General Stone salutes James for the first time as Major Starkly. Everybody at the table starts clapping and congratulates James for his achievement. For the next few hours they share wings, mozzarella sticks and a few pitchers of beer. Stewart drinks his soda and Sam too, so that he doesn't feel singled out.

They all leave Shooters together laughing and talking to each other, except General Stone, he is still giving Stewart the silent treatment. They all walk back to the compound to get some sleep, because tomorrow they get ready to fly to space and start their dangerous quest for Shawn's father.

CHAPTER TWELVE

The AHR team heads to Kennedy Space Center early the next morning. It is on everyone's mind that they are about to start the quest in which they may not come back from. None of them seem to care, however, because they're going to rescue and bring home a person that means a lot to each and every one of them. Dr. Howard Higgins who is their leader, the team creator, and the person that they all go to for guidance when needed. And for one individual, he is a father. The amazing thing is that he has been thought to be dead for a year now.

They arrive at Kennedy Space Center by six in the morning. They have a quick tour inside the space shuttle that is already in place to launch twenty four hours from now. Inside the shuttle there are two rows of seats.

"Wow, there's a lot more room here than it looks from outside," Shawn says as he climbs the ladder to where his seat should be.

"It better be since we will be here for three days," Stewart says climbing up the ladder right underneath him. Shawn climbs into his seat with Stewart sitting right behind him. Tyler is the third guy in the shuttle.

"Hey Tyler! Who's going to be sitting next to me?" Stewart asks. Tyler tries to explain to them how to buckle themselves into the seat, but Stewart is not listening to him. Tyler doesn't answer him, so Stewart, acting like a child, asks him again.

"I think Franks. Why?" Tyler finally answers. Stewart shakes his head.

"Nope. That's not going to work. Sam must sit there because if this thing blows up tomorrow morning I want to be seeing Sam's face, not Frank's face, for the last time." Stewart continues to ramble on by saying nothing intelligent, which he does when he gets nervous.

"Stewart, will you please shut the hell up," Shawn blurts out.

"I was just saying." Stewart calls back at Shawn. He is always trying to get the last word in. Tyler starts over again with the instructions of buckling them into the seats and this time Stewart stays quiet.

After the tour of the shuttle Tyler takes them both to the locker room where they see the space suits for the first time. The suits have their last names on them. They are all hanging on hooks in individual locker spaces. Shawn walks over to his and touches his name that is stitched on it.

"Are you two ready for lockdown?" Franks says trying to be funny. Sam pushes through him and up to Stewart.

"Are you ready?" She asks Stewart.

"I guess. It's not like we have a choice in the matter," Stewart says as he finally walks away from his astronaut suit.

The three of them follow Franks to the isolation room, where they will be for the next twenty four hours. They walk in and see James Starkly is already being attached to an I.V. line that runs into his arms.

"What's with the I.V.?" Shawn asks.

"We hook you up to an I.V. and put you under anesthesia for twenty four hours. This process thins your blood vessels to prepare your body to leave Earth's orbit," General Stone says from behind them.

Shawn looks around and asks, "Hey, General Stone, where's Tyler and Bobby?"

James Starkly sits up from his bed and says,

"They don't need to do this. Their DNA can travel through

space." He says as he lays back down in his bed.

"Then what are they doing while we are under?" Shawn asks while they are hooking him up to the I.V.

"Knowing Tyler, he's dressed like a NASA worker helping to load the shuttle with our supplies," James Starkly replies.

"Wait, why does he dress up as a NASA worker?" Stewart now asks.

"He likes to be secretive. He always thinks that somebody is watching him."

By now they are all hooked up to the I.Vs and are sealed in the isolation room. General Stone looks through the window as he watches them all pass out.

The next morning the team wakes up one by one. The last one to wake up is Stewart. Even drugged Stewart is still a pain in the ass to wake up. He actually needed to be woken up by someone.

One hour until launch Shawn and Stewart and the rest of the AHR team are all dressed in their space suits. Before they hop on the shuttle they have one last meeting with General Stone, so he can introduce the two pilots that will fly the shuttle to the space center.

"Gentlemen, I would like to introduce Sgt. Hal Cooper and his co-pilot Stacy Whiteman." Hal Cooper is a mid-sized man with brown buzzed hair and a thick brown beard. His co-pilot is much shorter, and bald on top of his head, with thick hair around the bottom of his head.

"Excuse me, General, I thought Tyler and Bobby are the pilots." Shawn asks.

"They are for the Blackbird Shuttle to NORA. But the public on earth loves watching the shuttles take off and these two gentlemen will be the two in the public's eyes, not you guys." General Stone explains that the AHR team will never be in the eyes of the people on earth.

The team finishes their last briefing and heads to the family room. This is a big wide open room with tables, the walls and ceilings that are all painted white. They enter the room and inside are James Starkey's wife and his two children, an eight year old boy and a four year old girl. Also in the room is General Stone because even the General can't go on past this point. The wives of Cooper and Whitehead are also in the room.

Stewart and Shawn stand off to the side, along with Tyler and Bobby. Sam is sitting with her father at one table, and Cooper and Whitehead sit at another table with their wives. Even Franks has his older brother, Sonny Franks, and their eighty-four year old mother. She acts like she is a twenty six year old girl.

"Hey Shawn, Stewart, come over here, please," James Starkly yells. Shawn and Stewart both look at each other, then walk over.

"Shawn and Stewart, I would like you to meet my wife Rose, my son Coby, and my daughter Misty." Both Stewart and Shawn say hello to his children and shake Rose's hand.

"Honey, Shawn is the son of Doctor Howard Higgins. I guess you can say Stewart is his son, too."

Little Coby walks up to Stewart and tugs on his hand. Stewart takes hold of one of the chairs and kneels to one knee.

"Yes, little man?" Stewart says to the very small child.

"Are you going up to space with daddy?" Coby asks.

Stewart says, "Yes I am,

"Are you scared? Stewart looks up at Shawn, James, and Rose. He leans close to Coby. He whispers,

"Yes…yes I am very scared, but I have your daddy to keep me safe." Coby calls out,

"Don't be ascared, it will be a-okay, Stewart." Everybody starts laughing. A red flashing light goes off above the door to the bridge that leads to the space shuttle, letting everyone know it's time to begin boarding. James hugs and kisses his wife and children.

Hal Cooper and co-pilot Stacy Whitehead are the first two to exit through the doors to the shuttle. They are followed by Tyler and Bobby. James and Franks say their one last goodbye to their families and walk across the bridge. Stewart and Shawn are waiting for Sam, but the General is kissing and hugging his daughter as hard as he can before he finally lets her go. Sam walks over to Shawn and Stewart where they are waiting near the door. As the three of them prepare to walk across the bridge, General Stone calls out "Stewart, can you hang back for a second? I would like to talk to you?" This is the first time he said anything one on one, ever since finding out that he was dating his daughter. Stewart slowly walks over to General Stone, unable to tell what the General has in store for him. Shawn and Sam stop dead in their tracks. They wait for Stewart.

"You two can leave, I want to talk to Stewart alone," the General says to them. Shawn starts to walk away, but Sam doesn't budge. Again, the General tells her" Sam, I said to leave and close the door behind you." The door closes behind her and all the families have left the room, leaving only Stewart and the General, alone in the room. The General turns his attention back to Stewart.

"Listen Stewart, you need to promise me something. Can you do that?" Stewart for the first time doesn't make a joke and just nods his head yes. General Stone continues.

"I love my daughter very much, and unfortunately she has fallen in love with you. So you have to promise me you will bring her home safely to me. Sam is all I have left in this world." Stewart never has had to make such a promise, but he puts his hand out and says, "I promise to bring Sam home safe." The General takes Stewart's hand and pulls him in, giving Stewart a big hug. He lets him go to meet up with the other members of the team.

It takes everyone about forty-five minutes to get buckled into their assigned seats. Stewart got his wish, allowing Sam to sit across from him rather than Franks. Tyler is with the pilots helping out. James is sitting across from Shawn, Franks and Bobby are in the back row behind Stewart and Sam.

The team can hear mission control go over all the instruments with Hal and Stacy, followed by the loud roar of the shuttle engines. The shuttle begins to shake and vibrate throughout.

"Hey Shawn, don't you get sick on me because I'm going to get hit with your vomit," Stewart says to Shawn through the headset. Franks joins in on the headset and says, "That's funny, Stewart, I was just going to say the same thing to you." Stewart attempts to give Franks the finger, but as the engines rise to the correct temperature the shuttle begins to shake even harder.

Mission control starts to count down from twenty and the sound of the engines begins to scream louder as the shuttle violently shakes. Within their headsets a countdown continues with "ten, nine, eight, seven, six, five, four…" The members on the shuttle can feel the thrusters shooting to the ground, the shuttle is shaking twice as hard, "three, two, one." G-forces throw everyone Instantly back into their seats, as the shuttle takes off. Then they hear through their headsets that the shuttle has cleared the towers.

They are all stuck in their seats while the shuttle shakes for eight minutes until they are through Earth's orbit, at which point the shuttle releases its extra tanks.

Tyler helps unbuckle Shawn and Sam helps Stewart. The second Sam unbuckles Stewart he begins to float up out of his seat.

"Stewart, come look at this view," Shawn says as he gains buoyancy. They both take a look at Earth through the porthole window of the shuttle.

"Earth Looks different from up here. It looks like a giant snow globe," Shawn says to Stewart who floats next to him.

"It's hard to believe we live on something so beautiful," Stewart says back to Shawn.

Sam, who is already out of her spacesuit, floats up behind both Shawn and Stewart and says, "It's amazing right. The earth looks so clean and pure up here."

Shawn and Stewart say simultaneously, "It is definitely beautiful." Stewart stares at Sam clad in her normal blue activewear worn underneath the actual space suit. Sam's suit shows all of her curves.

"Wow, not as beautiful as you, Sam," Stewart says as she helps him out of his suit. They hand off their suits to Tyler and Bobby to be put away in storage.

"Wait, give that back." Stewart says to Tyler who is holding his suit. Stewart acts like he is swimming to make it over to Tyler.

"Let me have that back for a second." Stewart takes the space suit back from Tyler and rips off a Velcro patch that he put on his space suit.

"Wait! What are you doing?" Tyler screams.

"Relax!" Stewart says as he goes back to tearing off the patch. Inside is his personal IPad.

"What's that?" Sam asks.

Stewart hands the space suit back to Tyler. He holds the IPad up in the air.

"Never leave home without it," Stewart says to everyone.

"It's not going to work," Shawn says to Stewart.

"Why not, the satellites are even closer to us now than on earth." Stewart says as he points outside the shuttle. He starts up the IPad and instantly he is hooked up to the internet. "See, it's quicker than it is on earth," Stewart says with a big smile on his face.

"This will make these two days go by a lot faster," he continues, waving his IPad in the air.

"When did you put that in your suit?" Sam says as she snatches it out of his hands.

Meanwhile in the front of the shuttle Hal Cooper and Stacy Whitehead set the shuttle on auto pilot on course to the International Space Station.

CHAPTER THIRTEEN

The two days could not have gone by any faster for Shawn and Stewart. The anticipation was so high it was killing the both of them. They both want to get to the space station, and most importantly, they want to save Howard Higgins, Shawn's father.

On the third day they finally dock at The International Space Station, five hours later than what they had planned for. They were aiming to dock at the station at eight thirty Thursday morning, but didn't dock until one in the afternoon. The delay makes the transferring of the AHR teams' supplies even harder. Now they have less time to do it in.

The Blackbird Shuttle is the AHR team's space shuttle they use to fly to NORA, the moon reflects, shimmering off its jet-black exterior.

Seating seven comfortably it has a large cargo bay, a small sick bay, and a small computer room that seats two, which helps fill the rest of the shuttle. The team needs to finish switching cargo in less than ten hours so they can make the space warp to enter NORA's atmosphere.

The United States Space Shuttle docks and its passengers are anxious to exit. The hatch to the shuttle opens. a gush of air releases. Then out of nowhere the head of the Russian cosmonaut Boris Volkoff pops in. He has been living at the space station for a year now. Stewart, wanting to desperately get out of the shuttle so badly, takes his hand to Boris's head and pushes it up out of the way.

"Hey, watch who you are pushing there, kid," Boris, in a deep Russian accent, screams at Stewart who suffers from cabin fever, climbs up the small ladder into the space station for the first time. He puts his hand out to Boris, but the short, scruffy looking man wants nothing to do with the courteous act at first. Reluctant Boris introduces himself. He is a fast talker, which makes it hard for Stewart to understand him, so Stewart just nods his head. Once Boris stops talking, the two shake hands.

"Mighty strong grip you got there," Stewart comments afterwards, rubbing the pain out of his hand.

Shawn exits the shuttle next.

"You always were a little weak there, Stewart," Shawn says. He shakes Boris's hand, and he, too, rubs the pain out of his hand afterward.

"You were saying, Shawn," Stewart says back, continuing to rub his hand. Stewart helps Sam out of the shuttle, not that she needs help; he just uses it as an excuse to get close to her. Bobby follows them out next. Franks is the last to exit because Tyler and James are suiting up in their space suits in order to unload the space shuttle because the crane is getting set to start coming their way.

"Wow, Franks, you've gained weight since the last time I saw you my friend," Boris says, laughing.

"No, it's muscle," Franks quickly responds to Boris. Stewart walks by Franks and playfully pats his stomach.

"No, you're right, it's fat," says Stewart as he walks to the door with Shawn and Sam to see more of the space center. They all walk up to Henry White, an American astronaut, medium build, very short black hair, and the face of a fifteen year old with his clean shaved face.

"Boris, I'm starting up the crane right now," he announces.

"You tell me you don't have the crane up and going already Henry?" Boris screams walking out of the narrow hallway.

"Hey, where are you going?" Stewart asks Boris walking through the door.

"I'm going to get into my astronaut suit to start stacking the crates into the Blackbird Shuttle," Boris quickly responds.

"Do you need help?" Stewart asks.

"Sure," Boris replies, not really paying attention to what Stewart is asking him to do. Shawn is not paying any attention either, because he's too busy watching the crane starting to move towards the recently landed shuttle, where Tyler and James wait in the open cargo bay.

"Cool, I'll go get my suit from the shuttle," Stewart continues. Sam hears Stewart talking now. Stewart walks right past her.

"Wait, where are you going"? Sam says trying to get Stewart's attention, but she is failing miserably. They both walk past Shawn redirecting his attention away from Henry who's controlling the crane.

"What's going on? What are you doing?" Shawn asks her.

"It's Stewart, he's going to get his space suit."

"Why?" Shawn questions. Stewart has now come back with his space suit in hand.

"What are you doing with that?" Shawn asks Stewart, who is in a rush to get past both of them while they purposely block his way.

"I'm going to help Boris load the Blackbird shuttle; to help save time. Plus, I want to try space walking," Stewart says to them both.

"Why don't you go get your suit and we'll switch back and forth?".

"Why don't you get your suit too?" Stewart tells Sam who's visibly afraid at the thought of leaving the space station.

"No, that's okay, I'll stay here where it's safe." They both go through the door together to a waiting Sergio Kozlov, who is also a Russian astronaut. He has greasy, short, reddish brown hair, and a thick red beard.

"Are you the one I'm supposed to help get ready to go and help Boris load the Blackbird Shuttle?" he asks. Stewart raises his hand with Shawn racing in from behind.

"What's this? I thought you were going alone, who's he?" Sergio says to both of them.

"I'm going out there and Shawn is my relief," Stewart says to Sergio. At this point Sergio doesn't even care anymore because his buzz is wearing off from the rum he had earlier. Both Stewart and Sergio go to the hook up room. This is where the person gets strapped to the shuttle so he is able to spacewalk. Stewart, all ready to go, is literally pushing Sergio out of the room. Stewart gets to the shuttle

"When I leave the room, push the red button and when that door opens hold on to the rail making your way to the Blackbird Shuttle," Sergio is explaining things to Stewart needs to know, and Stewart is listening intently to every word so he doesn't float away in space. At the same time he is eager to get out there. Sergio leaves and air locks the room. Stewart pushes the red button and the door slides open. Instantly he feels the cold darkness of space rush against his body. He takes a second to take everything in and pushes off into space grabbing onto the rail before he floats away. He isn't very adept at spacewalking so he starts to doggy paddle to theBlackbird Shuttle.

"You're not swimming in a pool out there," Shawn says, talking to Stewart through the headset. Stewart finally stops doggy paddling and starts slowly hopping to the Blackbird shuttle's cargo bay.

"About time you got out here, Stewart," Boris screams through the headsets.

The crane makes its way back with more crates. Shawn heads back to Henry White, who is carefully operating the crane. If Henry makes one mistake it can be dangerous for all of those involved. Just a year ago he lacked the patience to operate the crane. All that changed when he flipped his fastback Ford Mustang speeding on Highway 61 Even though he only suffered minor cuts and bruises the accident left enough mental scarring to make him stop pushing the pedal to the metal and keep life inside the speed limit signs. Shawn, still standing by Henry, looks out at Stewart in space.

"Do you see me? I'm floating in space! The view is great out here. You're going to love it," Stewart squelches to Shawn doing backflips. Watching from inside the Space Station Sam is visibly nervous, mouthing, "Stewart, please stop! Stewart!" Screaming in a high-pitched voice "You're gonna hurt yourself or Boris! STEWART STOP!"

. She walks away angry, mumbling under her breath.

"I think you pissed off Sam. She just left grumbling under her breath." Shawn is now trying to relay Sam's actions and the tone in her voice to Stewart over the headset.

While Shawn continues to wait and watch Stewartload the Blackbird, Sam heads to the space station's communication room. The team has to move all their supplies to the Blackbird in eight hours, each transfer takes a tentative thirty minutes, depending on how heavy the load is. The heavier the load the slower the crane goes.

Meanwhile Sam finds her friend Crystal Washburn sitting in the communication room. Crystal is a United States astronaut. She is one of the astronauts who has been living at the space station the longest. Sam sits down next to her and keys Stewart onto one of the monitors. Crystal turns to Sam to warn her that General Stone iis on the camera phone. Sam is oblivious to her.

"Oh my god it's true, Samantha Stone has finally been bit in the ass by the love bug."

"What! That's not true. Where did you hear that?" Sam argues, trying to divert the question and play it off, while keeping one eye on Stewart. Crystal connects Sam with General Stone. His face appears on the monitor.

"There you are, darling, you look tired," Stone says. Sam is not paying any attention to her father while he talks. She ignores him, but he continues, "Why were you guys so late to the space station? What went wrong?" The general keeps talking and Sam continues ignoring her father. It goes on for about an hour. Sam notices that Stewart is coming in from the Blackbird. She stops her father mid-sentence.

"Listen, dad I got to go, lots to do, love you." Crystal disconnects with General Stone. Sam stands up.

"Yeah right, you don't have a crush! You spent that whole time watching the monitor." Sam's face starts blushing.

"Fine, his name is Stewart. He's the guy out with Boris bringing the supplies from shuttle to shuttle."

Sam tells Crystal that she will get Stewart so they can meet, and runs out to find him. By the time she gets there, Stewart is taking over the headset to Shawn, who's out with Boris.

"It's fun out there in space, isn't it?"

Sam stands behind Stewart waiting for him to stop talking. Stewart lets Shawn get to work before Boris starts yelling at him. He turns around to Sam.

"I heard you were worried about me, are you getting soft on me?" Sam smacks him lightly in the chest.

"NO!" she says, laughing.

Henry is behind them, and he starts laughing. Sam walks over to him and says in a mean tone,

"Is there something that is funny, Henry?" She is standing right in front of him looking up at him. Stewart grabs her and pulls her to him.

"Don't worry, Henry, her bark is louder than her bite," Stewart says with Sam in his arms.

"Shut up, I'll kick your ass," Sam says, but Stewart says nothing, he just kisses her while Henry works on moving another load to the shuttle.

"Come, I want you to meet a friend of mine," Sam says to Stewart.

"Sure, I would love to, but I've got to be ready to switch with Shawn or Boris."

Sam's face tightens up. "What? You're going back out there?" Sam pushes away from Stewart. He tries to grab her. She pushes him away with anger.

"Listen, I have to. I need to do my fair share of work, so I'm switching with Shawn and Boris. Besides, Tyler, James and Franks are switching in and out on the other shuttle loading the crane." Stewart is trying to explain, but Sam isn't listening.

"Why does it have to be you? Where's Bobby?" she frantically says. Stewart kisses her to stop her from talking.

"Listen, Bobby is in the Blackbird prepping it for the trip to NORA. So do you want to stand here bitching about something that you won't be able to change my mind on, or you can take me and show me off to you friend?" Sam thinks about it for a second, realizes that he's right, and drags him off by his hand.

"So this is him," Crystal says to Stewart.

"Stewart this is Crystal," Sam introduces the two in an effort to break the ice. Stewart sits down because he notices the monitor showing the Blackbird loading dock.

"So do you think you will get all the crates in time?" Crystal asks Stewart.

"I think we will. So where are you from Crystal?" Stewart asks to try to get to know her.

"I'm from Dallas, Texas. My family is very much into oil, and I have two brothers," Crystal pauses to let Stewart speak.

"So your family is into oil and you are an astronaut, how did that work out?" Stewart asks Crystal who pauses to think of a good answer.

"Well my dad has my brothers to do the oil thing, and I always loved looking up at the sky in our horse fields, and I pursued it." Stewart doesn't have a response right away. Finally he asks,

"What do your parents think about your decision to be an astronaut and not follow in the family business of oil?" Crystal doesn't answer Stewart right away, but with some emotion in her voice she finally replies,

"My mother was ok about it, but my father was against the idea. He wanted me to be with the family. My youngest brother, Luke, loves the idea of going up into space, but my other brother Harry and my father bullied him into the family business. He tried with me but my mother helped me to follow my dreams." Crystal stopped talking just enough to give Stewart a chance to ask another question.

"Have you talked to your father since becoming an astronaut?"

"No, I don't talk to my father and Harry, my brother don't' talk to me." Stewart says nothing, so

Crystal blurts out, "It's a good thing I'm up here in the space station," to try and lighten the mood.

Sam laughs with Crystal, but Stewart is more interested in what's going on outside with Shawn and Boris. He is waiting for Boris to let him know that he needs a rest. Crystal and Sam start talking back and forth among themselves.

"Hey Stewart, Boris is ready to come in. He would like you to get ready because after the load they're working on him coming in."

Stewart hops out of his seat and runs out. Sam can barely keep up with him. She helps Stewart climb back into his space suit so he's ready when Boris comes in. Sergio comes into the room.

"Good, you're ready I don't have to go chase after you," Sergio says, slurring his words, with the smell of alcohol coming off his breath. He attaches the line to Stewart's space suit. Sam comes behind Sergio to check if the line is attached properly. She kisses Stewart one last time before he heads out. On the United States shuttle Tyler is being replaced by Franks. They continue to switch back and forth in order to race against the clock and make the space warp to NORA. Stewart gets the word that Boris wants to come in. Sam hurries out of the room so Stewart can push the red button to open the bay door. The switch goes forth without a hitch. Sam was on her way back when Tyler stopped her.

"Hey Sam, can you wake me up when it's my time to go back out there?" Sam agrees to wake him up because she already has to wake up Boris, and besides she feels like she's doing her part. She goes back to the control room so she can watch and speak to the guys. As she enters the room she hears Crystal laughing hysterically, and banging her fist on the table.

"What's so funny?" Sam asks.

"It's Shawn and Stewart. First Stewart tried to shove Shawn out the cargo bay, and then they started to harass Franks and James about moving too slowly." Sam looks at the monitor right when

Stewart and Shawn are setting up to sumo wrestle.

"Hey, if you two don't stop I'm going to-" Stewart cuts her off and says,

"You can't do anything from inside there." The two of them charge at each other and collide. They both fall down causing Sam and Crystal to start laughing.

"Hey Shawn, can you power bomb Stewart for me?" Sam asks. As the two of them continue watching the monitor they can't stop laughing. Shawn does try to power bomb Stewart but loses him as he lifts him up. Stewart starts to float away a little bit and he swims back to the shuttle.

"In coming! Look behind you! The crane is coming back," Sam warns the two goofballs so that they don't get hit by the crane. The two of them take a little bit more time unloading their first load together.

"Look who is taking forever unloading the crane now. Come ladies get moving."James and Franks start busting on Stewart and Shawn, which makes Shawn and Stewart want to move a little faster. This went on the whole time these four were out there. For every group that went out, they continued pushing one another to move faster.

The six men switched back and forth for eight hours. Bobby also helped out, getting in and out of both shuttles.

Stewart is trying to sleep in a sleeping bag that was hanging on the wall.

"Hey, sleepyhead, it's your turn to switch with Shawn," Sam says softly, because he has been going on and off for seven hours now. Sam also goes to wake up James, who is in the same area sleeping in another hanging sleeping bag. She leaves the room to go get coffee for the both of them, with the hopes of helping them wake up. When she comes back the two of them are out of their bags and sitting on a bench in the middle of the room.

"Here you both go." Sam hands them each a cup of coffee.

"You'll make a good wife someday, Sam," James says as he takes the cup from her.

"Hey, watch it pal," Sam says back to James. Stewart just drinks his coffee down like it's a cold glass of soda.

"Wasn't that hot?" James says to Stewart who is cringing in pain.

"Yes it burns all the way down."

James starts shaking his head in disbelief. "Well I guess we should go finish loading the shuttle."

Sam walks out with both of them following her. She has been getting the team anything they need to carry on with their jobs. James heads one way while Sam and Stewart head the other way. Sergio helps James get into his suit while Sam helps Stewart get into his own suit, so this way they both can switch with their parties while the crane is moving the crates.

The switch went off without any problems. Shawn is exhausted, and the clothes under his suit are soaked. Sam helps him up and walks him to his sleeping bag. She waits outside the room so the two men can change their clothes and she goes in when they are done to help them into their bags. She hooks I.V'S to each of them to help them sleep and get their energy back. She's been doing this the whole time to each of the team members as they switch.

The team finishes with two hours left. All six men are exhausted and hungry. Sam and Crystal set up a table of dehydrated food bags so they all can relax, and eat together. Shawn and Stewart get their first taste of dehydrated food.

"What's this?" Stewart asks as Crystal and Sam hand him silver pouches.

"Just add water and eat it, it's really good," Sam says.

At this point Stewart doesn't really care; he's so tired he would eat dirt.

"Hey you're right, this is pretty good," Stewart says. Shawn offers him a taste of his food and Stewart gives Shawn his.

"Well aren't you two the sharing type," Crystal says

"Too bad they're sharing the same food with each other," Sam says as they all start laughing at Shawn and Stewart. The two of them continue to share the same meal as if nothing was said.

"You two did really well out there," Boris says. "I always thought Americans were fat, dumb and lazy until I met James and Franks. Now you two come up here and do what you did. Maybe there's hope for you Americans after all." Boris leans back in his seat with his legs spread out. "Yup, there might be hope for you yet."

"No, there's no hope," Stewart says quietly for only Shawn to hear.

Are you married Boris?" Stewart asks. Boris sits up in his seat.

"Married? No, not me. I have a sister named Vera, who is younger than me, but not married. You can say I'm married to my work. How about you Stewart, are you married?"

"He better not be," says an eager Sam.

"No I'm not married, maybe one day, though," Stewart says as he looks at Sam.

"Wait, you two are dating?" Boris asks as he points back and forth to Sam and Stewart.

"What does General Stone think about that?"

"Why is that the first thing everybody says when they find out we are dating?" Stewart says out loud so anybody sitting there would answer him.

"He's a hard ass, and the one thing that irks him the most, is protecting his daughter from everything."

Stewart looks up at Sam who is not saying anything. She looks at everybody in the room and says, "He's not that bad. Besides, my father actually likes Stewart."

They all start to get up and leave one by one, muttering,

"Sure he likes Stewart." As each of them leave they place their hands on Stewart's shoulder.

"Really? Come on guys, my father is not that bad." Sam starts to think for a minute.

"Ok, he is that bad." Sse says.

"That's comforting," Stewart says as he gets up from his seat. He goes up to Sam, wraps his arms around her and says, "Don't worry your father can't scare me away." Sam wraps her arms around

Stewart's waist. They hold each other for a while and then leave holding hands. With the Blackbird fully loaded, the crew tries to get some rest before they take off for NORA.

While the AHR team sleeps, Bobby remains awake. He is preparing the shuttle for its flight to NORA. Hal Cooper, the pilot of the U.S. shuttle, is helping him.

There's only thirty minutes until the team leaves, so Sam gets her father on the big screen monitor, and asks Crystal to leave her alone.

"Hi dad, how are you doing, not drinking I hope?"

Stewart walks in right after the comment she made, but the General thinks Stewart heard the comment.

"Who is that behind you?" He frantically asks.

"That's Stewart, daddy." Stewart looks into the camera.

"Hi, sir. How are you doing?" The General is not pleased with Stewart taking up his time with his daughter, and ends up losing his temper.

"Stewart, get the hell out there so I can have alone time with my daughter."

Stewart backs away from the camera's view.

"Daddy, stop that, Stewart didn't do anything wrong to you, so don't yell at him like that," Sam screams at the screen. Stewart says bye and leaves the room. Sam is furious with her father, but she says nothing, because she realizes this could be the last time she speaks to him. Because they speak to each other when she reaches NORA and the space warp closes. So she lets it go, and the both of them talk right up to the point when Stewart slowly walks back in.

"Sam, we're leaving in fifteen minute," he informs her. Stewart was just about to leave when the General screamed out his name.

"Come to the screen, Stewart, so I can see you," he begins. "Listen Stewart, I'm sorry for the way I acted earlier, I was out of line."

"Thank you daddy for apologizing listen I Iove you and talk to you in a few months"

"I love you too sweetie. Stewart, you both keep each other

safe. Plus I know you two are ready to free Doc Higghins."

"We will daddy. Goodbye." They disconnect with him. Sam finds Crystal and hugs her goodbye, and then goes with Stewart to meet everybody else. Stewart and Shawn start to put on their space suits.

"What are you two doing?" Boris asks.

"We are putting on our suits," they both say together.

"You don't need your suits. They stay here. The Blackbird is totally oxygenized to where you don't need suits inside."

Both Shawn and Stewart both feel pretty stupid and they both quietly take the suits off. Before Boris completely gets in his space suit they both say their goodbyes to him.

Inside the Blackbird, Bobby and Tyler are starting up the engines, which take time to warm up, but not as long as the United States Shuttle. James and Franks are sitting behind the cockpit. Sam is also in the shuttle, in the communications room which sits across from a small medical room.

Hal helps Stewart down into the shuttle. He goes to help Shawn down and Shawn says to him, "Hey Hal, it was nice to meet you. I hope you and Stacey have a safe trip back."

Hal is surprised over Shawn's comments.

"What? We're not leaving. We are here until you guys come home, and we all fly back to Earth together." Then he wishes Shawn luck on his trip and his mission to rescue his father. He helps Shawn down into the shuttle and closes the hatch, sealing the air inside.

Shawn sits in with James and Franks and he starts to hear the engines grow louder and louder. His heart starts to beat, and his hands are gripping the arms of the seat he's sitting in.

"Are you ok over there?" James asks Shawn.

"I'm fine," Shawn says quickly back to him. Stewart walks in with Sam, and hits the back of Shawn's chair, which makes him jump clear out of his skin.

"Wow, what's wrong with you?" Stewart asks.

"He's trying not to be scared," James tells Stewart.

"I'm not scared, he just caught me off guard when he hit the back of my chair. James and Franks start laughing at Shawn. Shawn quietly sits in his chair ignoring them.

Over the speaker Tyler tells them all that they are going to take off. They all sit in their chairs ready to blast off. Then they hear a large sounding bang.

"Is that supposed to happen?" Shawn asks,

"No, that's new." Franks is a little scared now. They hear the banging sound again.

"What's going on up there?"

Tyler explains that the lock won't release them and they have to cancel the mission. Boris, from inside the space station, jumps into action. He goes into the room with the exit bay door, grabs an axe and instead of latching himself, holds the cord in his hand and pushes the red button to open the door. When the door opens Boris jumps to the top of the Blackbird, but when he lands he loses his footing and drops the cord. He quickly hooks the shuttle with the axe so he doesn't fall off. Still, with the axe hooked into the side of the Space Shuttle Boris swings himself, floating effortlessly, down to the locking station which is blocked by ice. In eye blinking reflexes, Boris nudges himself closer to the side of the ship and an access door handle, releases the axe from the side of the Space Shuttle and grabs the handle, throwing the axe wildly, whacking away at the ice. With the ship lopsided all systems ready for take off except for the one lock Boris continues to chop away at the ice. Each swing Boris throws all his energy from the shoulder forward so he can get the momentum ro free the last lock. With each momentous throw forward he can sense his white-knuckle grip begin to loosen slowly. Boris, flat-footed on the housing of the Space Shuttle's hull, can feel the ship readying itself propel itself into space. Boris' dead on forward momentum deflects chunks of ice into space, small shratnellike pieces chink off Boris' faceshield. Boris instinctively shifts his head out of the way, dink, dink, dink. Tiring, he throws his body weight into what he assumes will be his last hit as the ice chunk rumbles beneath his feet, shifting right, then left, gaining stability. In his own effort for stability Boris slams the axe head into the shuttle's hull, climbing up the shuttle and back to from whence he started. In a weakening moment his white-knuckle grip loses itself to the access door handle. Boris hangs, free floating effortlessly attached by the axe head to the ship's hull and the wooden handle Boris is incrementally to its smooth end into space. Boris watches his fingers disconnect from the handle. In the same instant his arms flail in space searching for a handhold but finds none. Instead, his rapidly swimming arms knock against the back of his helmet and the air hose secured to the oxygen system connection sprouting out of the ship's interior walls at odd intervals.

Voiceless Boris floats away into the never ending spectrum of space.

Stewart gets up and heads up where Tyler and Bobby are.

"What's Boris doing?" he asks as he watches Boris chop away at the ice.

Without notice the shuttle releases and Boris falls with it. This time he drops the ax and hits the shuttle hard, which pulls the oxygen hose out of his helmet. Boris starts grabbing for it to hook it back up, but starts sliding off the side of the shuttle. Within seconds the lack of oxygen shatters his face shield and kills him instantly. His body floats away, never to be seen again.

Stewart is in shock over what just happened. He doesn't hear Tyler screaming at him to take his seat. Sam hears Tyler yelling at Stewart, so she comes and brings him to his seat. His face is pale as a ghost as he sits down.

"What's happening? What's wrong?" Shawn asks.

"Boris, he's dead," is all Stewart can say. The news puts them all in shock, and all of them remain silent. Then, all of a sudden, the shuttle takes off through the Milky Way.

The space warp is just outside the boundaries of the galaxy. It looks like a giant spiral, the center of which is black and grey. The outer part of it is purple with what looks like white puffy clouds that flash from constant lightning. The Blackbird races towards it. The shuttle begins to shake and then the shaking stops and then they all hear, "Welcome back, Blackbird."

CHAPTER FOURTEEN

"Thank you, Scanvokia" says Tyler. The team is still in shock over the death of Boris Kozlov. Stewart the only witness, suffers most. Sam, sitting next to Stewart, holds his hand for comfort not knowing what to say to comfort him.

"Scanvokia, how's the weather down there, old friend?" Tyler asks as they approach NORA.

NORA is the smallest planet in this galaxy, it's even smaller than Earth. It looks similar to Earth, however instead of blue water there is red water. There is also a lone giant land mass with a few islands scattered on NORA.

"There's a major storm moving in off the ocean. The wind is picking up and the rain is starting now, so be careful entering orbit, it's going to be hairy." Scanvokia is saying this to Tyler just as the Blackbird enters NORA's orbit. The shuttle begins to shake again, and the loud rain bangs off the outer shell. But before too long the Blackbird is in NORA's horizon skies.

Shawn walks up to the front of the shuttle to look at NORA from above. All he can see is the tops of trees and a giant rock mountain. Then the shuttle turns right in its descent to the ground, and a giant cyclical building, five stories high, with a ten foot high barrier wall that surrounds it, becomes visible. Inside the large compound is a small runway which the Blackbird aims to land on.

Once landed the shuttle pulls into a big hangar that is

connected to the main building. Two big cargo bay doors open up to let the shuttle pull inside. It comes to a stop. A group of soldiers mixed with Noraians greet the AHR team.

Tyler is the first to leave the shuttle. Colonel Roger Baker greets him. Roger Baker is a very heavy man. The size of his head makes it look as though his hat is three times too small. His thick, black beard covers more than half his face. Standing beside him is an average sized man, Major Greg Burns. He is Colonel Baker's assistant. He is hated by all the lower class soldiers, both human and Noraians. On the other side of Baker is a being from NORA. His name is Scanvokia.

"Colonel Baker, it's nice to see you again," Tyler says as he shakes Baker's hand.

"The apartments are all set up for one Shawn Higgins and Stewart Collins," says Major Burns, who usually talks for Colonel Baker because the Colonel has become very lazy in his command. Tyler basically ignores Burns, and turns to his friend, Scanvokia. They have been friends for life, kind of like Shawn and Stewart's relationship.

Shawn steps off the stairs from the Blackbird.

"You must be..." Colonel Baker cuts off Major Burns from speaking, and steps in front of him, like Burns isn't even there. It looks like a human eclipse happening in front of Shawn.

"I'm Colonel Baker," he puts his short arm out to shake Shawn's hand, but his stomach is out so far he's pushing Shawn away. Shawn quickly shakes his hand. Tyler saves him by taking him to meet Scanvokia. Scanvokia turns into his human self so he can talk to Shawn. When Noraians are in their true form they're unable to communicate with humans. Noraians in their natural form can talk to others through their minds rather than speech. Scanvokia turns into a built figure with blonde hair, a clean shaved face that shows the dimples on his cheeks.

"Nice to meet you, I'm Scanvokia, but you can call me Brad Winters."

Shawn shakes his hand and introduces himself. "I hope you

don't mind," he says, "but I would like to call you by your true name, Scanvokia." Scanvokia smiles from ear to ear and says,

"Wow, your father chose to call me by my true name, too."

"What's surprising about that, it's your name, right?" Shawn says to Scanvokia with Tyler laughing beside them.

"All humans have called me Brad, but you and your father." Scanvokia goes on by saying,

"That tells a lot about a family." Shawn tries to introduce Stewart, but he is still upset over Boris, and blows by everyone with Sam at his side.

"Sorry about that, he's not himself right now. Boris Kozlov just died and my friend Stewart saw the whole thing."

"Wait, what Boris died? How did it happen"

"He died freeing the Blackbird shuttle from ice."

"Sounds like something Boris would do. I'm gonna miss him"

"That says a lot about you, Scanvokia."

"What do you mean?" Scanvokia asks.

"Means you are a caring Noraian, I like that."Colonel Baker is huffing and puffing, breathing heavily behind them.

"That's not right, sir," Major Burns says,

"He should respect his superior officer."

Just then James, holding his army satchel and a yellow envelope, goes to hand it to Colonel Baker. Major Burns takes it rudely from James instead.

"What's this?" Burns notices James's Major pin and speaks with a tone of disgust.

"They made you a Major now?" asks Burns as he rips into the yellow envelope. He pulls out the contents and reads them to himself.

"Why that's crazy," he goes on, "He can't do that".

"What does it say?" Colonel Baker says in his deep crackly voice. He rips the papers out of Burns's hands and reads them himself.

"Why that's unheard of, he can't do that." Baker storms over to Tyler, Scanvokia, Shawn and James who are talking amongst themselves.

"He can't do this. This is my control post. Who is he to tell me who I'm able to give orders to?" Baker's face is bright red with high blood pressure. He throws the papers on the ground and storms off with Major Burns following closely behind.

"What was that all about?" Shawn asks.

"Oh, he just read that he has no power over you and Stewart under the orders of General Stone, his final gift to the both of you," James says, and then he walks over to Franks who is helping Bobby and some of the soldiers unload crates from the Blackbird.

"Are you ok? Do you guys need a hand?" James asks.

Franks is visibly shaken over his friend's death, although he is trying to hide his emotion in his work. James sticks around for a while until Major Burns comes back barking orders to the soldiers, making them work harder.

"I want to be unloaded in ten minutes, and I want the supplies to start being delivered to them all," Major Burns continues to scream at them like he usually does. Shawn turns around from all the yelling.

"Where's all that noise coming from?" Tyler looks over at Burns yelling at everybody.

"Oh that's Burns yelling again. Trust me, you'll get used to it. Thanks to Stone he and Baker have no power over you and Stewart." Shawn is thankful for that and is relieved and happy until Tyler says,

"I want you to remember something. Burns might not be your boss, but I am, and you need to understand that." Tyler puts his hand on Shawn's shoulder smiling over what he just said, and it brings a smile to Shawn's face. They both walk away into the five story compound leaving all that noise from Major Burns behind them.

On the fifth floor Sam and Stewart are just unlocking the door to Stewart's apartment. All the apartments were built the same. The living room is what they walk into first, then a small kitchen with plumbing and electricity. There's even a small balcony leading straight off it. There's one big bedroom with a master bath.

It was a very simple design and very easy to build. It took a little under fifteen years for the building to be complete.

Stewart walks in, not even taking a second to look around, and sits on the couch. Sam has to turn on a light since Stewart didn't. Stewart is unable to shake the feelings and sights he saw when the tragedy occurred. Sam tries to sit next to him. She tries to comfort him in his time of grief. She talks to him, but Stewart only gives one word answers. Then there's a loud knock at his door. Sam gets up to answer it.

"Sorry, we must have the wrong apartment," Major Burns explains.

"Wait, who are you looking for?" Sam quickly says before Major Burns walks away.

"Stewart Collins." Sam opens the door all the way and says,

"This is the right apartment." Burns yells at the two soldiers to bring the six small crates in here. Stewart remains on the couch while Sam directs the two soldiers on where to put everything. While they bring the crates in, Major Burns walks over to Stewart who hasn't moved since they arrived.

"My name is Major Burns." He puts out his hand towards Stewart, which Stewart ignores. This makes Burns' vein pop out of his neck.

"Oh, I see you're the quiet type. You just let the woman do all the work." After Burns makes the comment to Stewart he looks over to the soldiers to show them he's still their boss.

Stewart says nothing as he gets up, grabs Burns by his green army uniform, and punches him right in the face, knocking him quickly to the ground. Burns scrambles to get to his feet and storms out of the room.

"Ok, I feel better now," Stewart says as he rubs his hand. Sam just laughs along with the two soldiers, who happen to be carrying in the last two crates into the apartment. As the two soldiers leave, Stewart says to Sam.

"Who was that clown?" Sam walks over to him and says,

"That clown was Magor Greg Burns. I think you just punched

your superior boss out." Stewart rubs his hand and says, "Well I guess I just made a lasting impression on him. But on a good note, I feel a lot better."

Sam goes over to Stewart, hugs him and tells him sweetly, "I'm glad you're okay. I'll help you unpack." Stewart and Sam start to unpack his crates. The first thing Sam comes to she opens.

"You wrapped your guitar in your leather jacket?" Stewart runs over to Sam, grabbing the guitar out of her hand.

"Is it okay?" He throws the leather jacket on a nearby chair, and quickly plays a few quick chords. Sam starts laughing.

"What's so funny?" Stewart asks Sam, who is still laughing.

"I bought you a guitar. I figured you would leave yours home." Stewart is blown away by the thought of someone else buying him a guitar.

"Thank you, but why?"

Sam simply states,

"I like hearing you play, and like I said earlier, I didn't think you bought yours."

Stewart gives Sam a kiss for what she did and is like a little kid in his eagerness to go see it. As they continue unpacking Shawn knocks three quick times on the door and walks in.

"Hey Stewart, unpacking already? You want to come over and help me unpack?" Shawn picks up the guitar and starts playing it.

"Wait, you play the guitar too?" Sam asks as she walks in from the bedroom. He stops playing.

"I do, Stewart taught me a long time ago." Stewart walks from the kitchen with three cans of soda and hands one to each of them.

"He wasn't the easiest person to teach, but once he got comfortable he actually got pretty good." Stewart sits on the love chair.

"I'm so pissed " forgot my guitar is back on Earth," Shawn says as he plays Stewart's guitar.

"Don't worry, you can play mine."

"Why?" Shawn stops playing.

"Sam bought me one and brought it with her." Stewart grabs

Sam and pulls her down on him and he kisses her on the cheek.

"That was nice of you," Shawn says to Sam.

"I love hearing him play, now I can hear you both play together, and then Stewart is going to teach me to play." Stewart hugs her, and agrees.

"You got to be better at learning than Shawn was." Shawn throws a pillow at him.

"So did you meet Major Burns?" Shawn asks Stewart, who has Sam laughing on top of him. She gets up and Shawn looks at her, then Stewart

"What did you do?" He says to Stewart. Sam stops laughing and says,

"He just punched him out."

"What?" Screams Shawn.

"Well I guess it's a good thing Sam's father gave me and you immunity, but you might have to answer to Tyler for your actions."

The three of them hang out for most of their first night on the planet NORA.

"Well I'm going home," Shawn says, getting up to leave.

"Wait don't you need our help to unpack your things," Sam asks Shawn as he heads for the door.

"No, I'll unpack things as I need," Shawn says, walking out and goes back to his own apartment. Sam stays until Stewart falls asleep and then she leaves for the night.

CHAPTER FIFTEEN

The sun rises the next morning in the full red sky. It begins to shine over NORA's red sandy land. The red ocean water is rushing in from the ocean's current hitting the rocky cliff wall, as dark clouds start to fill the sky. Trees and grass patches spreading out across the land start to sway from the wind that is picking up. Shawn wakes from the wind blowing against his bedroom window on the fifth floor apartment. He stumbles out to his balcony, hitting the corner of the couch on his way outside. He is startled by the presence of Stewart who is already standing outside on his balcony, drinking a cup of coffee.

"Wow, what are you doing up, and where did you get that coffee?" Shawn says as he wipes the morning snot out of his eyes. As Stewart sips his coffee, he lights one of his rolled cigarettes.

"What, did you bring them from home?" Shawn asks Stewart, who is continuing to drink his coffee looking at the landscape as the wind continues to blow things everywhere. Being up so high they can see the tops of trees swaying back and forth. There is a thick line of trees that surrounds the compound. In the far distance they can see one side of an old volcano with two waterfalls coming out of it. Shawn asks again where Stewart got the coffee.

"You need to relax and let a person answer your question when asked it." Stewart goes to drink his coffee when Shawn reaches over the balcony railing and grabs the coffee and drinks it himself.

"This is good. Where did you get it?" Shawn says as he takes another sip of the coffee.

"Sam dropped it off before she went to the gym," Stewart explains while he attempts to get his coffee back.

"Can I have that back please?"

Shawn takes one last sip and tosses an empty cup at Stewart, the wind takes over the balcony. They both start to look at the coffee cup flying with the wind until they hear Sam's voice from behind Stewart.

"Thank god Sam is here," Stewart says as she walks up behind him. She gives him a quick kiss and says hi to Shawn.

"So are you two ready to get a bite to eat?" Sam says to the two of them. She knows they are both hungry.

At the same time Shawn and Stewart both reply,

"I'm going to take a shower." They both run off leaving Sam standing out on Stewart's balcony. Twenty minutes later Sam and Stewart head next door to get Shawn, who is still in the shower.

"Shawn!" Stewart calls out; yet there's no answer from Shawn, so Stewart screams out again. Then they hear him coming from the bedroom.

"I'm coming," Shawn screams. He comes out of the bedroom and starts going through the two crates in the living room, throwing clothes all over the couch that Sam is sitting on. After she unburies herself from Shawn's clothes, she asks him, "Are you sure you don't need help unpacking?"

Shawn, still looking for his sneakers, continues to throw things everywhere. Stewart comes in from his balcony.

"What could you have been doing out there with that weather?" Shawn asks as he is still throwing stuff everywhere.

"I was smoking a cigarette, why?" Stewart says. His leather jacket is soaked because it has started to rain. Shawn finds his black Adidas sneakers and asks Stewart where he threw his cigarette.

Stewart hesitates then blurts out, "I threw it over the balcony."

Shawn is disgusted with Stewart's actions. He starts looking through all the crates again.

"What are you looking for now?" Sam says. Shawn doesn't answer, but finds an ashtray and hands it to Stewart.

"Do me a favor and use the ashtray."

Stewart takes the ashtray. "Hey this is from Jan & Lib's Hi-Tops."

"Yes, I know. I grabbed a few ashtrays and a small crate of rum."

"I'm so glad you grabbed the rum because I took a small crate of whiskey from Libby too." Shawn and Stewart smile.

"She is going to kick our asses when we get home." Shawn says.

" No, she won't, you guys will be gone for months. She won't even remember. She will be happy to see you both."

"She will be happy but she is going to whip our asses for taking her liquor. It's like taking her money and she doesn't forget that.

"I guess we will be bartending at the bar for a while for free." Stewart says.

Sam, who has been folding Shawn's clothes while he and Stewart argue like little school girls, asks,

"Can we go eat now? Or do you two want to sit here and argue some more?" She starts to walk out with Shawn and Stewart following behind.

They walk down the hallway to the stairs leading them to the second floor, where the cafeteria is located. As they grab their trays the soldiers that are online let the three of them cut in front. As they walk out to the sitting lounge all the soldiers, both humans and Noraians, all stand up and start to clap.

"Do you know why the soldiers are standing and clapping at us?" Shawn asks Sam.

"I don't know, this is new," Sam says back to him.

Stewart is standing behind them already picking food off his plate and eating. The three of them go sit down at a table with James, Franks, and Tyler.

While Stewart is eating, a soldier walks up to him and says, "From all of us soldiers we want to thank you for punching Major Ass Kisser Burns."

The soldier walks away. Everybody at the table starts to laugh except for Tyler. Then they all see Tyler looking at Stewart from the other end of the long table. He stops laughing.

"Stewart, I want to talk to you later," Tyler says. The rest of the table taunts Stewart for getting into trouble. Stewart is not paying any attention to any of them while he is eating his egg sandwich.

"Today we're leaving the compound to visit the high priests," Tyler tells them.

"Is there anything we need to know?" Shawn asks.

"What do you mean?"

"Stewart and I don't know anything about your planet or the people that live on it."

"Ok, where do I begin," Tyler says, attempting to put Shawn's mind at ease. "When my people are in their true form they can talk amongst our kind using just our minds. The only way they can talk to you is when they're in their human form. When we are in our Norian form we have great strengths, but when we are in human form we have your weaknesses." Shawn and Stewart are drinking their coffee listening to every word he has to say.

"Don't worry, the whole team will be with us."

"Tyler," Sam interrupts,

"I have to stay here and work on a few things, is that ok?" Her voice is really rattled and the only person that picked up on it was Stewart.

"Ok, I'll let you stay behind this time but this would have been your first time out too. If you have something to do, you have something to do." He gets up from the table and says to everyone

"We leave in an hour so be down in the garage in forty minutes."

Right before Stewart meets everybody down in the armor garage he stops at Sam's apartment on the fourth floor. He knocks several times and when there's no answer he walks in and sees Sam balled up on the couch.

"Didn't you hear me knocking? Stewart asks. Sam doesn't answer him.

"Sam, is everything alright?" Stewart is very concerned over the way Sam is acting. Still Sam doesn't answer him again which makes Stewart lose his cool with her.

"I don't know what's going on with you, but I also know for a fact that you have nothing to look into either." Stewart was going to continue when Sam jumped up from her position and started yelling," Get out of here! You think you know it all, so good, get out!"

Sam keeps yelling at him as she's making him walk backwards to the front door. She backs him all the way to the wall and she kicks him out slamming the door in his face. Stewart stands outside her door for a few minutes, hoping Sam opens it, but she doesn't.

Stewart heads down to the armory garage where he is witnessing both humans and Noraians in their true form working on a black metal armored all-terrain vehicle. He walks around this massive truck that is two sizes larger than a Hummer.

"What is this thing?" Stewart asks Shawn, who is standing over by Tyler.

"This is the AHR mobile war machine," Tyler tells a distracted Stewart.

"I was just about to show Shawn the truck, you can come along if you want to." Tyler starts pointing things out like the armor piercing windows throughout the truck. He goes to the front of the truck and lifts the hood.

"The engine is mostly human designed."

Shawn climbs up onto the front bumper to get a better look.

"This is a Roush Ford engine. This looks like it is all human made," Shawn states to Tyler as he's now pointing out engine parts. Tyler starts to explain.

"The engine is designed by humans, but the material comes from NORA. Which means it's strong enough to get up over twice the amount of heat, which makes it more powerful over anything it encounters, and it is three times faster than normal speeds."

Shawn is blown away by this, but Stewart is still standing on the ground thinking about Sam. They both climb down and head around to the side where a door splits in the middle. One half goes up and the other down. The three of them climb into the truck. A normal size man can walk around inside comfortably. It seats ten, four up front, and six in the back. They walk to the middle row of seats.

"These two seats turn into one man armor defense guns," Tyler tells them. He pushes a button and the seat spins around and sits outside fully armored, with a metal armor wall sliding over to cover the gap in the side of the truck.

"That's cool," Stewart says.

"Shawn's father designed it. He also designed this." They follow Tyler up front where they enter through a doorway.

"This is a state of the art computer system stocked with a full navigation, sonar and G.P.S."

Stewart sits in one of two spinning computer seats.

"Now this is really cool," he says as he starts up the system.

"Tyler, we are all ready to go whenever you are ready," James says as he sticks his head in and out of the truck.

"Okay, let's go get ready," Tyler says as they both follow him to go get changed into their black cargo pants. Some of the team members wear long or short sleeve shirts. They all wear black helmets and black cargo boots, and this makes Stewart very happy. While walking back to the truck Shawn stops at three matching bikes. He sits on the first one in line.

"Now this is cool." Tyler walks back towards Shawn who is still sitting on the bike.

"This bike has the same armor as the trucks and the same that covers the compound. On either side of the bike's foot stands are machine guns and electric ray guns. Push that button on the handle bars."

As Shawn does what he was told, an armor glass pops up like a snowball over the driver. When activated it feeds oxygen in so the driver can breathe. Shawn pushes the button again to deactivate the glass ball.

"If you think that is cool, when we get back today I'll show you our one man shuttles."

The rest of the team is already packed and loaded waiting in the other armor truck. Shawn sits up front with Tyler, Stewart is at the computers, James and Franks are in the gun seats, and Bobby and other soldiers fill up the other remaining seats. Major Burns gives the orders to open both the armor garage doors and the main gate of the whole compound from up in the watchtower. Tyler starts out into the jungle and Burns closes the doors behind them

"So how far is this place?" Shawn asks. Tyler doesn't answer him because he is focusing on driving. There are no roads on the terrain of NORA, but it has many trails that the team made to get around. Tyler reaches one of the wide-open trails and can answer Shawn's question that he asked earlier.

"It will take about an hour through these woods."

"Where are we going?" Shawn asks as he's being thrown around in his seat.

"We're taking you to see the high priests. They are like the presidents of all the planets in our galaxy. They watch over and foresee things on each planet. Some are from our planet and some from others that are strong enough to represent themselves."

"Where are they now?" Shawn asks.

"They don't live in a giant white house like your leaders. They live in a giant volcano that erupted a long time ago. It's believed that the volcano's lava formed our lands and through time the red sands covered the land, the trees came much later."

"Can the volcano erupt again?" Shawn says in a worrisome tone.

"Don't worry about that. When the volcano erupted a giant fifty foot tidal wave capped the volcano. Now there is water rushing through the volcano and not lava."

Tyler stops talking for a bit because he has to avoid some fallen trees in the trail.

"There's one more thing, just outside of the volcano is a village where my people go to gather and get what they need to survive. My people don't have money like you on earth. We make the things we need. The people that make or gather the material get to pick first." Tyler was going to go on, but Shawn asks,

"And this works?"

"We realized if we didn't do these things we would have died as a race and our civilization would have died a long time ago. It can get crazy down there because it's first come, first serve, so when the supplies are gone it takes three or four days to make or gather more. That's one of the reasons why we travel with the whole team."

After some time battling the elements, big and small roaring rivers, rocky steep hills, and fallen trees everywhere, they come to rest on top of one of the hills, looking down at a grassless opening with two rivers coming from two waterfalls that dispense water from the water filled volcano. There are four waterfalls that release water from the volcano, some bigger than others. All four of them release back into the red ocean. This mighty volcano has been turned into a giant fire hydrant. It's also the most holy place in NORA. The battle truck comes to a stop, and everyone gets out one by one.

"Listen I don't have to tell the original crew this but Shawn and Stewart I want you ttwo to stay close. Don't lose sight of us."

While the two of them receive instructions by Tyler the rest are gathering their gear they might need for this small journey. They start to make their way down to the small village that sits on the grassless area. It has three small buildings to protect the resources and goods they have gathered or made. There are also five mid-sized tents barely covering the items that sit underneath them, like fruits and vegetables and meats from the creatures that are on NORA. There are building materials scattered all about. This is one of the busiest times for the village because all the Noraians meet in the village to get their weekly resources, So, they're all scrambling about making it very crowded., As they start to walk into the crowd with everybody bumping into each other. Most of the Noraians are in their true form; sparkling glowing figures.

The AHR team stays closely together as they walk through the crowded village. Shawn and Stewart trail behind the group looking at everything they come across, not listening to Tyler's instructions at all. As people are pushing and bumping into them, knocking them every which way. While Shawn is working his way through the crowd he feels a sharp pain in his arm.

"That hurt," Shawn says, rubbing his arm.

"Are you ok?" Stewart asks, because he heard Shawn scream out.

"Yeah, I'm fine someone just poked me with something as they were walking by."

As he walks through the crowd he starts to notice a small red dot forming on his arm. They finally get through the packed village and Shawn still finds himself rubbing his arm, but this time letting no one see him doing it.

They all head up the rocky path to the entrance of the volcano. Shawn and Stewart are finding it hard to keep up with the rest of the team because they can't help themselves from stopping and looking around Stewart stops and bends over to pick something up.

"Holy crap." He screams out "Shawn come quick look what i just found?" Stewart says holding the item out for him to see"

"Is that a diamond there is no way that is real?" Shawn says as he grabs the small diamond out of his hand. Shawn starts looking over the diamond

"Holy crap Stewart this is a real diamond." Stewart not paying attention to him anymore

"I'm rich, they are everywhere ." Shawn realizes Stewasrt is picking up these small diamonds laying on the ground like rocks on earth. Shawn starts picking some up in the area that they are in.

"SHAWN, STEWART! LET'S GO! James screams out finally getting the attention of Shawn and Stewart who start walking to James showing each other there diamonds they just picked up

"What do you have there?" James asks.

"Hey James guess what? We're rich, rich I say." Styewart says. Shawn and him are all smiles.

"Rich, huh hate to damper your parade but you're not rich because you can't keep the diamonds.

"Why not, they were just laying around free game," Stewart

says looking back at all the diamonds laying about on the ground.

"Are you kidding me right now Stewart, If it was that easy I would have brought them home to my family."

"Then why don't you take some of mine? I got plenty." Stewart says as he hands him diamonds. James looks down at the handful diamonds Stewart just gave him

"I hate to do this to you Stewart but I have to." James throws the diamonds away.

"Why, why can't we take them home?" Shawn asks.

Because it would throw the balance off on Earth now you're rich where are you going to say you found the diamonds. Sorry guys, I tried the first time I saw them too. First thought was ``My kids are set." Shawn starts picking the diamonds out of his bag in handfuls eventually showing James.

"Look you happy, I have none left." Shawn pulls his bag back.

"Ok, come on Stewart, drop them." Stewart says nothing, he turns around dumping the diamonds out onto the ground.

"Oh my god Stewart, tell me that's not the only thing you brought on this mission is your laptop and a sandwich."

"It's ham and muenster cheese, want half? It has lettuce, tomato and spicy mustard on it." Stewart waves it in front of James face before throwing it back into his bag.

"Plus I have my laptop," Stewart puts that back in his backpack" I think I'm well-prepared for this mission.

"Believe it or not James this is Stewart prepared for Stewart camping one time he brought a rubber duck." James looks at Stewart shaking his head.

"I remember that duck, didn't you throw that thing in the fire?'

"Yes, yes I did happily, I might add."

"Come on let's go, they're waiting for us." James says as he leads Stewart and Shawn to the volcano entrance. They're the last three to show up at the entrance where two Noraians stand at their posts speaking away in there true form. Tyler, before turning in to his true form to talk to the guards says,

"Everything ok?'

"Yes we are good." James quickly says. Tyler turns into his true form.

Wow I still think that's freaking awesome.

"My name is Zeakeo Vinn. I'm here to see the high priests. They're expecting us."

Shawn starts to hear voices. He looks around, but sees nobody there. He is drawn away by Stewart tugging on his arm and realizes he is speaking to him.

"Shawn, come on, we are going into the volcano."

Shawn, following Stewart into the volcano, realizes Tyler is in his human form following them into the base of the volcano.

"Shawn are you ok?' Tyler asks at a confused Shawn

"I'm fine." Shawn quickly tells him, wishing he could tell Tyler what just happened but the trust isn't there yet.

CHAPTER SIXTEEN

Inside the volcano the walls are supported with thick metal beams, which resemble the veins of a human body. The old tunnels that run throughout the volcano have arches from carved out wood for each entrance that the Noraians made by hand. As the team follows Tyler and Bobby through the tunnels, Shawn and Stewart follow closely behind looking at their surroundings. The caves are filled with candle light since there isn't electricity in the volcano. In some spots there's no light because there's too much moisture due to the water that runs through the volcano walls.

"Do you hear that?" Stewart says to Shawn.

"I think it's the water rushing through this thing like a high power air system." Shawn, being so drawn in by the volcano, is brought out of it when Stewart puts a damper on things by saying, "Imagine if one of these cave walls collapsed, the water would rush through here so fast we would die. At least it would be quick."

Shawn is not responding to Stewart's crazy nervous rants. They all exit the caves into a large room. It is wide open and very bright filled with wooden and metal boxes being used as furniture. While they walk further into the room one of the Noraians approaches them. Tyler and Bobby turn into their true forms, but are still wearing their uniforms. The other figure is wearing a white robe and is holding a large metal staff with a diamond ball at the top of it.

"Are these the two men that we heard so much about?" Shawn once again starts to hear whispering in his ears. He starts looking around to see if he can see anybody talking, but he sees nothing out of the ordinary. Stewart sees that Shawn is bothered by something again.

"Hey, are you ok?" Stewart asks.

Shawn doesn't answer him right away. He is still looking around. He looks at James and Franks who are guarding them from behind. Shawn finally answers Stewart when the whispering has stopped.

"What? Yeah, I'm fine," he says as he rubs both his ears.

Just then Tyler and Bobby turn back into their human form. So does the third man they were talking to. He has turned into a white older man, has shoulder length grey hair, and a dusty grey thick goatee around his small sized mouth. He turns toward Shawn and Stewart and starts speaking in a rough, crisp voice.

"My name is Titus. I have traveled far and wide. I have seen many different beings across this galaxy. I am one of ten priests that help patrol this galaxy. At least I thought I saw everything but when Zeackeo brought me your father Shawn he utterly astounded me. When he told me about his idea to form a team using aliens and humans I knew he was different. I knew he really wanted to protect people. Then I heard of you Shawn. Your father talked about you all the time, even talked of you to Stewart Like you were his own son like Shawn here." Shawn and Stewart really have nothing to say listening to Titus explain their history.

"I'm sorry about your mother. I knew her very well like I knew Zeackeo. Your mom was very smart and driven, but when she met your father it made her very strong, it made them both very strong. Wish she could have met you. She would have been even stronger. Titus stops talking for a second "Maybe sometime that could happen just maybe." Titus says silently to himself. I'm sorry for what happened to your father and for dragging you both up here into our battles. But we think you, Shawn Higgins, are the key to everything that's-" Tyler coughs to interrupt Titus from talking. Titus stops talking, looks at Tyler, and then continues to tell his story.

"As I was saying, we think you are the key to rescuing your father and bringing him back safely. The high priests give our full support when you go up against the Tri-Vinn soldiers and their leader, Brackeo Vinn, in the battle to save your father and the other Noraians he has held in captivity for all these years."

Titus starts walking to a room that is off to the left. Bobby and Tyler follow behind with Shawn and Stewart behind them. James and Franks are still guarding the perimeter. In the room Titus continues to talk.

"The Tri-Vinn soldiers have been seen near the mines on the other side of these lands. We think Brackeo Vinn has them digging for something, but we don't know what is so important in the old mine. We believe your father and the other prisoners are being held deep in those mines. We were told recently by one of our spies deep within the Tri-Vinn soldier inner circle that Brackeo Vinn is looking for the Albac Blade." Shawn steps forward. "Wait. What's the Albac Blade?"

Tyler starts to explain. "It is said that whoever cuts themselves with the tip of the Albac Blade will gain the power of each element from each planet in our galaxy, including NORA. But the Albac Blade is just a myth our father's told us as a kid."

"Wait, didn't you tell us that Brackeo was your brother? Maybe he believes your father's stories." Shawn says.

"Brackeo must have found something," Titus begins in his deep voice, "for him to have his soldiers dig through the old mines."

"Do you remember any of the stories?" Stewart asks.

Tyler tries to remember the old stories that his father once told him.

"The only thing I can remember is that there are six different keys that the person needs before entering the chamber where the Albac Blade lies. Even if a person finds all six keys, the chamber is in the most dangerous place ever."

"Brackeo must have found one of the keys or thinks there's

one in those mines," Stewart says to everyone.

They all continue to talk, trying to figure out what Brackeo could be after, or what he might have found.

"We should think about heading back to the compound. It's getting late."

Tyler agrees, says goodbye to Titus, and they leave. They go back through the same way they entered the volcano. By now the crowd of people has left, leaving behind empty old wooden buildings and the three man-made tents. They all head back up to the truck and before Shawn gets in, he looks over the nearby cliff and stares at the red ocean water smacking against the cliffs below.

"Shawn, are you ready to go?" Tyler asks.

Shawn hops in the back of the truck letting Bobby help Tyler drive back in the dark.

On the way back they get attacked by the Tri-Vinn soldiers. As they were trained to do, James and Franks both spring into action using the gunner chairs to fight off the enemy. Shawn sits in the back with the soldiers feeling helpless. Stewart is locked in the computer room because when the gunner chairs are activated the computer rooms seal up. The truck is getting hit by armor shells and electric bombs. James and Franks are shooting back at the Tri-Vinn soldiers with loud gun fire. One of the blasts knocks the AHR battle truck off the dirt trail. Shawn runs up front to where Tyler and Bobby are. He tries to look out the front window to see if there are any Tri-Vinn soldiers in the nearby woods.

"What can I do?" Shawn asks.

"Shawn, I see you." Shawn jumps a little bit and starts looking around for where the voice just came from but no one is there.

"Shawn, are you ok?" Bobby asks as he notices Shawn is off.

" What? Yes, 'm fine"

"Then hold on, we're getting out of here," Tyler says, as he finally drives the AHR truck out of danger, leaving the attack by the small group of Tri-Vin soldiers behind them. James and Franks deactivate the seat guns, releasing Stewart from the computer room.

"What was that?" Stewart nervously asks.

"That was the Tri-Vinn soldiers," Franks says back to him.

"How did they know where we were?"

"I guess we have a spy in our base," James says.

They all look at each other thinking about the fact that there might be someone leaking information to Brackeo and his soldiers.

The team arrives several hours later than expected. The guards in the watchtower announce that the team is back. They open both doors so that they can pull into the cargo garage. Inside is a frantic Sam pacing back and forth, which she has been doing for about an hour now. The team exits the truck one by one. All of them are beat and exhausted. Shawn gets out and heads to the bikes in the back of the room. Stewart changes out of the combat gear and is approached immediately by Sam. He walks past her right to Shawn who is looking at the bikes.

"I'm going up to the apartment, you coming up later?" Stewart says to Shawn, with Sam quietly waiting behind him.

"I'll be up later."

"Bring food," Stewart says quickly back to Shawn as he walks away with Sam at his side trying to get his attention. Tyler then stops Stewart.

"Oh, by the way, for punching Major Burns I'm putting you and Sam on guard duty tonight, starting at midnight. Sam you got guard duty because you didn't stop him from punching Burns," he says to her before she could complain. Then Tyler walks over to Shawn who's kneeling in between two bikes.

"So do you like them?" Tyler asks Shawn, who is comparing parts between bikes.

"There good and all," Shawn says, standing up, "The bubble is really cool, but I think I can make some modifications to it." Tyler looks down at one of the bikes.

"Go ahead," he says, "You're part of the team. Make any modifications on anything, just run it by me first, if you don't mind, that goes for you to Stewart if you want to make modifications on anything AHR team related i'm fine with it please run it by me first."

"Thank you Tyler." Stewart says before he walks away with Sam still trying to get his attention but fails miserably.

"Yeah, thanks Tyler, that's pretty cool." Shawn says to Tyler and was the first step in building any kind of trust with Shawn.

"Hey, I want to show you something over here," Tyler says as he's walking over to three one man shuttles and three two man shuttles.

"What's this?" Shawn asks, as he looks down at these black and silver bullet shaped ships, with small wings on both sides of the body and three small back fins.

"These ships are what we use to travel quickly to the other planets around NORA."

"How is that possible?" Shawn says back to Tyler, who is opening up one of the ships to show Shawn inside.

"Well, the metal that we build everything with here can withstand massive amounts of heat and can take a lot of damage. So we built all the motors and steering assemblies out of it, too." Shawn climbs into one and gets comfortable in the one man pilot seat.

"This ship must weigh a ton with all this metal," he says to Tyler.

"The metal is very light and durable."

"Wait a minute," Shawn says, messing around with the controls, "These are the same controls on the simulator."

"I was hoping you would realize that. What do you say we take them out for a spin tomorrow with Bobby?"

Shawn turns on the motor and starts to hover a few feet off the ground. Tyler backs up out of the way from the hovering ship.

"Okay, that's enough, bring it down now." Shawn brings the ship down slowly, listening to Tyler's advice. Scanvokia walks over to Tyler and Shawn in his true Noraian form, which Tyler sees and turns into his true form.

"I need to talk to you," Shawn hears softly in his ears. Scanvokia realizes Shawn is in the cockpit and turns into his human form so that they can talk to Shawn.

"Sorry Shawn, I didn't see you sitting in there," Scanvokia says to Shawn, who pops up out of the ship.

"That's okay Scanvokia," Shawn says as he starts fumbling with his words.

"How are you doing tonight?" Scanvokia asks Shawn, who is out of the ship and is starting to think he's going crazy in his head because he's starting to hear voices more often. All he wants to do is get out of there before anyone notices anything is wrong with him, so he quickly says, "Listen I'm going to go, I'll see you tomorrow morning." Shawn is trying to get out of there, but before he does Tyler stops him and asks, "Hey are you okay?"

Shawn hesitates at first, but then answers him, "No, I'm fine I'm just very tired." Then he walks away.

Back upstairs in Stewart's apartment, Stewart is now just coming out of the shower with Sam sitting on his bed.

"I'm sorry for being a bitch earlier, but I was scared, and when I'm scared I have always talked to my father and no one else." Stewart sits down next to Sam on the bed.

"What were you scared of?"

Sam doesn't answer him right away, in fact she stands up from the bed and she runs her hands through her hair in a nervous motion.

"I was scared of leaving the compound and I made a bullshit claim and you called me out on it and I got defensive again, I'm sorry for that." She sits back down next to Stewart. "So do you forgive me?"

"I forgive you, but we have to work on that little issue you have. Before our mission next month."

Shawn, standing in the doorway of Stewart's bedroom, announces, "Am I interrupting something here?"

"Yes you are, so come back later," Stewart sarcastically says to Shawn, who turns around and heads back into the living room. Stewart and Sam join him shortly after. As they are eating the pizza Shawn brought up from the mess hall they start talking about things that happened today.

"Did you hear what James said to me right after the attack earlier tonight?" Shawn says to Stewart.

"Wait, you guys were attacked, by who?" Sam asks.

"Coming back tonight we were attacked by the Tri-Vinn soldiers," Shawn says to Sam.

"Aren't you glad you didn't come today?" Stewart says to Sam who is now even more disappointed in her actions. Shawn takes a bite of his pizza and says, "Why weren't you there with us today?" Stewart can see that Sam is struggling with an answer for Shawn, so he blurts

out, "I had her stay back to collect some data that we needed right away, you know boring computer stuff." Then he changes the subject.

"You were saying something about James saying something right after the attack." Shawn gets up to grab a notepad and comes back.

"Oh right, he told me that the team thinks we have a leak."

Sam is annoyed with what Shawn is saying. "How is that even possible? This whole thing is like the army, one tight family."

"That might be so, and I hate to say it, but there's a rat in the family," Stewart says, hoping not to start another fight with Sam.

"If there is a snitch on the team or in the Earth compound, we have to find him or her before they spill about the mission," Sam says.

"What are you working on over there?" Stewart curiously asks Shawn, who has been drawing something in the note pad since he got up and grabbed it. Shawn doesn't answer him; he gets up and sits next to Stewart and Sam on the couch.

"That's great, Tyler said we can make any changes to the vehicles in the garage so I started to draw my changes. I wanted to go to the team's war truck." Shawn shows Stewart a horrible drawing of the team's truck. Then it shows Shawn's additions.

"What is this thing called a treasure map? God you suck at drawing."

Shawn starts getting defensive over the rude comment Stewart made about his drawing and Sam laughing.

"Can you do any better? I basically drew it on the way up here" Shawn says. Stewart gets up.

"You know I can." He heads in his room and grabs his personal laptop and sits back down. He starts up one of his design programs, downloads plans from the base main computer of the truck and says,

"How about that, is that better?" Shawn just looks at Stewart who is sitting back on the couch lighting a cigarette smiling.

"Ok, now you're just showing off for Sam."

"Yes he is," Sam says as she's smiling at her man for being smarter than them all. Stewart sits back up and Shawn immediately gives him an ashtray. Then they hear someone knocking at the door. Sam gets up to answer it.

"Hi Tyler; Hi Scanvokia. What are you both doing here so late?" Sam says.

"Can we come in, please?" Sam lets both of them in.

"What are you two doing here this late?" Shawn asks them both.

"Well we were alerted to a break in on some of our plans and the signal led us here."

Shawn starts looking over at Stewart who is looking in the other direction until Shawn hits him in order to get his attention.

"Oh well, that was my fault," Stewart says.

"What did you need the plans for anyways?" Tyler asks. Shawn was about to start to explain when Stewart blurted out,

"Wait a minute your computer tracked my personal laptop?" He walks around from behind the couch and grunts. "I'll have to change that so that it won't happen again." Scanvokia laughs out loud.

"You'll probably do it too," he says as he goes and sits next to Tyler on the love seat, across from the couch.

"So Shawn, you said you have new ideas for the battle truck. Can I see them?" Scanvokia asks. Stewart, slides the laptop to the far side of the table so everybody can see the screen. They all discuss

Shawn's plans for changing the battle truck in this way. Shawn starts off by saying,

"I want to add a third axle right under the entrance to the front half of the truck. That way, when we are under major attack we can disconnect and have a better chance of getting all our computers and information out of danger. And I want to add more fire power."

Tyler gives Shawn permission to make the changes to one of the two battle trucks to see how they will help the team in combat. Tyler and Scanvokia get up to leave for the night, but before he leaves Tyler says

"Oh by the way, you two have guard duty in an hour so don't be late. Remember I'll check on you later to see if you're both out there, so don't try skipping it."

"You were serious about that?" Stewart asks. Tyler looks at him and simply says, "Yes."

As soon as Tyler and Scanvokia exit, Stewart turns to Shawn.

"We are going to do a hell of a lot more than that, right?"

Shawn smiles ear to ear, "Of course, I had to tell Tyler something to get permission to work on one. First, I want to cut a hole on top of the back of the truck to put a gun on top of the roof, something like a tank would have on it. What I want to do is set the back part up as a defense base so when we have to disconnect there will be enough defense to survive, because I felt useless back there tonight and that's not going to happen again." They discuss more ideas until Stewart and Sam have to go on guard duty for the rest of the night.

Stewart and Sam show up fifteen minutes late because Stewart had to stop and get coffee from the mess hall. Tyler is waiting in the guard check in room. The room is very small. Half of it is a cage where they lock up the weapons. The guards carry them for protection when they are on duty. Tyler is not happy with Stewart and Sam, and his voice is raised when he starts talking to the both of them.

"Why are the two of you late? I told you both to be here by

midnight and here you are twenty minutes late."

Stewart cuts off a furious Tyler.

"Excuse me, Tyler, sir, I think we are only fifteen minutes late." Stewart smiles over his wise ass comment until Sam elbows him in his side.

"Do you think this is a joke or something," Tyler yells in their faces, "Your father is a General, you should know better, Sam!" Stewart apologizes after seeing how mad Tyler is, but it doesn't change Tyler's mood. He hands them both a weapon.

"Cool, a forty five magnum, this is my favorite gun," Stewart says, pointing it like he is going to shoot it.

"Good," Tyler says in a much calmer tone,

"Because it has just been issued to you, Stewart, I hope you will treat it with a little bit more respect than you show others at times." Tyler then tells Sam that he wants them to walk around the compound and report anything out of the ordinary.

"Remember I will be checking in on you both throughout the night." Tyler leaves the room and lets the two of them sign in. Stewart places his gun to his side so his leather jacket covers it. Meanwhile, Sam has her gun in a side holster that connects to her belt. They start by patrolling the five floors of the compound starting with the fifth floor, and going floor to floor. Stewart is drinking his coffee while Sam holds the flashlight.

On the third floor the two of them run into Major Burns, he is heading to his room for the night.

"Major Burns'" Stewart screams out,

"Can I please talk to you for a second?" Burns turns around to see who is talking to him, and covers his face when he notices that it's Stewart who is calling out his name.

"Please don't hit me again," he says as he continues to cover his face.

"I'm not going to hit you, I just wanted to apologize to you for that." Stewart puts out his hand out for Burns to shake, but Burns is not willing to accept his apology. He turns away and heads to his apartment. As the door shuts all they can hear are the six locks each being individually locked. Stewart and Sam start laughing because of all the locks Burns has on his door. They both decide to go to the mess hall to get another coffee and a hot chocolate for Sam before they make their rounds in the armor garage and outside around this huge compound.

After searching the armor garage they head outside to begin their patrol. Shortly after they go out the rain begins to fall.

"Great, now it's raining," Stewart says as he cups his lit cigarette in his hand. Sam notices a figure standing in the distance. As they approach the figure, Stewart steps on and snaps a twig that lies on the ground.

"Who goes there?" The wet young human screams with his gun shaking in his hand.

"At ease soldier, put down your weapon," Sam screams. The soldier puts down his weapon and Sam and Stewart approach him. He is wet and very cold.

"Are you alone out here tonight, soldier?" Sam says.

"Yes ma'am. The Noraian soldier that was scheduled to be on guard duty with me called out."

"How long have you been on duty?" Stewart asks the soldier, who is staring at Stewart smoking his cigarette.

The young male soldier looks down at his watch. "About ten hours now," he says, still looking at the cigarette.

"Do you want to go get something hot to drink? Sam and I will wait here until you get back."

"No," the soldier quickly answers, "That's ok, I have to stay here. If I leave my post I'll get docked pay."

"How about this, tell me what you want and you can stay here with Stewart and I will go get you something?"

The soldier is shocked that Sam, Generals Stone's daughter, is offering to get him something on a shift. He doesn't waste any time asking

" I Will take a large coffee, thank you MrsHiggins". Sam walks off to the mess hall and Stewart lights another cigarette, noticing that the soldier is watching him again.

"Would you like one?" Stewart holds out his silver cigarette case and the young soldier takes one and says

" Thank you Stewar collins."

"You know my name, how is that?"

"Oh the whole compound knows you and Shawn Higgins, Doc Higgins son and then you punishing out Major Burns

"What's your name?" Stewart asks as he lights the soldier's cigarette. The soldier takes a drag of the cigarette

"My name is Sully Miner, Jr. I'm from Seattle, Washington." Sully takes another drag of the cigarette as he answers Stewart's question.

"How long have you been on NORA for?"

"I've been here for a year. I was top five in my boot camp and they offered me this gig."

"What about your family? When was the last time you saw them or even talked to them?"

"Well I get letters from them all the time. Mail gets brought to us every trip the Blackbird makes."

Stewart is listening to Sully, but his attention has shifted on two figures standing together in the distance. Sully finally realizes that Stewart is looking past him and he turns around to see what Stewart sees. Stewart starts walking towards the two figures. As they get closer Sully notices

"That's Colonel Baker." Sully was going to call out to Baker when Stewart notices that Baker is talking to Major Burns. He pulls Sully behind one of the small supply buildings that sit all around the complex.

"What are you doing? That is Colonel Baker and Major Burns."

Sully, trying to get past Stewart kicks some stones around by his feet and gets the attention of Baker and Burns which make them run off. Stewart notices that they each ran off in different directions. Stewart and Sully both walk back to Sully's post where Sam is just arriving with coffee for the both of them.

"Here you go soldier," Sam says as she hands him his coffee.

"Thank you, Sam Higgins."

Sam and Stewart continue on their guard duty, leaving Sully thinking Stewart is a little bit crazy. They continue back up to the five floors where they come across Major Burn's apartment. Stewart notices that the light is on so he begins to knock on the door. Burns answers the door half asleep.

"What is it, what do you want with me at this hour?" Burns screams at Stewart who is trying to say something.

"Have you been outside since we saw you last?" Burns doesn't know what to say because he is half asleep.

"No, I didn't leave this apartment all night, now get out of here before I tell Tyler about this and you two will be on guard duty for the whole time you are here."

Burns slams his door shut sending an echo down the dark hallway. Stewart is standing in the same spot thinking of earlier events until Sam pulls him away. For the rest of their shift Stewart doesn't mention what he knows because he has no proof. Plus he was very tired and he wasn't sure what he had seen.

CHAPTER SEVENTEEN

The next few weeks were very stressful times on NORA. The Tri-Vinn soldiers have been attacking more frequently all across the planet. The earth compound and the AHR team have been defending attacks from the Tri-Vinn soldiers every day. Sometimes it is very difficult to defend off some attacks because Shawn and Stewart had one of the battle trucks apart for their changes.

Shawn and Stewart have been helping defend off the Tri-Vinn soldiers. Shawn has been flying the bullet ships, helping Tyler, Scanvokia and Bobby attack from the air. Stewart has been sharpening his skills in shooting different weapons with Sam, James and Franks on the ground. Stewart also has been getting better in self-defense because basically he's been getting his ass kicked by Sam everyday. He's also been helping Shawn, been working on the battle truck between his lessons and guard duty with Sam. Stewart also has been keeping an eye on Colonel Baker and Major Burns to see if he can validate what he saw that night with Sully, but he hasn't been able to so far.

"Where's Shawn? I thought he was going to help you finish the battle truck this week?" Sam asks.

Stewart comes out from underneath the truck.

"He was here until there was another attack he, Tyler, Scanvokia and Bobby took two of the two man bullets and flew out there to see if they could help."

While Stewart and Sam are talking, part of the garage ceiling opens up.

"Here he comes now."

Stewart waits for all the bullet ships to land before he attempts to go see Shawn. He goes over to Shawn's ship with Scanvokia sitting in the back, clearly upset, and lifts the top open for him. Shawn unbuckles his belts to climb out of his ship.

"What happened out there, how much damage did the Tri-Vinn soldiers do this time?"

"It's not good, we got there too late," Shawn answers as he zips his flight suit down to his waist.

"Got there too late for what?" Stewart asks.

"You did well out there tonight," Bobby says. Tyler nods his head in agreement, but doesn't say anything. He is obviously upset over what happened tonight. Tyler and Bobby leave for the night.

"What happened out there tonight?" Stewart again asks.

"Tonight Brackeo sent his soldiers to destroy the village. By the time we got out there all the buildings were burned to the ground. There were burned supplies and dead Noraians throughout the village. We started a giant fire in the center of the village and threw the remains in. Each body Tyler threw in hurt him more and more. He said nothing the whole way back."

Stewart and Sam are listening to Shawn and they feel upset over the news. Shawn, in his normal fashion, changes the subject and turns it on to the battle truck.

"So how far did you get on the battle truck?" he asks.

"I have almost got the hydraulics hooked up to the axle and tires, but the wiring will take some time. I gave the list of parts you gave me to one of the soldiers to get for us. He said he would have them by tonight."

Shawn climbs underneath the truck to see the work Stewart has done.

"So what are the hydraulics for?" Sam asks Stewart.

"Well, it's a surprise for all, we're almost done and we want to show everybody at once."

Sam understands.

"Can I help with anything? Shawn comes out from underneath the truck.

"She can help you on the wiring."

Sam helps run the wires with Stewart through to the front of the truck and after that she leaves for the night. Shawn and Stewart fall asleep down in the garage trying to get the battle truck done. They awake to Colonel Baker quietly talking to Major Burns. They see the both of them just outside the side door to the garage. Stewart starts to sneak up to the door to hear them talking. Shawn follows because he wants to see what's up. By the time they get to the door the conversation is almost over.

"Put the two boys in the same patrol team next time," Baker says to Burns. Baker's voice is much deeper and it seems to be that Burns is agreeing with Baker's orders.

Stewart peeks out the door to see if the figure is really Burns and Baker but they are already walking away in the dark. Not seeing if it really was Burns or Baker gives Stewart more doubt. Baker's back is turned to Stewart peeking at him. Shawn pulls Stewart away, and they quietly run back to Shawn's room for the rest of the night.

Major Burns starts banging on the door of Shawn's apartment, waiting for someone to open it, but no one does. After a while Major Burns unlocks the door and notices both Shawn and Stewart sleeping on the couches. Burns starts to scream at them both.

"Get up now you two, and get your butts to Colonel Baker's office."

"Wow, the whole thing was a dream and I'm back home with my drunken mother screaming at me," Stewart says as he opens his eyes and sees Burns standing over him.

"Nope not a dream, but Burns is very close to my drunk mother."

"Ha-ha, very funny you bum, now get up and go," Burns continues to yell until Shawn nudges him out of the way and helps Stewart up.

"You can't touch me, I'm a superior officer."

"Not over us," Stewart says as they walk away from a red faced Burns. Burns kicks the nearby garbage can down on the ground and storms off behind them.

Shawn and Stewart walk into Baker's office with the entire AHR team already in there waiting. Colonel Baker, stands in front of his desk waiting for Shawn and Stewart to arrive, finally begins to speak.

"I'm glad you two finally decided to show up."

Burns comes rushing in after them all out of breath.

"I found them in Shawn's apartment sleeping, Colonel," he says, kissing Colonel Baker's ass once again.

Stewart goes and sits next to Sam.

"You two fell asleep in the garage working on the battle truck didn't you?" Sam asks. Stewart nods at her. Sam then hands Stewart her coffee.

"You look like you need this more than me," she says to a half asleep Stewart.

"Thank you," Stewart says as he gives her a kiss on her cheek.

"So now that everybody is here let's get started," Colonel Baker says. Colonel Baker sits behind his desk and starts speaking.

"Over the recent attacks in the village; the High Priests and I feel that we should have scheduled flyovers in order to prevent this from happening again." Tyler has heard enough as he gets up and walks out of Baker's office.

"Excuse you, Tyler, the Colonel isn't done talking."

Tyler turns into his normal form and lifts Major Burns up off his feet and places him aside. Then he turns back into his human form.

"I'll take the first patrol," Tyler says to the Colonel and walks out.

Baker turns his attention to Shawn and Stewart.

"When are you two going to finish my battle truck?"

Shawn now realizes that Stewart is about to go on one of his rants towards Colonel Baker. He stands up and tells the Colonel,

"The Battle truck will be done later today." He grabs Stewart by his shirt and drags him out of Colonel Baker's office before he can say anything at all. Sam gets up and follows them out, and then James and Franks follow her, with Bobby behind them.

"Wait, Colonel Baker is not done talking, get back in here now," Major Burns screams at the team, but they pay him no attention, because once Tyler left the room the power over them left, too, which gets Colonel Baker even more furiously mad. His face turns bright red. He slams his big fat hand on his desk.

"Oh, sit down now Burns."

Burns cowers down into the seat like normal and takes the brunt of Colonel Baker's fury. The whole AHR team is in the garage with Shawn and Stewart.

"Hey, do you two need a hand finishing the battle truck?" James and Franks ask.

"No, we're almost done. We have some final programming with the computers that Sam and Stewart are finishing up and I have to do a few things. Thank you, though," Shawn says.

Right before Franks and James leave, Major Burns races in.

"Listen up! Colonel Baker posted the patrol shifts and we are going to have two people on patrol per shift, and Shawn and Stewart are going together. James you're going with Tyler next time out, and Brad you're going with Bobby." Major Burns is smiling ear to ear whistling as he leaves the garage.

"You can't pair us up like that," Scanvokia starts screaming at Major Burns as he walks out the garage and gets farther away from them all.

"Hey Scanvokia, we'll be fine. It's only patrolling in the air, what could happen?" Stewart asks. Sam is standing nearby shaking her head in concern of the fact that Shawn and Stewart got paired together.

"Ok enough of this, Stewart takes Sam inside the truck and finishes the computers."

James realizes Shawn is a little stressed out so him and Franks stay back and help them anyway. Shawn is over by the truck struggling with one of the tires, so James takes his jacket off and walks over and helps him out. Shawn looks at James and smiles for his help.

"So I guess we are staying now, but I am hungry," Franks says as he throws his hands in the air out of disgust." Oh fine, I'll help too," he says, but by now he's just talking to himself.

The AHR team works together to finish the battle truck by nightfall. It's not until morning, when Tyler comes back from his patrol, that Shawn and Stewart are ready to test what they can on the battle truck. Tyler walks up to the both of them and before he can say a word, a soldier comes up to the three of them.

"OK Shawn and Stewart, your two man ship is ready for you guys whenever you are ready."

Tyler looks at Shawn. "Are you planning on going somewhere?"

"No. After you left yesterday Colonel Baker posted patrol teams and Stewart and I are next."

Tyler is very angry over the fact that Shawn and Stewart are going out together, but he can't do anything about it now because there has to be someone out on patrol.

"Shawn let me or Scanvokia go with you instead of Stewart?" Tyler pleads with Shawn.

"No, listen we will be fine. I want to go with Stewart. I'll take the normal route that I took with you and Bobby."

Tyler finally agrees after some time of convincing.

"I want you to check in every half hour. How long is your guy's shift for?"

"Nine hours."

Tyler is not happy with this decision, and he's not alone. Sam is furious about the decision, too.

"Listen. The minute you start feeling tired you both fly back."

"Listen to Tyler," Sam chimes in, "It's dangerous out there."

Shawn and Stewart climb into their flight suits and head toward the waiting ship with Sam and Tyler both following them and giving them instructions the whole way. As they both climb into the ship Sam and Tyler buckle them in and still continue to feed them both instructions.

"Mom, Dad, please. We will be ok," Stewart says to both Tyler and Sam, who finally shut up.

Shawn and Stewart both give the hand signals to close the ship up tight. Shawn turns on the ship as Sam and Tyler back away. The ship starts straight up toward the opening in the ceiling.

"Are you ready for this?" Shawn says to Stewart who is entering the ship's computer system.

"I guess I'm ready. You do know how to fly this thing right?"

They fly off into the distance as the ceiling closes behind them.

Back at the compound, Tyler runs to Colonel Baker's office, pushing by Burns who is at his desk outside Baker's office door.

"You can't go in there," he says to Tyler as he is being pushed out of the way. Tyler bursts through Colonel Baker's door anyway.

"How dare you come running in on me like that! Who do you think you are?" Baker starts screaming as he stands up from his chair.

"Why would you put Shawn and Stewart on the same shift? They are sitting ducks out there if anything happens." Tyler is now screaming at Colonel Baker who is still standing behind his desk.

"Well, if that's the way you feel, I guess you better stop bothering me and make sure they come back safe. Burns, get in here now."

Burns comes fumbling in the room pulling on Tyler to leave. Tyler doesn't care for Burns tugging on him so he pushes him to the ground and storms out of Colonel Baker's office.

"Get up you piece of garbage and get me my lunch." Colonel Baker is now throwing things at Burns, who is trying to get to his feet to exit the room.

Shawn and Stewart are more than half way through their shift flying over the coastal areas of NORA, where there are many homes right off the cliffs and even on the beaches. Some are really big, and some are small. Some even sit up in the trees. As they fly over the cliffs and come to the wooded area their visibility is at an all-time low. Shawn doesn't have the skill level to fly in the wooded area so they take a quick fly over. Over the radio is the voice of Tyler.

"How are you two doing, you have been out there for six straight hours."

Tyler waits for a positive response from Shawn. Finally he is able to hear his voice over the speaker.

"Roger that, base. We are about an hour out, but we are back over the village now and all is clear. Now we're heading back to the coastal area."

Shawn and Stewart start to head back to the coastal area when Stewart notices some Noraian civilians fighting below.

"Did you notice that?" Stewart asks Shawn.

"I did. We're turning around now, hold on." Shawn turns the ship around and lands the ship in an open grassy field.

"Call back to the compound and let them know what's happening." They both unbuckle from the ship. Shawn climbs out leaving Stewart in the ship calling back to the compound. He walks over to the Noraians they saw fighting from above. As he gets closer they stop fighting and slowly step away from each other. He notices a very large and tall Noraian figure behind them. It is wearing a long brown robe, standing approximately fifty feet away. Shawn stares at the figure and watches its actions, then he sees the figure glance at the ship where Stewart is in conversation with Tyler back at the base.

"Destroy the ship now," Shawn hears in his head. Shawn turns to Stewart and starts screaming.

"Stewart get out of the ship now, Stewart get out!" Shawn screams, running towards the ship. Stewart finally hears Shawn screaming and gets out right before the Noraian soldiers blow it up. The blast throws both of them from their positions. Shawn looks back for that mysterious Noraian figure with the robe, but he is gone along with the other Noraians figures. Shawn runs over to Stewart who hasn't moved from the position he landed in after the explosion. This concerns Shawn, causing his emotions to soar. He runs towards Stewart.

"Stewart, are you ok?"

Stewart just lays there. Shawn, who has partial hearing loss from the blast, slides on the ground next to Stewart's unconscious body. He turns Stewart's body onto his back and notices that he has blood dripping from his forehead.

"Stewart wake up, please wake up Stewart!"

Stewart opens his eyes for a second, only to fall unconscious once again. Shawn notices the ship is still on fire, so he tries to pick up Stewart but then realizes he is too weak to do so. He looks around to see if there is any shelter for the both of them, but being in the middle of a wide open field he sees none. Then he notices near the tree line on the outskirts of the field lies a giant boulder, which they can hide behind if the ship explodes.

After some time Shawn's hearing returns to normal, the ringing stops, and with the rest of his energy he drags Stewart over to and behind the boulder. When Shawn gets his breath back he starts setting up camp.

By the time Stewart wakes up, Shawn has already got a fire going and something cooking over it.

"What happened? How long have I been out?" Stewart frantically asks Shawn, who is sitting next to the fire.

"A few hours, how do you feel?"

Stewart sits down next to the fire.

"I'm fine, I just have a headache and I'm a little banged up."

Shawn turns the cooking creature above the fire.

"What is this?" Stewart asks as he feels his head.

"You were bleeding so I wrapped your head with your sock," Shawn says quickly before Stewart could react.

"What? My sock? Why did you use my sock?"

"Would you rather I use my smelly sock?"

Stewart thought about it for a second and finally thanked Shawn for helping him.

"So what are you cooking?" Stewart asks Shawn, looking around the small campsite again.

"I'm glad to see you listened to me all the times I dragged

you camping against your will," he continued before Shawn could answer his question. Shawn spins the creature a few times.

"I don't know what they call it here. To me it looked like a hairy deer but it was black and had no antlers."

Stewart is trying to look at this thing over the fire, but when that doesn't work for him he starts poking it with a stick.

"How did you catch the thing?" he asks as he continues to poke at it.

"Well I was collecting wood for the fire, when I came across it and shot it with my gun. Then I carried it back here, cut the legs and head off it, connected the body to this stick and started cooking it." Stewart continues to rub his head." Do you think they'll find us tonight, Shawn?"

"I don't know if they can find us in the dark and the fire from the ship is almost out."

An hour passes and Shawn and Stewart are just about to eat.

"You made it, so you try it first," Stewart says as the two men continue to hold the piece of meat in their hands. Shawn is just about to eat it when they both notice lights above them. They watch the lights land in the field. As each one reaches for their guns, or any nearby weapon in Stewart's case, they soon recognize that it is the other two ships from the compound. Tyler and Scanvokia walk up on Shawn and Stewart who remain sitting by the fire, holding their weapons to try and defend themselves.

"Are you two ok?" Tyler asks.

"We are fine," they both reply.

"What happened?" Scanvokia asks.

"Don't really know. On our way to patrol the shores when we saw a few Noraians that seemed to be fighting. There were three of them on one. We landed the ship and Stewart stayed behind in the ship to contact the compound as I approached them."

Tyler and Scanvokia sit next to the fire as Shawn continues on.

"They stopped fighting with the one Noraian, without me making a single move. They all looked back at a bigger, taller Noraian that wore a long brown robe."

Tyler stops him. "Are you sure that the one with the robe was taller than the rest?"

Shawn takes a moment to think.

"Yes, the one in the robe was definitely taller than the rest of them. Then, I noticed that they were looking towards the ship and Stewart so I screamed to Stewart to get out of the ship. Then the ship blew up." He leaves out the detail about the voices he is hearing inside his head. Scanvokia turns to Tyler. "Do you think it was Brackeo?"

Tyler stands up. "It was my brother you saw today, that's why I wanted you to fly with Scanvokia, Bobby, or myself. Baker should have never paired you two together."

Shawn and Stewart look at each other. They both take a deep breath.

"Why didn't he take us, why just leave like he did?" Shawn asks Tyler.

"I don't know." Tyler looks at Scanvokia. He then looks up to the sky and around the darkened land.

"Well, it's too late to head back now. Scanvokia and I will secure the ships and let Sam and the rest of the team know that you are both okay."

A few minutes later both Scanvokia and Tyler come back. They are both carrying a black duffle bag. In the bags are medical supplies and food.

"Here, let me take a look at your head, Stewart."

Stewart lets Scanvokia take a look at the cut on his head and bandage it up right; not with a sock. When he finishes he sits next to Stewart on a nearby rock.

"Thank you, Scanvokia, for patching my wound up," Stewart says as he rubs his head.

"Do you mind?" asks Scanvokia, as he refers to the meat that lies next to the fire.

"Go ahead. Shawn and I were unsure if it was safe to eat."

Tyler and Scanvokia start to eat, but first they each hand a piece to Shawn and Stewart. Shawn and Stewart wait to see both

Tyler and Scanvokia eat before they take a bite. Shawn and Stewart take a bite and quickly spit it all out to the ground.

"Come on, that's good meat," Scanvokia says, as he bites into more of his own piece.

"I'm not eating that," Stewart says, as he washes the taste out of his mouth with water and tosses the rest of his meat to Scanvokia. Shawn does the same and tosses his piece to Tyler. Shawn then looks through one of the bags for anything else to eat. Finding only fruit, two apples and three oranges, he tosses two oranges and an apple to Stewart, only keeping one each for himself.

"Fruit! Is there anything else in there?" Stewart questions.

"Nope, just fruit," Shawn quickly responds to Stewart.

"This sucks. This won't happen again, I promise you that," Stewart mutters under his breath as he begins to peel an orange.

"God, I wish I had a cigarette right now," Stewart says aloud, still complaining.

Tyler sits up.

"Oh right, Sam gave me this to give to you when I saw you." Tyler pulls Stewart's silver cigarette case out of his pocket.

"No way! She didn't?" Tyler hands Stewart his cigarette case.

"Oh, I love her," Stewart says as he takes one out and lights it with the fire.

"She's a keeper," Shawn says from the other side of the fire.

Stewart agrees. He lies back down and finishes peeling his orange. Throughout the night Scanvokia and Tyler take watch. None of them actually go to sleep. They stay up talking and making jokes as they listen to the creatures all around them. Shawn and Stewart ask what each noise is and if it's dangerous. This night also brought these four team members closer. So whatever Brackeo's plan was, it definitely backfired.

CHAPTER EIGHTEEN

When the sun rises the next morning, Scanvokia, Tyler, Shawn and Stewart head back to the base. Once they land back inside the garage, Shawn leaves for his apartment, visibly shaken up over what happened the night before. Stewart sees Sam sleeping on a couch that she had some of the soldiers bring out for her. He goes over to the sleeping Sam and gently wakes her with a kiss on her lips, which makes her jump until she realizes it's Stewart. She gives him a giant hug pulling him down on top of her.

"Thanks for the cigarettes," Stewart says, and Sam hugs and kisses him. Stewart doesn't tell Sam about running into Brackeo-Vinn because he doesn't want to worry her and make her more afraid to leave the compound.

The next week and a half stay quiet. There are no attacks by the Tri-Vinn soldiers. With two days left before the team leaves to rescue Shawn's father from Brackeo-Vinn, the team goes over the plan with Colonel Baker and Major Burns, as well as Scanvokia, right up to the day before the rescue.

Stewart walks into Shawn's place finding him sitting on his balcony.

"Hey there, are you hiding out here on your balcony? What's been on your mind lately?" Stewart asks as he sits down next to Shawn. Shawn is clearly upset when he answers Stewart.

"Why didn't Brackeo kill us or even capture us at least?"

Stewart doesn't say anything.

"I can't believe this is all happening tomorrow. After all these years of thinking my father is dead and tomorrow we're going to save him on another planet." Shawn turns to Stewart who is smoking one of his cigarettes looking up at the sky.

"What do I say to him?" Shawn looks towards Stewart hoping for friendly advice from him, Shawn hasn't been able to himself. Stewart takes another drag off his cigarette.

"Do you know what I'm going to say? 'Hi dad! Nice to see you!' Then I'm going to give him a hug."

Shawn laughs." That's good, make sure you say that with your shit eating grin, he really loves that." The two lifelong friends share a good moment together before Shawn continues.

"Listen, I really appreciate you going through all this with me, putting your life on the line like this."

Stewart was going to stop Shawn from talking, but let his friend unload some bottled up emotions.

"I know you have always been a big part of my family, Stewart. I've always thought of you as my brother and I know for a fact that my father always thought of you as his second son. Hell most of the time, I always thought that you were his favorite son."

Stewart stands up, takes a really big final drag of his cigarette and throws it away over the balcony and Shawn again yells at him for doing it. Stewart ignores Shawn's rant and says,

"That's why I'm here. You and your father have been the only family I've ever had, and when we thought Doctor Howard Higgins, your father, and you can say my father, was dead I was crushed. I felt that I lost a big part of me, like I died too, just like a big part of you was lost, as well. But if anything happened to you and I wasn't there to help you or die with you I could never live with myself." Stewart goes on, "You and I might not be blood brothers, but I bet we are closer than most true blood brothers out there." Shawn gets up from his chair and gives Stewart a hug.

"Ok let's stop this loving crap." Stewart pushes Shawn off him.

"Speaking of loving, where is Sam tonight?" Shawn asks as he receives a slap in his chest by Stewart, whose face is bright red over Shawn's question. Stewart lights yet another cigarette.

"She's sleeping. She has been working really hard this past week getting ready for tomorrow. She wanted me to wake her up so I'm going to head over to her place later. We have plans to hang out together tonight." Stewart says.

"I was meaning to ask you something, before we got on the shuttle. What did General Stone say to you?"

Stewart takes a drag of his cigarette looking out over the land of NORA.

"He told me that he is ok with me and his daughter seeing each other. He also made me promise that I would bring his daughter home safely to him." Stewart stops talking and continues to look across the land smoking his cigarette.

"Well what did you say to him?" Stewart takes another drag of the cigarette.

"What do you think I said? I told him that I would bring his daughter safely home. It was the biggest and last promise I will ever make to anyone except you, your father, and Sam." Shawn has been staring at Stewart the whole time.

"I'll help you keep your promise."

"Thank you" Stewart thanks his best friend which causes Shawn to thank Stewart for helping him here on NORA. They both look up at the sky, the same way they do back on earth. But looking at the sky on NORA is overwhelming because one of the planets that surround NORA in space comes so close, it looks like it's in NORA's sky.

"You know your father was right, it's like you can reach out and grab it."

"Listen, tomorrow we are going to get our father and put an end to all this. We need to reunite the family."

Stewart throws another cigarette over the balcony and Shawn was about to yell, but stops himself when he sees Stewart light up another cigarette.

"What's going on with you? I never see you chain smoke

unless there's a problem."

Stewart says nothing at first, he just leans against the balcony railing.

"I'm worried about tomorrow, I keep thinking about the rat," he finally says.

"What rat?" Shawn questions.

"James said a while back, when we were ambushed by the Tri-Vinn soldiers, he said to us that he thought there was a rat in our Company." Stewart throws a third cigarette over the balcony. Shawn is not paying any attention this time as he is deep in thought about having a rat on the team.

"Who do you think the rat is?" Shawn asks.

"Colonel Baker," Stewart blurts out.

"That's crazy. It's not Colonel Baker, he is a jerk but not smart enough to be a spy. If anybody, I would say Burns, he is weak minded and will do anything if yelled at." Stewart Starts laughing " I know that's true."

"Very funny you punched Burns out and put a target on our backs early ." Stewart is still laughing.

"I guess you're right," Stewart says, but in the back of his mind he still suspects Baker. Stewart notices the time and realizes he was supposed to wake Sam up an hour ago. As he leaves for the night he tells Shawn to be safe on patrol with Tyler tonight. For the last week Shawn has been going on patrol with Tyler for safety.

Shawn leaves shortly after Stewart to head down to the garage to meet Tyler.

Meanwhile, Stewart is knocking on Sam's door. After a few knocks Sam opens the door wearing a tight, long, red dress, her hair put back in a ponytail, but no makeup or shoes.

"Wow," Stewart says as he looks at Sam. "If I knew we were going somewhere tonight I would have dressed up myself."

The apartment is full of nothing but lit candles. "Come in," Sam says. She is very nervous, but like Stewart, she never shows it. Stewart was fine until he saw all the candles lit everywhere. The dining room table was already set up for a romantic dinner for two. There was a bottle of wine chilling on ice in the center of the table. Stewart pops open the wine. Sam sits down as Stewart pours the wine in each glass.

"Everything looks great. I honestly didn't think you knew how to cook."

Sam takes a sip of her wine. "Please, I didn't cook this, I got it from the kitchen downstairs."

Stewart sits down at the table, gulping down the wine he just poured for himself. During dinner the two talk about anything and everything. They share laughter and jokes, as they polish off the first bottle of wine. After their meal, they both head for the living room where Sam brings out a bottle of Jack, changing things up a little.

"Have I told you look wonderful in that dress," Stewart tells Sam. She starts displaying the dress by spinning slowly around which makes her dizzy and disoriented she falls onto the couch and Stewart. While sitting on Stewart, Sam starts kissing his neck and moves to softly kiss him on his lips. Stewart doesn't stop her, but after a while Stewart slightly pushes Sam away. He speaks up.

"Are you sure you want to do this?" Sam says nothing as she gets up. She tries to drag him to her bedroom, but he stops her and grabs her tight. He pulls her back on top of him .They continue kissing, Sam starts kissing on Stewart's neck again. But this time she starts softly biting his neck and earlobe. Stewart starts squeezing Sam's butt cheeks as she starts rubbing against his body. Both of them continue kissing. Stewart starts kissing Sam right below her ear and continues down her neck slowly. As he kisses her down her neck he slowly begins to move the strap holding Sam's dress on, down her arms as he follows with kisses. Sam suddenly stops him and pulls up the strap

"Let's go to the bedroom," she says as she kisses Stewart slofly on his lips. She stands and Stewart holding her hand stands up and lets Sam lead him to her bedroom. Once Inside the room Sam turns Stewart around to where his back is facing her bed. Sam starts kissing Stewart on his neck once again, as she is all close up on him unbuckling his jeans. With one gentle kiss and a push Stewart falls on her bed. Sam tugs at the bottom of Stewarts jeans, ripping them right off him. Stewart adjusted to the center of her bed as she climbs on top of him. Sam starts kissing Stewart as he is grabbing at her ass revealing her pink silk boy cut underwear. They continue to kiss. Sam pulls off her dress revealing her breasts where Stewart starts kissing each of them. Sam rubbing against Stewart, which is helping her get more in the moment after a little bit. Sam's underwear gets pulled off by Stewart and Sam follows by pushing Stewart down on his back where they start enjoying each other pychally and very passionately. About an hour later they both lay next to each other sweaty. They lay together holding hands. Until Stewart runs out naked to grab his cigarettes out of his jacket.

"Woo-hoo, you go boy!" Sam is busting Stewart's nude body as he runs back into bed. Snuggling together in bed Stewart and Sam share a cigarette together.

"What if the General found us like this?" Stewart jokingly asks.

Sam takes the cigarette from Stewart.

"Oh, he'd probably kill you." Stewart takes back the cigarette.

"That sucks, but it would be totally worth it."

Sam rolls on to him, takes and puts out the cigarette, then starts kissing him all over again.

"So you want to go again?" Sam stops kissing him and says,

"Round two," and they have sex again falling asleep in each other's arms for the night.

CHAPTER NINETEEN

Back down in the garage Shawn has been waiting for Tyler to show up for their patrol duty.

"You're late," Shawn says to Tyler as he walks in the garage.

"Sorry about that. I was handling last minute things before tomorrow's mission."

"Any changes that I need to know about?"

It takes some time before Tyler answers.

"No, it's nothing like that." Shawn downplays it for now and walks over to the two man ship. Then out of nowhere Tyler says,

"Hey, tonight I was thinking we will take separate ships." Shawn thinks the idea of taking separate ships is weird, but nothing about tonight has been ordinary,

"Sure, if you think that's best."

"Ok, good I'm gonna get you strapped in then I want you to follow me. Once in the air I'll give you more instructions." Shawn listens to every word. Tyler finishes strapping him into the seat, Then the top closes. Shawn is in his ship ready to take off. Tyler runs over to his ship and quickly gets strapped in and ready to go; second nature every time. He lifts the ship off the ground and the garage roof opens letting them both fly out.

"I feel the more practice you get, the better a pilot you'll become," Tyler explains.

Shawn has second thoughts about his decision in making it

as a pilot.

"Ok Shawn, listen we are going to go through some drills while we patrol ok?" Tyler says over the radio.

"Bring it on." Shawn confidently says back. Shawn does well on the first set of drills in controlling the ship in different defensive maneuvers and even offense against Tyler.

After several hours of patrol, with complete radio silence between Shawn and Tyler, Shawn hears,

"We're going to take a detour, follow me." Shawn has been feeling funny about Tyler's actions tonight, and this detour is not helping matters any, but he follows Tyler in his descent. As Shawn tries to keep up with Tyler in the dark foggy forest, his ship constantly bangs against tree limbs from all sides. Shawn tries to avoid a big tree limb but loses control of his ship, and before he knows it he starts smashing into the ground. The ship begins to slide for a bit, taking down small trees and whatever gets in its way. When the ship finally stops. Shawn is in a daze. It takes him some time to get his composure back. He unbuckles his belts before opening up the ship door. He is being cautious, never knowing if he has to start running. When the door opens he notices three Noraians surrounding his ship. As they get closer Shawn starts to hear the voices within his head.

"Who is he?"

"Where did he come from?"

Shawn stands up before the three Noraians get to him. As his legs fully extend he is able to see about six to eight more coming towards him. He reaches for his sidearm but it's knocked from his hands by one of the first three that approach. Shawn is then grabbed and thrown a good distance from his ship. He tries so hard to get up fast, allowing him more time to get away, but the Noraians react much faster.

"Grab him; we will take him to Brackeo."

"And we will get rewarded, yes we will."

The voices in Shawn's head are getting louder, and easier to understand. By now there was no place to run, and there's about twelve Noraians surrounding him. All Shawn is thinking about is seeing his father sooner rather than later. He closes his eyes not knowing what they were going to do to him. With his eyes closed tight he hears footsteps racing in from behind. He opens his eyes to two dead Noraians lying around him. There are hundreds of electrical rays shooting around him as he tries to move and duck for cover behind a nearby rock. After a while the sounds around him go quiet. Shawn slowly peeks around the rock and sees Tyler holding out his hand in order to help him up. Shawn rejects Tyler's offer for help and gets up on his own.

"Let me guess, Tri-Vinn soldiers," Shawn says to Tyler, wiping the dirt off his clothes.

"Why were they here? Where are we Tyler?" Shawn stares at Tyler while asking the question. When Tyler doesn't answer, Shawn starts screaming.

"Are you working with the AHR Team, or are you working with your brother, Tyler!" Shawn takes a few steps back from Tyler when he doesn't answer him again.

"Why did you bring me here to a Tri-Vinn camp?" Shawn hollers at Tyler. Tyler takes a few reluctant steps towards Shawn.

"It's not like that. If you follow me I'll explain. We have to keep moving, it's not safe out here."

Tyler starts walking away, giving Shawn a chance to choose to follow or not. Shawn looks around and hears noises that he never heard before. So he decides to walk quickly toward Tyler, making sure he always stays just a step behind.

"Where are you taking me?"

"You were supposed to land fifty feet that way." Tyler starts pointing in front of them. They continue to walk through the black wooded area. The fog is rolling in off the ocean.

"Why did we come here tonight? Why did we stop the patrol to come here?" Shawn is trying to get any information from Tyler that he possibly can. The silence remains until Tyler finally responds,

"Your father is being held not too far from here."

Shawn pushes Tyler from behind and pulls out his sidearm gun. Shawn aims it at Tyler.

"What do you mean my father is being held close to here," he exclaims. He points the gun closer to Tyler who is not moving on the ground, but instead just looks up at Shawn.

"Are you working with your brother, Brackeo?"

"No! Please let me explain," Tyler quickly explains. He gets up slowly brushing the leaves from his clothes. Shawn is still pointing the gun at him.

"Listen, I'm taking you to my family home. The place I grew up in."

Tyler walks away from Shawn who is still pointing the gun. Shawn decides to put the gun away and follow Tyler, but remains at a safe distance, unsure if he can trust Tyler anymore.

"My brother and I played in these woods as kids, Shawn looks around the dark woods as Tyler is talking.

"Where my brother Brackeo is holding your father, is in the mines not too far from here. Our father worked in those mines until his life was taken within. So after all the material was sucked from those mines they closed them down. My brother and I, along with our sister, used to play down there all the time."

"Wait, you have a sister, where is she?" Shawn asks. Tyler takes a deep breath and says,

"She died when we were young."

"Sorry," Shawn replies.

"The death of my sister changed my brother Brackeo for the worse; he started chasing fairy tales of ultimate power. Stories that our father told us as kids. Then my brother took the one place that we all could be with our father, the mines, and he turned them into his vindictive and evil base. He turned the one place I had special times with my sister and him and he turned it into things as evil as him." Tyler looks down at the ground and takes a deep breath of disgrace. They come up to a medium size log cabin. Tyler turns to Shawn, who is still standing behind him.

"Excuse me, Shawn" Tyler changes into his true form and then walks into the cabin with Shawn right behind him. Then Shawn starts listening to the conversation between the two shiny Noraian figures talking.

"Mom, this is Doc Higgins's boy." Before anything else is said the figure quickly walks over to Shawn and wraps its arms around him. Tyler switches back to his human form.

"Don't be alarmed, this is my mother, she means you no harm." Shawn just stands still as Tyler switches back to his true form in order to finish talking to his mother.

"Momma, stop hugging Shawn, leave him alone." The figure holding Shawn turns into her human form, still hugging Shawn. Now Shawn can see this very old woman with stringy gray hair hanging down her back. Her skin is full of wrinkles and age spots. When she's in her human form she's very weak and absent minded, which would explain her standing there hugging Shawn completely naked. But when she is in her true Noraian form she is a little bit aware of her surroundings and aware of what she is doing.

"Mother, please stop hugging Shawn now."

Tyler runs over to the two of them with a red robe and a cane trying to separate his mom from Shawn.

"Mother, put this on now," Tyler says. The old lady grabs the robe and puts it on. She takes the cane from Tyler.

"Mom let me help you sit down." The old lady pushes her son away.

"Hush up boy and leave me alone." She struggles to walk over to Shawn with her wooden cane.

It's ok dear, you're safe here. Please come sit down over here with me."

Shawn doesn't hesitate at all. He sits in a chair next to the old lady's rocking chair. Tyler helps his mother to her chair. Shawn speaks calmly to the old lady.

"Nice rocking chair." As she sits down, her rough voice begins to speak

. "Your father made it for me; he brought it all the way from earth." The old lady starts to cough repeatedly.

"Are you ok, mother?" Tyler says, as he quickly raises to his feet and repeats himself.

"Are you ok, do you need something?" The old lady swats Tyler's hands away. "I want you to hush-up," she says to Tyler, and turns her attention back to Shawn.

"Excuse me ma'am-"

The old lady cuts Shawn off from speaking." What's this ma'am stuff?"

"What would you like me to call you?" Shawn says with some hesitation in his voice.

"What would you like to call me, dear?"

Shawn is almost surprised in her answer. "Well how about your real name?" Shawn politely asks. The old lady starts to rock slowly in her rocking chair.

"Well dear, my name is Florminsky Vinn."

"Well then, it's nice to meet you Flor...min...sky." Shawn struggles with the pronunciation of her name, and is visibly embarrassed by it.

"That's ok dear, it's a hard name to say. I will give you a chance just like I did for your father when he couldn't say my name right either."

Shawn feels a little better knowing his father messed up in saying her name, and then Florminsky goes on.

"What if you could call me anything you want, what would it be?" With no hesitation Shawn says,

"Abby." Florminsky looks at her son Tyler and smiles.

"Your father picked the same name for me, why is that?"

"That's my aunt's name, my father's sister." The old lady continues rocking in her chair.

"Well then, it's official, my human name is Abby," she proudly says. Over time Abby starts getting tired, and she starts to repeat herself.

"You remind me of your father, and my daughter would have loved you."

"Mom stop this right now," Tyler screams out. "Sorry Shawn,

ever since we lost my sister, my mother just won't let her go." He helps his mother up out of the chair.

"Come on, mother, time for bed." Tyler helps his mother into the other room. Shawn starts looking around. He looks at the way the cabin is built, and how each thing is placed inside. Tyler comes out of the room.

"What are you looking at?" Tyler asks.

"Oh nothing, just the way you build your homes."

"Yup. Metal beams for the frame of the house and trees make up the walls. It was my father's idea, then everybody copied his design in making their own homes. He worked in the mine to make the metal, so why not use it to build our house?" Tyler walks around the house with Shawn following him as he shows Shawn certain things.

"My brother and I helped build this place with my father. The only thing we all did without fighting or drama. I made contact with your father right after mine had died. Your father helped me move on from the passing of my own father, but my brother Brackeo didn't want anything to do with that. All he had was them damn mines. He was always about the darkness, and sadness. I think it overwhelmed him and his soul, just like my father. Then the death of my sister drove my brother over the edge, and my mother and I lost him forever at that moment." Tyler started to get a little emotional as he talked about his family. Shawn stops him because Tyler is visibly shaken, so the only way Shawn knows to help is to change the subject.

"What are we going to do now that I crashed the ship and there is no time for you to fly back to the base and come back to get me?" Tyler gathers himself.

"Shawn, follow me." Shawn follows Tyler to the back of the house.

"What's this place?" Shawn asks. Tyler starts moving pieces of cut wood used for the fireplace inside the house. He slides part of the wall out of the way, and continues to walk down a flight of stairs. At the bottom he flips a switch which lights up an open space.

"My brother doesn't know everything around here." Tyler walks over to a giant computer and turns it on. Shawn walks over to four bikes.

"Hey, aren't these the bikes that are back at the compound?" Tyler, still turning on the computer, turns to say, "Something like them." He walks over to Shawn while the computer is starting up, and starts pointing out the changes he made on these bikes.

"These bikes are untraceable on radar, and they have a little bit more speed, as well as weapons."

Shawn continues to look over the bikes while Tyler heads back to the computer. Tyler activates the transmitter.

"Soldier, get me Colonel Baker and get me Scanvokia right away." The soldier on duty is surprised by the urgent call and starts to fumble around.

"I said now, soldier, this is important!" The soldier jumps out of his seat.

"Sorry sir, right away sir." The soldier runs out to Colonel Baker's quarters. Scanvokia hears the noise from nearby and walks into the computer room to see what's going on.

"Good, there you are, Scanvokia. Get the team, we have to change things around a bit for tomorrow."

Scanvokia leaves the room to collect the other team members and as he exits the room he runs into Major Burns.

"What's this all about? Why is Tyler demanding to wake up Colonel Baker at this time of night? I stopped that soldier from waking up the Colonel. So what's so important?"

Burns keeps repeating himself because Scanvokia has always made him nervous, but this time he is trying to stand tall in his convictions.

"Burns, you fool, go get Colonel Baker now, we have to change the rescue plan for tomorrow."

Burns doesn't want to break, but eventually he does and leaves to get Baker. Suddenly Scanvokia runs in.

"I have my best man gathering up the team."

"Good, my friend. Listen, there's no time. Shawn and I will

not be able to get back there tonight. I want you to take a battle truck-" Shawn stops him.

"Have him take the one Stewart and I built."

"Are you sure it's ready?" Tyler asks.

"Trust me it's ready."

Tyler turns his attention back to Scanvokia.

"Take the new one out, and take your best soldiers with you to protect Bobby and the Blackbird. I want you to take the team with you to the pick-up spot and let them walk in from there. It's the safest way into the mines." Tyler continues talking. Bobby is the first to arrive.

"Bobby, I'm going to have Scanvokia help you protect the Blackbird."

Bobby, like always, agrees. James arrives next.

"James, you are in charge tomorrow. I want you to lead them safely into the mines from the pick-up spot." James tries to remember where the spot is.

"You remember when we camped out a while back? I brought you into the mines."

"Ok, I remember." James says to Tyler. By now the rest of the team is in the room. Franks is half asleep and Stewart and Sam come in together.

"What happened, are you ok?" Stewart asks.

"I'm fine," Shawn says, "I crashed the ship, and I'm not coming back tonight." Stewart is not happy over this decision.

"What do you mean you're not coming home? And you crashed two of them now?"

Colonel Baker comes in screaming through the door.

"What? You crashed another ship? This is unacceptable, young man."

"Colonel Baker, shut up, that's not important right now." Baker's face turns bright red.

"Why, I never," Baker says to himself.

"So what are these changes for tomorrow?" he asks with interest in his voice. Stewart is watching his every move. Tyler starts to tell Baker, but Shawn, who is off the camera's view, signals him not to.

"Nothing really, Scanvokia is going to drive the battle truck instead of me. I'm sorry I jumped the gun, but I also knew you wouldn't want to be told by anybody else but me," Tyler says to Baker to cover up the fact that Shawn was telling him not to share everything. He storms out of the room with Burns on his tail.

"Listen team, tomorrow is what we all have been working for. Tomorrow we go out there and make our leader Doc Higgins proud. I want you to be safe and smart in all of your actions. Good luck and please be safe." Tyler is trying to give his team one final pep talk before they start their mission tomorrow morning.

"Guys, let me talk to Stewart and Sam alone." Shawn asks everyone else to leave the room. Tyler goes to check on his mother. Once he leaves, Shawn turns his attention back to Stewart and Sam.

"Why can't Bobby or Scanvokia come and get you?" Stewart quickly says.

"Because it's too late for that." Shawn's voice is not full of confidence.

"Where are you? I'm coming to get you!" Stewart says frantically.

"Will you please shut him up, Sam?" Sam. puts her hand over his mouth.

"Thank you, Sam. Listen, I'm safe. I'm actually at Tyler's childhood home not too far from the mines. Something is going on here, and we have a spy amongst us. I thought it was Tyler, but I was wrong. I am starting to think you were right in calling Colonel Baker the traitor. That's why I had Tyler only tell him things he already knew."

"What? You thought Tyler was a traitor?" Sam says.

"Yes, it wasn't one of my best thoughts. Besides, he has been acting suspicious since we got here."

Sam shakes her head in disbelief of the thought of Tyler being the traitor.

"Listen, I was wrong, but let's move on. You both have to be on your toes tomorrow, and take care of each other and I hope that we will be all fine. We need a little luck, so Stewart please wear your leather jacket." Stewart laughs, but he is still not happy about the whole thing.

"I'll be fine. Listen, go back to sleep, and remember, look out for each other, and I'm only a call away."

They disconnect.

Sam takes Stewart back to her place. It takes her some time to get Stewart back to sleep, but when she finally does, she falls asleep shortly after.

Back at Tyler's house, Tyler comes back to the bunker but Shawn is not down there anymore. Tyler goes looking for Shawn, who went into the woods. Tyler comes upon him just off his property, sitting on a big rock, looking off the cliff at the black sky. Shawn realizes that Tyler is behind him.

"The star patterns are different here. No big dipper or little dipper," Shawn says.

"You made me worried. You can't run off like that in these woods, it isn't safe. Tri-Vinn soldier's camps are all around here."

Shawn continues looking up at the sky. "Sorry. The great big silver planet in your sky is unbelievable. It's like you can grab it right out of the sky."

"Your father used to say that all the time when he looked up at our night sky." Shawn keeps looking up at the planet, which is closer than the moon is from Earth, but not by much. Tyler lets Shawn look up at the planet for a while because it seems to calm him down.

"We should head back now, it's not safe here." Shawn follows Tyler back to the log cabin, where Tyler falls asleep. Shawn stays up for a while listening to all the different sounds around him, and eventually falls asleep, as well.

CHAPTER TWENTY

The next morning Stewart and Sam, as well as the rest of the AHR team, are up before the sun rises over the NORA landscape. Bobby is finishing packing the Blackbird for its return trip back to the Milky Way Galaxy. The team leaves four hours before the sun rises. They have a five hour trip to the mines. Bobby will leave four and half hours later with a plane full of soldiers to help protect the Blackbird while it's on the ground.

While the AHR team travels to their destination, inside the computer room Stewart and Sam sit, talking to Tyler, and Shawn who are in Tyler's little hideaway.

"Listen Stewart, I'm sending you a map of the mines. This will help you guys get through the mines if James forgets the way or you get separated from them."

"Ok, cool I'll put it on my PND "portable navigation device."

"Good luck guys, see you all soon.

They make it to the pick-up spot a little after four in the morning. The sun still hasn't risen in the sky. As they park, the Blackbird lands on top of a hill. Bobby, who's now in charge while James isn't there, says, "Soldiers, secure the perimeter." Stewart has a few tricks up his sleeve. He tells Scanvokia to park the new and improved battle truck right at the hill's slope. He goes into the control room and pushes the red button.

"Boy, I hope this works." Quickly the back of the truck

separates from the front. The back tires fall forward to where the body rests on them. A cannon gun flips up on top of the portable base on wheels. The front part could drive safely away, but not this time. Right now it's staying behind to give extra cover for the Blackbird. It is placed on the other side of the shuttle protecting the back side; this part of the truck also has guns on it. The soldiers set up barriers all around the top of the hill, and at the edge for extra protection. After the AHR team helps set up protection for the shuttle James leads the team down into the dark foggy woods, leaving Bobby and Scanvokia in charge of the shuttle.

James takes the lead with Franks heading up the rear. After a half hour of walking through the darkest, creepiest part of woods they get close to the mine entrance.

"The entrance to the mines is right up ahead," James says to the group. They all move through the woods as quietly as possible. James quickly notices a Tri-Vinn soldier camp and signals everyone behind him to duck down.

"What's going on James?" Franks asks. James points out that the mine entrance is behind the Tri–Vinn camp.

"I count eight." Franks tells him.

"Doesn't anyone notice that they are wearing green United States uniforms?" Stewart points out.

"Well I guess we definitely have a traitor on our side," whispers Sam, who was the one person that didn't want to believe that there was a traitor in the United States Army.

"Hey, we can try the captured bait trick, if you'll be the captured one, Franks?" James tries to offer a suggestion, but the idea of being the decoy sends Frank on a rant.

"Fine you big baby, I'll be the decoy," James says.

"I'll have two of the Noraians act like Tri-Vinn soldiers, and I will be the captured one. They will parade me right up to the camp allowing us to get inside," James proudly explains. He feels confident with his plan until Stewart puts in his two cents.

"Let me see, you want to use yourself as a human shield? That's the stupidest thing I have ever heard." Stewart raises his voice at the end of his statement and everyone begins to hush him to be quiet.

"Listen, this isn't a movie. You're probably going to get shot or even killed! You have a family to think about," Stewart says to James, who momentarily reconsiders his plan.

"You don't have to worry about that because Franks is a really good shot. Besides, when the fighting starts you and Sam are heading toward the mine entrance." James hands Franks his weapon belt and his custom built machine gun.

"Hold on to these, I will collect them soon." James walks away with the two Noraian soldiers. About ten minutes later they start to see James walking with his hands up and behind his head. The Noraian soldier is poking James from behind with their weapons, trying to make it seem realistic. Once they reach the camp the rest of the group, including Franks, Sam, Stewart, and a mix of Earth and Noraian soldiers, move forward to target the camp. They enter the camp, walking into an immediate double kill. Two Noraian soldiers are shot by Tri-Vinn soldiers leaving James standing alone. Franks, along with all the others, open fire, which gives James enough time to grab a weapon off the ground and take cover.

After a while the Tri-Vinn soldiers are overtaken by the AHR team. Stewart is about to join the celebration when he glances over to see dozens of Tri-Vinn soldiers coming out of the mine entrances. James picks up one of the electric ray guns that the first group of Tri-Vinn soldiers had, but gets pinned down before he can defend himself. Franks makes it back to Stewart, Sam, and the other half of the soldiers.

"Where did all of those soldiers come from?" Stewart questions with a slight hint of fear in his voice.

"I don't know, but apparently we walked right into a trap," Franks screams over the shots he's firing at Tri-Vinn soldiers.

"How did this happen?" Stewart screams back to Frank's.

"I don't know, but we have to find this rat before he or she gets us all killed." Frank starts firing back trying to give Sam and Stewart a chance to get into the mines. Just then the ground starts to shake.

"What is that, an earthquake?" Stewart asks running to hide

behind a fallen tree.

Just then, giant lizards march toward them carrying more Tri-Vinn soldiers. The lizards came quickly as they left, bringing more soldiers.

"Oh crap, that's not good," Frank says.

"What?" Stewart screams.

"Don't worry about it. I need you to get ready to leave," Franks screams to Stewart. Stewart and Sam hesitate at first because of the shooting. They crawl around the fighting and undetected, sneak into the mine's entrance. After Stewart and Sam are inside the mines Franks attempts to get to James who is pinned down by one Tri-Vinn soldier armed with an electric ray gun. Slithering along the ground using the wooded environment as camouflage Franks finally reaches James.

"Here, I thought you would like these," Franks unlatches James' weapons belt so James can get back into the battle. James slaps his forty five caliber pistol on the ground for Franks.

James screams," That's much better," firing his weapons back at the Tri-Vinn soldiers.

Left with nothing but the radio at his hip. Franks radio's Scanvokia for help, only to discover that the Tri-Vinn soldiers are attacking there, too.

"I have some bad news, and some even worse news," Franks says, who is ducking to reload James' forty five caliber pistol.

"What?"

"Well first we have no help because Scanvokia and Bobby are being attacked over there, which means we are in the middle of an all-out war." James looks at Franks and says,

James winks at Franks, "Good, I wouldn't have it any other way," and returns fire.

Stewart and Sam are in the dark mines. The only light they have is the PND's dim display Stewart holds. They both walk close together to ensure that they will not get separated. Going deeper into the mines the tunnels are extremely slippery and tighter in some spots. Eventually, they come to a point where there are some lights set up. In their minds they believe it may mean they are one step closer to the bottom of the mines.

Just on the outskirts of their peripheral vision Stewart and Sam come across three Tri–Vinn soldiers on patrol. Stewart tumbles ideas around, thinking of ways to get around them. Sam gets up and walks towards them, and when she is in reach of two of them, one shot each takes them both down. Stewart grabs the third. He throws the soldier into the mine walls knocking him out.

"Come on, we have to hurry, when he wakes up he's going to alert more soldiers." They run hurriedly through the mines trying to get to the bottom as fast as they can.

Back outside the mines James and Franks are still pinned down by the Tri-Vinn soldiers. The soldiers that traveled with the AHR team are almost all gone. The soldiers left continue to diligently fight.

"We have got to get moving. I fear Stewart and Sam might be walking into another trap. They'll have no chance." While battling the Tri-Vinn soldiers, James realizes that they are the only ones shooting.

"Stop firing, stop firing!" James screams walking out into the open.

"Where did all the Tri-Vinn soldiers run off too?" Franks asks as he walks out to James. They are looking all around for the Tri-Vinn soldiers searching for answers,:

"Why did they leave?" asks Franks. James looks around and says,

"I don't know, I bet Stewart and Sam have reached the bottom of the mines."

"Well, we have to get to them before those damn Tri-Vinn soldiers do."

They run into the mines with the six remaining soldiers, two humans, and four Noraian soldiers.

At the bottom of the mines Sam and Stewart have reached the security system. It's guarded by ten Tri-Vinn soldiers. They sit out of sight, quietly calculating a plan of action to eliminate the guards. Startled from behind, scared to death Stewart nearly blows their cover.

"Relax, rookie," Franks whispers.

"What's the problem? Why are you two just sitting here?" Stewart grabs Frank by the chin and turns his attention toward the ten soldiers near the computers.

"Oh my bad, wait here," Franks, James and the last six AHR soldiers kill the ten Tri-Vinn soldiers quickly. Afterward Stewart and Sam work on the security system to free the prisoners. Stewart starts to break into the system, but he keeps getting shut out. He tries and tries again. By now, he is getting frustrated. At that moment, James notices Tri-Vinn soldiers sneaking in the mine tunnels towards their location.

"We got trouble, the Tri-Vinn soldiers are coming this way!" James screams, opening fire on them. Franks is just about to help his friend when more soldiers come from the other direction.

"We got more coming this way too!" Franks makes a gesture toward the other entrance, and shoots at the soldiers coming in on his side.

"Not to put any pressure on you two, but can you hurry up please?" Franks screams at Stewart and Sam.

Stewart is struggling with his part and starts to worry. He is having a hard time hacking into Brackeo's firewall for his security computers.

"Stewart, will you please relax, and breathe, because you can do this," Sam says with an encouraging tone, but for the first time, Stewart doubts his ability on computers.

Franks and James are trying their hardest to block the soldiers from getting to Sam and Stewart.

They are using every trick to keep the Tri-vinn soldiers from entering the security chambers. The bodies of the Tri-Vinn soldiers are piling up at the entrances of the chamber, still they keep coming. Stewart lights a cigarette to help gather his thoughts. Puffing away he gets in a groove and begins making progress on Brackeo's firewall .

CHAPTER TWENTY ONE

Shawn and Tyler make their way to the other side of the mines after sunrise. The plan was to give the AHR team members a chance to accomplish their mission first. The two of them had no problems getting to the mines on Tyler's two battle bikes, considering the fact Tri-Vinn soldiers were too busy with the other team members. Preparing to enter the mines, Shawn freezes. A battle echoes off in the distance.

"Hey, don't worry about them," Tyler says, "They're safe and you know they can handle themselves. Besides, we have our own mission, so please don't lose focus." Shawn agrees, but hesitates as his mind is on Stewart.

"Stay close, Shawn, parts of these mines are slippery and dangerous."

They both enter and head toward where Shawn's fathers is supposed to be, as well as the other prisoners. Tyler is the only person who knows these mines other than Brackeo.

Their travels only get harder. They are forced to deal with the elements of the mines, and the Tri-Vinn soldiers that are scattered throughout. But Tyler and Shawn have learned how to work as a team, and take the soldiers out as quickly as they come upon them.

"The holding cells are up head," Tyler whispers to Shawn. As they get closer to Shawn's father they run into trouble. Tyler gets hit from behind. Shawn is surprised by what just happened and reacts by throwing a rock at the soldier that is attacking Tyler, distracting him enough to give the advantage back To Tyler. As Tyler gets back to his feet, more soldiers rush in. They knock into Shawn bumping him to the ground because there target is Tyler. Shawn picks up another rock and starts hitting the Tri-Vinn soldiers. One of them grabs Shawn and throws him a good distance into the mine wall knocking him unconscious for a bit. Tyler sees that Shawn is down, which causes him to take all his anger out on the soldiers attacking him. One by one he defeats them. When he finishes, his instinct is to run straight to Shawn, who is just waking up.

"Are you ok?" Tyler asks as he puts out his hand to help Shawn up off the ground.

"I'm fine." After the latest attack Shawn and Tyler make sure they stay alert as they continue to head through the many tunnels. Tyler signals Shawn to let him know that they're right outside the room where his father is being held. Tyler notices that there is no one guarding the prisoners because of the unique way they are being held. All the prisoners are in body-sized notches that have been carved out of the mine walls. They are seven feet in height and five feet in depth. If the prisoners fall they will be electrocuted, and die from the amount of voltage that would course through their bodies. The prisoners must stay standing at all times in order to survive. Unfortunately, two prisoners were too tired to stand anymore, and they fell to their untimely deaths. Shawn runs over to both men that fell, in hopes neither one was his father. Thankfully they aren't.

"Shawn, your father is over here." Shawn runs over to the notch in the wall that holds his father. He was just about to reach for his father, when Tyler stopped him.

"Don't do that. That electric current will kill you. We have to hope that Stewart and Sam can disarm the electric field." Tyler stresses the fact to Shawn over and over again. Shawn takes out his walkie-talkie.

"Stewart, do you read me?" Shawn starts to worry when his friend doesn't answer, but then Sam's voice comes across the radio.

"Shawn, this is Sam, Stewart is still trying to break the system. He's having a little bit of trouble," Sam says, as the sound of gunfire and screaming reverberates in the background.

"Stewart, I'm standing right in front of our father, he's unconscious, and could fall at any time but I see him."

"It's not like I'm under enough pressure," Stewart screams back.

"Wait, I almost got it. It is your turn Sam." Stewart says, the cigarette almost down to the filter burns in his mouth. Stewart takes the walkie-talkie from Sam. She starts working on the computer now.

"Hang in there buddy, we'll have our father soon," he says over the noise. "Listen Shawn, Sam will have the system down soon, but I got to go. We are under attack over here."

Stewart disconnects. Shawn screams into the walkie-talkie, but there's no answer. Stewart goes and helps James who only has one soldier left. Franks and three soldiers go to help, too, since there aren't any more Tri-Vinn soliders coming from their side. Stewart backs away to let Franks and the soldiers in to help them fight.

Sam is still typing on the keyboard to break down the final stage of the electric currents surrounding the holding cells.

"I got it!" she screams out. "The electric barriers are down." She turns around and notices that there is a single Tri-Vinn soldier at the other exit of the room, but none of the team members realize it. She tries screaming to get their attention, but it's too late. The Tri-Vinn soldier starts to point his weapon at Stewart and then he fires it. Sam jumps in the way of the shot getting her hit by the electric ray. She hits the ground head first, hard knocking her unconscious. Stewart turns to see what happened. He pulls his gun out fast and shoots the soldier, then darts over to Sam. She is bleeding from her head.

"Sam, please wake up!" Stewart clutches Sam to his chest.

"Guys we gotta get her out of here now. Her breathing is very faint." Stewart continues to hold her body close to his chest.

James sees what is happening and feels that staying there to fight is pointless since they just keep coming." Franks, help Stewart with Sam, and start heading down the other tunnel."

Franks tries to help Sam, but Stewart refuses to let him. Stewart picks her up and carries her down the tunnel with Franks leading and the remaining soldiers. James waits until his team is out before he drops two grenades and runs. The explosion kills some Tri-Vinn soldiers, and collapses the tunnel entrance giving them some time to get away.

Meanwhile, with the barriers down, Shawn catches his father's body as he falls to the ground. Shawn's father is a shell of what he used to be. He is very gaunt, skeletal skinny. He has salt and pepper hair, and his face is dirty with a rustic beard.

"Dad, are you ok?" Shawn tries to wake his father up from exhaustion and malnutrition. He pours his water on his father's face to try to wake him up.

"I'm not telling you anything, Brackeo! I told you before, just kill me!" Shawn's father is rambling on after being abused and starved for so long.

"Dad, it's me Shawn, wake up!"

"Shawn? Is that really you?" Doc Higgins asks regaining consciousness. Doc Higgins puts his arm around his son's neck to sit up. He takes many sips of Shawn's water and, gaining some strength stands and gives his son a big, tight hug. Then he shakes Tyler's hand and gives him a hug.

"How are you doing my friend.

"I'm sorry my brother " Doc Higgins cuts Tyler off.

This is not your fault ." He says to Tyler pouring all his attention back to his son.

"I can't believe you're here. I'm so sorry I kept this from you." Shawn's father pleads for his son's forgiveness.

"Not now, dad. We will talk later. Now let's get you out of here. Are you able to walk?" His father hugs his son again and says,

"Yes I can walk. I'll run if I have to. I'll do anything it takes to get out of here, now give me a gun, Tyler."

"Oh, just to let you know, you can thank Stewart and Sam for freeing you later," Shawn says, as he helps Tyler and his father get the other prisoners up and able to walk out of the mines. After a while Doc Higgins realizes what his son just said.

"Wait, Stewart is here on NORA too?" Doc Higgins exclaims.

"Oh by the way, they started dating too," Shawn says while he gives water to one of the prisoners.

"Who? Are you talking about Stewart and Sam? Oh, I knew they would hit it off. So, how's Stone taking the news?"

"Not good," Shawn says to his father, who is laughing as he helps the prisoner to his feet. Tyler walks over to Shawn and his father.

"The tunnels seem empty, and I think we should start going now." Tylers says as he just got back from checking ahead.

"Ok, then let's get moving," Shawn says. He helps one prisoner as his father helps another, and Tyler carries another as they lead the group out of the mines.

"So what's the plan to get us out of here?" Doc Higgins asks as they head through the tunnels.

"Bobby is waiting with the Blackbird in a safe location to fly us out of here."

They all race through the mine tunnels. As they come to an exit Tyler notices that his brother Brackeo-Vinn is standing on his two man space ship that he stole a while back from the earth compound. He is in his humanand is behind and above all his Tri-Vinn soldiers.

"Come out now my weak little brother or we will shoot you out," Brackeo Vinn screams to his brother who is trapped just inside the mine entrance.

"We are not coming out of these mines without a fight, Brackeo," Screams Tyler, I'm inside the mines.

Brackeo gives the orders to fire at the mine entrance, and the team takes cover behind the rock wall. Brackeo is laughing as his soldiers keep unloading on the mine entrance.

CHAPTER TWENTY TWO

Back at the Blackbird Shuttle, Bobby is pacing back and forth while Scanvokia is covering up the soldiers that died in battle. He places a cloth over each one as a sign of respect and honor.

"Sir, somebody is coming," a guarding soldier screams to Bobby. Scanvokia stops what he is doing to run and see who.

"Everybody on guard, somebody's coming!" Scanvokia screams as he runs through the camp, alerting everybody that is still alive.

"Everybody look alive," screams Bobby, who turns into his Noraian for. As the unit prepares for yet another battle, Bobby notices James's head popping up from the bushes.

"Hold your fire," Bobby screams out loud as he turns human again. James is followed out by the final three Noraian soldiers. Stewart is next, and he is holding Sam who is badly burned on her stomach and still bleeding from her head. Franks is the last person to exit the woods, watching their backs.

"Let me help, Stewart," Scanvokia says to him. Stewart, who is tired from carrying Sam the whole way back, refuses the help from Scanvokia. He struggles to carry Sam onto the Blackbird with Bobby following closely behind so he can start tending to her wounds.

"Where's the other group? They should have been back already," James asks Scanvokia.

"They haven't come back yet," Scanvokia answers him back quickly. Then off in the distance they hear gunfire and explosions. They are able to see black smoke rising in the distant sky. Franks runs into the Blackbird where Stewart and Bobby are treating Sam in the sick bay.

"You guys have got to come and see this." They all leave Sam on the bed pushing pain medicine through I.V.'s. Stewart kisses Sam on her forehead before he heads outside. Outside of the shuttle they still hear gunfire, and see a lot more black smoke filling the air.

"That must be the other team members. They must be in trouble. Let's go help them before it's too late," Stewart screams out, ready to run down to help them.

"No wait, you stay here with Bobby," Scanvokia says as he grabs the collar of Stewart's leather jacket to stop him before he runs off wildly.

"What? I'm not staying here," Stewart screams as he rips away from Scanvokia's grasp.

"Stay here with Bobby to protect the shuttle," Scanvokia says.

"Bobby has soldiers; he can take care of things here."

"What about Sam?" Stewart comes to his senses, and starts to think about the promise he made to Sam's father. He then realizes that he can't go and help Shawn this time.

"Don't worry we will bring them back safe, I promise. You take care of Sam." Scanvokia shakes Stewart's hand to give Stewart confidence. Right before Scanvokia is going to turn into his true Noraian form for speed, James approaches.

"Hey, wait. We are going with you."

"You won't be able to keep up with me, I'll go alone."

"We can keep up with you no doubt." Franks says to Scanvokia.

"We are going to," say the three Noraians soldiers that came back with James and Franks.

"Okay, let's go then," Scanvokia says as he turns into his true form followed by the three Noraian soldiers in their true forms as well. All six of them go bustling through the woods back towards the mines.

Bobby comes back out of the shuttle and walks towards Stewart who is still looking at the direction of the black smoke in the sky, praying that Shawn and his father are ok.

"Stewart, Sam is up and she's asking for you."

"How is she?" Stewart asks with concern, his voice trembling.

"She's going to have a nasty scar on her stomach. The infection will go away. She also has three stitches on her forehead which will give her a wicked headache for a while, but she'll live because of you. You saved her life, Stewart. You should be proud. I know I am proud of you right about now." Bobby shakes Stewart's hand.

"Go see her. I'll stand guard out here, and I'll come get you when I hear of anything, I promise."

Stewart runs in to be with Sam.

"Look who's up. You look great," Stewart says.

"Stop being a liar. I look horrible," Sam says as she hides her face. In her hands. Stewart sits down next to her on the bed and unlocks Sam's hands to reveal her face.

"I think you look beautiful, and I don't ever want you to hide your face again." This brings a big smile across Sam's face.

"Where's everybody else?" Sam says looking around to see if anybody is waiting outside the room.

"They're not back yet, but they're coming soon. Don't worry about that." Sam is starting to fall asleep from the medicine. She sits up slowly.

"You saved my life. love you for that."

"You saved me first. I love you for that." Stewart kisses Sam on her lips. She falls back asleep.

In the woods James and Franks are keeping up with Scanvokia and the soldiers on the ground. They are almost halfway back to the mines.

Meanwhile, back down at the mines Shawn, his father, and Tyler are barricaded just inside the entrance of the mines. They're trying to protect the badly beaten prisoners from the attacks of the Tri-Vinn soldiers. The fighting goes on for some time and Shawn, Tyler, and Doc Higgins are doing well for themselves protected by the mine walls. They have killed a lot of the Tri-Vinn soldiers in this battle. The three of them are doing so good they have Brackeo hiding behind his ship.

"Brother, stop hiding and come out to face me," Brackeo screams. Standing tall his long curly brown hair flows past his shoulders. He has a thick brown beard that covers half his face, and baggy brown leather clothes on.

"Come on out brother, let's finish this once and for all." Tyler takes a step out towards Brackeo.

"Wait, don't go, it's a trap." Shawn tries to convince Tyler to stay covered.

"Take your father and the prisoners to safety," Tyler says to Shawn as he walks out, turning into his true Noraian form. Brackeo realizes that Tyler is in his true form so he turns into his Noraian form. Brackeo, in his true form, is much taller than the other Noraians, even than his own brother. The two brothers start talking to each other through their minds. Shawn steps out of the mines even with his father trying to stop him, but when he can't stop him he follows him out.

"Why are you doing all this? We should be on the same team not fighting each other," Tyler says to his brother.

"How can you stand there and preach to me when you're the most dishonest person of us all, Zeackeo-Vinn? Oh wait, it's Tyler now."

Shawn listens to the two brothers arguing back and forth.

"You brother, are the reason our sister is dead." Tyler put his head down from the allegation his brother is throwing at him. "I did not kill our sister. You have to stop blaming me for that."

"There you go again. Lying, that's what you do best." Tyler takes a few steps towards his brother. "What are you getting at, Brackeo?" Tyler is getting tired of the games his brother is playing.

"You never told the boy did you?"

Tyler turns to Shawn quickly then back to his brother.

"It's not my place. It's his father's job to tell him, which was impossible because you had the boy's father."

Brackeo starts laughing which makes Tyler even angrier.

"You should not have kept it from the boy that our sister married his human father." Shawn's face turns white as a ghost. Brackeo now realizes that Shawn is listening in on his conversation with Tyler.

"I wasn't sure if you could hear me when I tried to kill your friend and he escaped from that ship. I had to be sure." Tyler is looking at his brother and wondering what he is talking about.

"What do you think about your good friend Tyler now? Or maybe you would like to call him Uncle Tyler."

Tyler quickly looks at Shawn because he finally realizes that Brackeo has been talking to Shawn, and not to him. Tyler also realizes that Shawn can hear them talking.

"I'm sorry Shawn." Tyler quickly says. Shawn is blown away from the news he just heard. Tyler is enraged over what his brother just did. He turns back towards his brother only to see him shoot Shawn, blowing a giant hole into Shawn's stomach and sending him flying back into the mine wall.

"No! Shawn!" screams Shawn's father. He runs over to the dead limp body of his son. He drops to his knees and cradles his son's dead body.

Tyler is in shock over what just happened and is grabbed by his brother Brackeo. He picks Tyler up by his neck.

"Why did you kill him? He's our family."

"He's not family and neither are you." Brackeo throws his brother hard into a giant boulder. Before Tyler can even respond, Brackeo is on top of him punching him over and over again. Doc Higgins, still cradling his son, realizes the remaining Tri-Vinn soldiers are moving in on them. He stands up, taking his son's side gun from his leg holster. As the Tri-Vinn soldiers get closer, Doc Higgins starts shooting at them, still standing over Shawn's body. Just then Scanvokia and the other three Noraians come flying from the trees, taking out the Tri-Vinn soldiers with help from James and Franks. Doc Higgins falls down to his dead son's body.

"Oh my god, Shawn!" James says. He and Franks look down

at Shawn's dead body.

Scanvokia and the soldiers attack Brackeo who is still punching Tyler deeper into the boulder. Scanvokia is the first to reach Brackeo. He jumps on the taller Brackeo, but is thrown off quickly. The other three Noraians hit Brackeo, one by one, and they get tossed away also. Tyler has crawled away from the boulder, but Brackeo grabs his foot and pulls him back.

"Going somewhere, brother?" Brackeo says as he continues to pull his brother back to him.

Scanvokia comes racing back and throws punches the back of Brackeo's head and body which gives Tyler time to get away.

"Scanvokia, I never liked you. You're a pest that I'm going to love squashing." Brackeo screams. He grabs Scanvokia towards him and punches him in the face a few times before throwing him through the trees. The other three Noraians soldiers come back again for Brackeo.

"Enough of this," Brackeo screams.

He grabs the first one and breaks his neck, and then throws him to the side. He grabs the other two soldiers, picks them both up by their uniforms and bashes them together. He throws them both over the cliff to the raging red water. Brackeo walks toward Tyler, who is badly beaten and can barely move. James and Franks start to point their guns at Brackeo to fire at him when they hear,

"Don't fire your guns, he's mine!" Doc Higgins almost has a heart attack, because his supposed dead son just spoke, and the hole in his stomach has healed.

"How is that possible?" Franks asks as both he and James point their guns to the ground and Shawn stands up.

"You were dead! How is that possible?" asks James.

"He's special," utters Doc Higgins as he looks at his son. Shawn looks down at his father.

"Get the prisoners back to the Blackbird Shuttle with Franks and James," Shawn says. Doctor Higgins doesn't listen to his son, but instead watches Shawn charge Brackeo.

"You stupid kid, you are no match for Brackeo-Vinn." Brackeo pays no attention to his badly beaten younger brother and shifts his attention to the charging Shawn. Shawn throws punch after punch at Brackeo, connecting with none of them. Brackeo grabs Shawn and throws him back towards his father.

"Are you ok Shawn?" Shawn looks back at his father and says,

"I'm fine, I told you to leave, I told you all to leave!" Shawn charges Brackeo again.

"You don't know when to quit, do you?" says Brackeo to Shawn. Shawn charges him once again. Shawn throws punches at Brackeo this time connecting with Brackeo's face a few times. Brackeo grabs Shawn and winds up to throw him off the cliff, when James shoots Brackeo in the arm he was using to hold Shawn. As soon as Shawn hits the ground Scanvokia comes out of nowhere and hits Brackeo with a punch of his own, bringing Brackeo down to one knee. When Brackeo stands up, Shawn hits him with a running spear straight off the edge. They both disappear over the cliff.

"Shawn," screams Doc Higgins running over to the edge of the cliff and sees only Shawn. He's holding on to a scruff of weeds protruding out of the rocks.

"Hold on, son, while I look for something to drop down to you."

Just then the weeds start to come loose from the cliff. Shawn's father panics.

James finds a rope and tosses down to Shawn just in the nick of time.

"Grab the rope!" James screams.

Scanvokia, Franks, and James pull Shawn up quickly.

When Shawn is at the top Franks says,

"You got some major league big balls on you kid." Shawn gives Franks a high five. They all laugh. Joy overwhelms them.

"Bobby, this is James. We're all safe. But we are going to need a ride out of here" James says through his headset.

"What about the soldiers?" Bobby asks.

"Scanvokia is going to be on his way back to drive the battle truck and the soldier's home."

Shawn tells James to have Stewart reconnect the battle truck so it's ready.

"Did you hear that, Bobby" James asks.

"I sure did."

They disconnect.

"Wait, connect the battle truck? What did you do Shawn?" his father asks.

"They actually made it better," says Scanvokia. He walks over to Shawn and shakes his hand.

"Until we meet again, my friend."

They stop shaking hands and Scanvokia turns his attention to Tyler who is badly beaten but standing.

"I'm sorry about your brother." They both shake each other's forearms and say their goodbyes.

Scanvokia turns into his Noraian form and runs back to the battle truck. Shawn walks back to the edge of the cliff. Tyler was going to join him when Doc Higgins stops him and goes himself.

"I should have told you, but I never knew how."

Shawn continues to look down at the water and says,

"I'm not mad dad; I wasn't ready to know, is all. But, I know now that I am special, and there will be no more hiding anything anymore." Before Doc Higgins can answer Bobby is above them and landing the Blackbird shuttle nearby.

"Come, let's go son."

As they walk to the shuttle Stewart comes running out to them and hugs Doc Higgins.

"No, I'm just fine, don't worry about me," Shawn says to Stewart till hugging Doc Higgins.

"Stewart, it's nice to see you, too, son"

"How's Sam?" Shawn asks.

"She's hurt, but she'll survive," Stewart says. They climb the retractable steps into the shuttle.

Bobby comes out." We have a problem. We can only fit two more."

Shawn, Tyler, Doc Higgins, and Stewart all look at each other.

They all want each other to get on the shuttle. Stewart has to go on because of Sam and Shawn tells his father to help Bobby fly the shuttle.

"I'll take Brackeo's ship with Tyler and follow you guys to the warp."

Bobby is screaming in the background to move it. Finally Shawn's father agrees and lets Shawn go.

"You better follow us, Shawn," says Stewart. He runs back into the Blackbird.

CHAPTER TWENTY THREE

The Blackbird waits while Shawn and Tyler take off in Brackeo's ship. Once they do the shuttle heads out to space.

"Shawn, this is Bobby, just follow us through the warp and we will see you on the other side."

Once Doc Higgins sees that his son is following them safely he goes back to see Sam and Stewart.

"Don't worry, Shawn and Tyler are following right behind us," Doc Higgins says to Stewart who is sitting by Sam's side.

"Hey, there beautiful," Doc Higgins says to Sam. She smiles and gives him a hug, and he gives her a quick examination.

"You'll be fine sweetie." He turns to Stewart and says,

"Take care of her while I go help Bobby fly us home." Doc Higgins leaves. Stewart reaches into his pocket for a cigarette and comes across a folded piece of paper. Stewart sits down next to Sam on the bed. He pulls out the folded paper getting the attention of Sam. In the background you hear Bobby and Doc Higgins talking to Shawn and Tyler over the radio.

"We are almost to the warp, Shawn."

The warp is open and in their view. Shawn and Tyler are flying close behind the shuttle.

Stewart unfolds the paper. He reads it out loud.

Dear Stewart,

You are my brother even though we do not share the same blood. You're the closest thing to family that I truly ever wanted. You've been my backbone through all of this. But, I hate to say that I haven't been totally honest with you. For the first time in our lives I've been keeping a secret. Maybe I was trying to protect you when you didn't need me to. Maybe I was protecting myself, I don't truly know. So here it is: lately I have been able to hear the Noraians talk to each other in their true form.

Stewart stops reading and looks at Sam who is even more surprised than Stewart.

"How can that be?" asks Sam.

Then they can hear Bobby say, "Oh my god here come some ships from the left side." Small ships attack the two shuttles heading toward the space warp.

"Shawn, watch out they are behind you," Doc Higgins screams over the radio.

They're reaching the space warp and head back to the Milky Way. Then they hear Shawn's voice over the radio. There is sadness in his tone.

"Dad, get them all out of here, and bring them home." He continues on by saying, "I'll distract the ships so you guys can fly home safely."

"No, Shawn, you follow us into the space warp. We are so close." Doc Higgins peads with his son to follow them, but Shawn turns left away from the space warp, leaving the Blackbird's trail. The enemy ships follow Shawn and Tyler back down to NORA's orbit.

"Shawn, please don't do this," Doc Higgins pleads with his son, but it is too late. They lose radio contact and the space warp closes behind them, leaving Shawn and Tyler back in NORA's galaxy. Stewart drops the letter as he looks down towards the ground over what just happened. Sam kisses Stewart on his cheek whispering in his ear.

"Finish the letter. Maybe it will help you."

Stewart takes a deep breath and picks up the letter from the ground and finishes reading.

> I didn't tell you because maybe you would think I'm crazy, or maybe I thought you would try to talk me out of what I have to do. I have to beat Brackeo or anybody else who is looking for the Albac Blade. I have to get the six keys before anybody else. I feel it's my destiny. Why else can I hear the Noraians talking? Please, my friend, take care of my dad like you took care of me. Our father will need you more than ever now. Sam, I know you are safe and sitting next to Stewart right now. Take care of my brother; he tends to get himself into all kinds of trouble. Stewart, promise me you won't fall off the wagon due to my actions. Sam, please take care of him. I will see you both really soon. Stewart, you completed your promise like I knew you would, so now it's time for me to complete the promise that I made to myself. I love you both very much, be safe, and always know that you are my brother and my best friend, the only one I have ever had. Take care, Stewart.
>
> -Shawn Higgins

Stewart is upset over what he just read. He puts his head down on Sam's lap. Tear trails run down his cheeks. Sam realizes that something's written on the bottom left of the page. It's in smaller writing than the rest of the letter in the bottom right hand corner, Sam reads it to Stewart'

"Family brings true happiness."

Stewart lifts his head up from Sam's lap. He wipes the tears from his eyes and softly says.

"Until we meet again, my brother."

Sam hugs Stewart. The Blackbird Shuttle jets to the International Space Station.

www.ingramcontent.com/pod-product-compliance
Lightning Source LLC
LaVergne TN
LVHW040140080526
838202LV00042B/2974